THE
END
BEGINS

THE
END
BEGINS

the seven trilogy
book one

SARA DAVISON

ASHBERRY LANE

Praise for The End Begins

"The first book in Davison's Seven trilogy grips the reader from page one and holds on until the very end. Meryn O'Reilly is a believable character, and—though dreadful—the story is plausible. The events unfold in a forward-moving way that allows readers to sympathize with Meryn and Jesse and understand the dilemmas they face. Thought-provoking, relevant and suspenseful, *The End Begins* is a must-read."

—*ROMANTIC TIMES*, 4 ½ Stars, *Top Pick*

"What would you do if the government outlawed the Bible? *The End Begins* depicts the response of a bookstore owner, the army captain duty-bound to arrest her if she breaks the law, and the family, friends and enemies in their lives. It's a compelling and scary read you won't soon forget."

—SANDRA ORCHARD,
Author of the Award-Winning Port Aster Secrets series

"Sara Davison takes 'what if' to a chilling level that is all too real. Yet wrapped in love, both human and divine, this novel gives us hope. Book Two can't come out soon enough."

—NANCY RUE,
Author of *One Last Thing* and *The Merciful Scar*

Published by Ashberry Lane, a division of WhiteFire Publishing
13607 Bedford Rd NE, Cumberland, MD 21502
www.ashberrylane.com
Printed in the USA

Canadian spelling is frequently used.

Published in association with the literary agency of Wordserve Literary Group, www.wordserveliterary.com.

ISBN 978-1-941720-19-6

Library of Congress Control Number: 2015948600

Front cover photo © 2010 Richard McGuire
Cover design by Roseanna White Designs
Photos from www.shutterstock.com
Edited by Rachel Lulich, Kristen Johnson, Amy Smith, and Andrea Cox

FICTION / Christian / Romantic Suspense

To Luke, my firstborn. Your sense of humour, kind heart, quirky way of looking at the world, and desire to serve the Lord and others bring me endless joy. I am eternally grateful to God for the gift of you.

To the men and women of the Canadian Armed Forces, who risk their lives to fight for justice, freedom, and peace here and around the world.
Thank you.

And always and above all, to the One who gives the stories and who is the beginning and the end of all things. It is all from you and for you.

Remember the former things, those of long ago;
I am God, and there is no other;
I am God, and there is none like me.
I make known the end from the beginning,
from ancient times, what is still to come.
Isaiah 46:9-10a

The End
And the Beginning

For the first time, the reverent stillness of the old limestone church didn't fill Meryn O'Reilly with peace. She raised her gaze to the gleaming wooden cross on the wall behind the pulpit. What would happen now? Even the air felt different, colder, in spite of the warm October day. On the way to church she had hardly seen a single person out walking, and only the odd car had passed by her. Everyone seemed to be taking refuge in their homes, as if it were safer, somehow, to stay out of sight. If that continued for long, she didn't know what would happen to her secondhand bookstore, but there were more important things to worry about this morning.

Meryn's best friend sat on the pew beside her. Kate clutched her daughter, Gracie, to her chest. Matthew, her four-year-old son, pressed close to her side, as though he could sense the tension in the sanctuary.

The minister climbed the steps to the stage. Although he was a young man, today his steps were slow. When he turned to face them, the invisible weight he carried bowed his shoulders. He clutched both sides of the oak pulpit. Thin light filtering through a stained-glass window cast an eerie rose glow over his lined face. "My friends, you don't need me to tell you that dark days have come to Canada. A group calling themselves Christians has claimed responsibility for—"

The doors to the right of the stage crashed open, shattering the hush that had fallen over the room.

Uniformed soldiers, carrying rifles, marched into the sanctuary and started down the aisle.

Kate's short red hair fell over one eye as she dug her fingers into

9

Meryn's arm. "They'll arrest us all." She pulled Gracie closer as other parishioners pushed past them, fleeing toward the back door.

More soldiers appeared in the back of the church, ordering any who tried to escape that way onto their knees. "Down on the floor!"

Meryn looked around wildly. What should they do? Her eyes fell on the little side door at the end of their pew. "Quick, Kate." Meryn grabbed her elbow and tugged her toward the opening. In all the fear and confusion in the room, no one moved to stop them as they slipped through the door. The shouts and cries faded behind them as they hurried down a dimly lit hall lined with old, wooden tables and stacked chairs. The hallway led to a set of stairs down to the basement. "We can go out the back exit."

She stopped at the bottom and waited for Kate to climb down, Matthew at her heels. "Why are they doing this, Kate?"

Her friend shifted Gracie to her hip so she could take Matthew's hand and help him down another step. "Ethan says Parliament convened an emergency session last night. They pushed through a bill to give the military virtually unlimited power to put down the terrorists responsible for the bombings."

Kate's husband was editor-in-chief of the local paper, the *Kingston Whig-Standard*. He'd been at the office for the last forty-eight hours, ever since seven mosques across Canada had been blasted from their foundations during Friday prayers. The deadly attacks on October 10, 2053, the worst on Canadian soil, were already known simply as 10/10.

A question rose in Meryn's throat but she bit her lip, holding it in for a few seconds.

The fear in Kate's eyes told her that she was not going to like the answer.

She pushed back her shoulders, steeling herself. "Do they know who is responsible?"

"They think they do." Kate's voice shook.

Meryn wiped the palms of her hands on her tan dress pants. "Who?"

Matthew hopped down the last step, and his little knees buckled.

Kate held up their clasped hands to keep him from falling. Her hazel eyes met Meryn's. "Us."

CHAPTER ONE

Meryan didn't move until a loud thud and a shout from upstairs yanked her from her stunned silence. "We need to get out now." She started down the winding hallway. When she reached the door at the back of the basement, she grasped the handle and pulled it open, wincing when the seldom-used hinges screeched in protest.

If any of the soldiers were outside the church, she'd just announced their presence. Meryn pressed a trembling hand to the doorframe and peered around it to scan the property.

No one was out there.

"Meryn?"

The panicked whisper set her heart pounding. She shut the door and scrambled back down the hallway.

Kate crouched in front of Matthew, struggling to hold onto Gracie and lift her son up with her other arm.

Meryn took the little girl from Kate. "What's wrong?"

"Matthew fell and hurt his knee. I'll have to carry him."

Footsteps thundered down the stairs.

Kate's eyes widened, but she scooped up Matthew and jerked her head toward a small storage room beside them.

In the dull light sifting through a tiny window near the ceiling, Meryn scanned the boxes piled high against every wall. A large, dust-covered wreath lay on top of the nearest stack of boxes marked *Christmas Pageant Costumes*. She pointed to a large cupboard in the corner of the room. "Try in there."

Kate wrenched open the door and squeezed into the tiny space, Matthew's skinny arms clinging to her neck and his legs wrapped around her waist.

There wasn't room, or time, for Meryn to try and fit herself and Gracie in too, so she ducked behind the door they'd come in, praying the near-darkness would offer them a small amount of protection. Her throat tightened when boots tromped past the open doorway and continued to the exit.

For a few seconds, they echoed faintly in the distance, then they started back. Whoever was out there drew even with their door and continued past.

Gracie let out a small cry.

Horrified, Meryn pressed a hand over her mouth. "Shh, baby. It's all right," she whispered in the little girl's ear. Had anyone heard? She strained to listen, but there was nothing but silence in the hallway. Suddenly the door she stood behind was yanked away from her. Meryn gasped, her eyes riveted on the rifle pointed directly at her chest.

She raised her eyes to the soldier holding the weapon. He was tall, but she couldn't make out any other features in the semi-darkness until he reached behind him, the gun still trained on her, and flipped the switch to illuminate the room. Meryn's throat went dry. She leaned against the wall. *God, give me strength. Keep us safe.* When the man didn't move, Meryn lifted her chin, fear giving way to anger as she eyed the weapon pointed at her and Gracie.

Something flashed through the jade-green eyes that probed hers. The soldier stared at her and Gracie, as though wondering what he should do with them now that he had them cornered.

Meryn was fairly certain she didn't fit the profile of a terrorist. Still, nothing could be counted on any longer. The three gold star shapes on his shoulders caught her eye, and she searched her memory. A captain.

Heavy footsteps reverberated down the hallway.

The captain lowered his gun. "My men are coming. Take her out the back door. Quickly. No one's patrolling out there yet. Go through the woods and you should be fine."

Meryn tightened her hold on Gracie. "Are you sure you don't want to arrest the two of us for blowing up those mosques?"

The corners of his mouth twitched. "Did you do it?"

She kept her eyes locked on his. "No."

"Then I think I'll take my chances." He jerked his head in the direction of the exit. "Go."

Meryn started for the opening, then stopped.

The man blew out an exasperated breath. "Do you *want* me to take you in?"

"No, but ..." Meryn brushed past him and opened the door of the cupboard. "Kate, come out. He's letting us go out the back door. Hurry."

Kate stepped out, clutching Matthew. Her eyes widened at the sight of the gun pointed in their direction.

"Hurry, Kate." Meryn put a hand on her back and gave her a gentle shove. "There are more soldiers coming."

The captain met Meryn's eyes over Kate's shoulder. "What if my quota for allowing fleeing suspects to escape is two a day?" He sounded more amused than annoyed.

The knot in Meryn's stomach loosened slightly. "Is it?"

His lips twitched again. "No."

"Then I think I'll take my chances." She forced bravado into her voice.

He waited until Kate and Matthew had nearly reached him before he lifted the gun to let them by. He lowered it again as Meryn approached, forcing her to stop. When he spoke this time, the amusement was gone. "Watch yourself. It's a whole new world now, and not every soldier will let you get away with that kind of defiance. And while you may not have blown up those mosques personally, just being in this building casts you in a suspicious light." He lowered his voice. "There's going to be trouble, and lots of it. My advice to you is to avoid it at all costs."

"Captain, today I had a rifle pointed at me for standing in a church basement with a baby in my arms. Will the kind of trouble you're referring to be avoidable, do you think?"

"You could start by not calling yourself a Christian."

"No, I couldn't."

He sighed and lifted the gun. "Just be careful."

She ducked beneath it and walked on weak legs out into the hallway, where Kate waited. Meryn held tightly to Gracie as they slipped through the back door and crossed the yard. She stole a look behind her as they reached the trees.

The soldier stood, framed in the doorway, watching them go.

Unsure if he could see her or not, she gave him a brief nod before following Kate into the woods.

CHAPTER TWO

"Is somebody out there?"

Captain Jesse Christensen spun around in the basement doorway as his commanding officer, Major Caleb Donevan, came up behind him. "Not that I can see."

Caleb slung his rifle over his shoulder. "Now that your back is turned, you mean? That sounds ... evasive. Let me take a look."

Jesse stepped aside as his best friend brushed by him. His back and neck muscles tightened as Caleb scanned the woods.

He turned to Jesse, his face grim. "What are you doing?"

Jesse shrugged. "Nothing."

"Exactly. You're standing here doing nothing while at least two adults disappear into the trees."

"Women. Carrying little kids." He shifted from one foot to the other under the intense scrutiny.

Footsteps thudded behind him.

Caleb looked over Jesse's shoulder and raised his hand. "Thank you, gentlemen. The basement is clear. Go back upstairs and help keep everyone under control."

Jesse glanced back as the three men he'd led to the basement retreated down the hallway. Taking a deep breath, he faced Caleb.

The major crossed his arms over his massive chest. "We are under orders to detain and question *every* adult in the building."

"I know."

"So you've just disobeyed a direct command. Can you help me out here by giving me anything close to a rational reason?"

"If you need to report me, report me." Jesse spun around and started down the hallway.

"Hey."

Jesse stopped and turned slowly.

Caleb strode forward, stopping inches from him. "Look, Jess, I don't have the stomach for this either. But we have a job to do, and we need to do it or there will be consequences. For us and for national security."

"I don't really think a couple of—"

"Stop."

Jesse clenched his teeth.

"Your job is not to think. Your job is to obey orders. Can you possibly do that from now on?"

He hesitated as long as he dared. "Yes."

"Good. I have enough to do these days without having to babysit you."

"Are you going to report me?"

Caleb exhaled loudly. "I get it, Jess, I really do. So I'll let it slide this time. But if anyone else saw them leaving, I'll have to file a report. Lieutenant Gallagher's watching us closely, and nothing would make him happier than one of his little rodents sidling up to him and hissing in his ear that you let a couple of possible suspects go while I looked the other way."

Gallagher. Jesse repressed a shudder. Ever since he'd been promoted ahead of the lieutenant two years ago, the man had been out to get him. "Understood." The two men looked at each other for a moment until Jesse dropped his gaze. "Sorry, Cale. I shouldn't put you in that position."

"No, you shouldn't." Caleb uncrossed his arms and punched him lightly in the arm.

Jesse lifted his rifle. "Do you really think this show of force is necessary?"

Caleb's jaw tightened. "It's not my job to think either." He glanced down the grey-bricked hallway, then lowered his voice. "But if it were, then I would say that, yes, this show of force is absolutely necessary. Those bombs going off on Friday have changed everything, including the rules. People died, Jess. Hundreds of people. And all the evidence points to the fact that it wasn't an isolated event—more could be coming.

"This Christian group, whoever they are, must be well organized to have pulled something like this off. They have to have a leader, training, supply sources, and plans. And we're situated halfway between Toronto and Ottawa, the biggest city in the country and the capital, both targets of those bombs, which means that chances are good the epicentre of all that is somewhere around here. We have to be vigilant. We have to take control of this area and not let anything—or anyone—slip by us. If we do, more people could die. And I know you don't want that. Neither do I—not if there's anything we can do to stop it. All right?"

"If you say so."

"I do." Caleb stepped back. "You talked to them, didn't you?"

"Who?" Jesse didn't meet his friend's eyes.

Caleb tilted his head and looked at him.

"Okay, fine. Yes, I talked to them. One of them, at least."

"What did she do, cry? Throw herself on your mercy?"

A small smile crossed Jesse's lips. "No, actually. She got mad. Probably because I was aiming a rifle at her daughter at the time."

"Hmm."

"What?"

"You're not going to do something idiotic here, are you? Because Kingston isn't a huge city, and we are going to be keeping a close eye on the Christians. Chances are you'll run into her again. You have to know that getting involved with one of them would be stupid at best, and career suicide at worst."

Jesse's head jerked. "Involved with her? I don't even know her. And did I mention she was holding her *daughter* in her arms? She's likely safely back home with her husband as we speak."

"I've never seen that look on your face when you're talking about a woman. It makes me very nervous."

"Don't be. It was nothing. Less than nothing."

"Just enough for you to risk being called out for insubordination."

"That was more about the kid."

17

"Sure it was." Caleb shook his head. "Can you focus on the job that needs to be done? And do it?"

"Yes. Absolutely."

"Good. Then let's get to it." He started back down the hallway.

Jesse shoved back a surge of worry as he fell into step behind him. The thought of the woman, dark hair flowing around her shoulders, her deep blue eyes defiant, flashed through his head. "She was pretty though," he said, not able to resist taking a parting shot.

Caleb whipped around to face him.

"Sorry." Jesse pressed his lips together.

"Not nearly as sorry as you will be if I catch you anywhere near her again."

Jesse didn't doubt it. He held up a hand. "You won't. No more thinking, about her or anything else. Just blind, mindless following."

Caleb stepped closer and clasped his shoulder. "I know I've been in Ottawa and I haven't had a chance to fill you in on everything that's going on, but it's bad. The group claiming responsibility for the 10/10 bombings—"The Horsemen" they call themselves—has ignited a firestorm I'm not sure even they anticipated. Christians have already been shoved so far to the fringe, it was inevitable they would be pushed over the brink at some point, and that might be what has happened. We can't fool around here. There's a lot more at stake than I can get into right now, but trust me on this."

"The Horsemen? Really? What's their end game, to touch off Armageddon?"

There wasn't a hint of amusement in Caleb's voice as his fingers tightened on Jesse's shoulder. "It's quite possible. And from what I've been hearing, they just might have succeeded."

CHAPTER THREE

The fuchsia and orange streaking across the evening sky sent flutters through Meryn's stomach, and she gritted her teeth. She used to love sunsets. Now that they hadn't been allowed out after dark for over a week, since the day of the bombings, they were a painful reminder that their hours of freedom were rapidly drawing to a close.

Meryn clutched her overflowing pail of blackberries in one hand and reached for Gracie's sticky fingers. Together, they shoved their way through the long grass in the ditch and climbed up onto the shoulder of the road. "Come on, Kate. We have to hurry if we're going to get back to my place before dark."

"My pail's almost full." Kate's voice drifted to her from behind a huge bush. "I'll grab a few more berries and then we can head back."

"Are you sure Ethan's okay with you and Gracie spending the night at my place?"

"I'm sure. He and Matthew were looking forward to a boys' night."

"Because I know he doesn't love it when you're not there."

Kate peered around the bushes, cheeks pink. "No, I guess he doesn't. It's silly, isn't it? I mean, we've been married almost five years."

"I don't think it's silly at all. It's sweet. But I'm glad he was willing for you to come and help me tonight."

"Well, he knew he'd get some jam out of it, so he didn't protest too much."

Meryn wrinkled her nose. "You do know I don't bake, right? Or whatever it is you do to berries to make jam. And may I also point out that there are countless jars of jam, already made, sitting on the shelves at the grocery store?"

"You said yourself that if things get much worse, it might get hard to buy stuff. We should start preparing for that now."

"You're right. We should." She scrunched up her face as she looked down at her pail. "Unfortunately, I don't have a clue how to begin."

"I'll show you. We have to learn to be self-sufficient somehow, even if, for some of us"—she threw a pointed look at Meryn—"domesticity goes against every fibre of our being." She disappeared around the back of the bush again. Meryn set down her pail and rubbed her berry-stained fingers across the front of her jeans before leaning down and swinging Gracie up into her arms.

The sun dipped lower in the sky as Gracie rested her head on Meryn's shoulder. The dying light fell over the field across the road, painting the stubble of cornstalks a gleaming golden-yellow. The chirping of crickets swelled.

For the first time in days, Meryn felt a moment of complete peace.

The sound of an approaching vehicle shattered the twilit calm.

Her arms tightened around Gracie when one of the now-familiar green army jeeps crested the hill and headed toward them. *Keep driving.*

The vehicle passed them, then slowed and pulled onto the shoulder.

What do they want now?

The door of the jeep opened, and a man climbed out and started toward her.

At least there's only one of them. She blinked as he approached. It was the soldier she'd encountered in the basement of the church.

Now that she wasn't distracted by a weapon pointed in her direction, she was able to take in what he looked like. His dark-green camouflage pants and jacket did nothing to hide a lean, muscular torso and arms. He wore a matching green beret over short dark hair, and his face and hands revealed the bronze tan of a man who spent long hours in the sun.

He smiled when he got to them, recognition flaring in his eyes. "Hello."

"Hi."

"Is everything all right?"

"We're fine." *Please go away.*

"Good. I thought I'd check it out when I saw someone standing here alone in the middle of nowhere."

"Like I said, we're fine."

The captain looked down at the berries, then back at her. "Actually, I was hoping we'd cross paths again. I wanted to make sure you were okay. After last week, I mean."

Meryn pushed back her shoulders. "If you mean have I recovered from having a rifle stuck in my face, then I suppose so."

He looked down at his boot and scuffed at the gravel before lifting his head. "Actually, what I wondered was if you made it through the woods and home all right, with no one else bothering you."

Warmth rushed into Meryn's cheeks. "Oh. Then, yes, we got home all right."

"And your daughter? She's okay?"

"My ..." Meryn bit back her surprise and hiked Gracie up higher on her hip. "She's good."

They both turned at the sound of rustling.

Kate waded through the grass in the ditch, moving toward them.

Gracie twisted around and held her arms out toward Kate. "Mama."

The heat in Meryn's cheeks intensified as Kate joined them on the side of the road and took Gracie from her. "A little confused, but fine." It took everything in her to meet the captain's gaze. The amusement on his face sent irritation rushing through her. "We should go."

"Wait." The amusement faded. "I wanted to introduce myself." He held out his hand and smiled. "Captain Jesse Christensen."

Meryn didn't move.

When the captain started to lower his hand, smile faltering, Kate reached out and took it. "I'm Kate Williams, this is my daughter, Gracie, and this is—"

Meryn grabbed her arm. "Don't."

"... Meryn O'Reilly."

Meryn let go of her and threw both hands in the air.

The captain nodded. "Ms. Williams, Ms. O'Reilly, Gracie, a pleasure to meet you. Can I give you a ride somewhere?"

"That's okay. Meryn lives—" Kate waved her hand in the direction of Meryn's house, but froze when Meryn elbowed her in the ribs.

The captain turned in the direction she'd indicated, lines creasing his forehead. "Where? In that red-brick farmhouse set way back from the road?"

Meryn frowned. "Have you been scouting us out?"

"No, I just drove by there and wondered who would want to be in such an isolated location. Do you live there alone?"

"Yes, she ..."

Meryn whirled toward her friend. "Honestly, Kate! Do you want to give him my family Bible so he can learn my entire history as well?"

Kate offered her a dimpled smile.

Meryn glared at the captain. "Is this an official interrogation?"

"No, of course not. I was just ... concerned."

"It's not really your job to be concerned about us, is it?"

"Actually, it is. My *job* is to ensure and maintain national security. And as you, and your property, are part of this nation, making sure you are secure is most definitely a part of my mandate."

"Until such time as you believe I have become a threat to that national security, is that it?"

"Exactly." He grinned and shoved his hands into the pockets of his uniform pants. "Of course, I don't anticipate that happening any time soon."

"Don't underestimate me, Captain."

The grin disappeared. "I'm going to pretend I didn't hear that."

Neither of them moved until Kate cleared her throat. "We should go, Meryn. It's getting late."

Meryn tore her gaze from his. "Yes, we should. As you know, we're not *allowed* to be out after dark." She didn't like the bitterness in her own voice, and the surprised look Kate gave her wasn't helping.

The captain stepped back, the dog tags around his neck jangling. "I'm sorry about that. We're hoping that's a temporary measure, until things quiet down."

"Until you have all of us under control, you mean," Meryn snapped.

"Subjugated and submissive. Or maybe arrested or killed. That would make things nice and quiet for you, wouldn't it?"

"Meryn!"

Kate sounded shocked, but the captain's eyes didn't look angry, just sad. "It's all right. I understand."

"No." Meryn pressed her fingers against her forehead and closed her eyes. Would she ever learn to control her tongue? When she opened her eyes and forced herself to look at him, the sadness was gone from his face. The intense look that had replaced it sent shivers racing across her skin. "It's not all right. That was extremely rude of me. None of this is your fault. Not entirely."

He smiled faintly.

Meryn took a deep breath. "I know you're doing your job. And I also know that you took a big risk when you let us go the other day. So, thank you."

"You're welcome."

Meryn reached for the pails of berries, but he stopped her with a light touch of his hand on her arm. She glanced down at it, then back up at him.

He dropped his hand. "I don't want to hold you up, but if you need anything, or if anyone gives you any trouble, I'd like you to contact me." He pulled a card out of his pocket and held it out to her.

For two seconds she thought about refusing it, but she'd been rude enough for one day. "Thank you. I'm sure we'll be fine though."

"I'm sure."

Meryn looked up at the softness in his voice. The eyes that met hers held something she had not expected to see there, given what he was.

Kindness.

She swallowed hard and closed her fingers around the card. Her thumb brushed his, and she snatched the card from him and stuck it into the pocket of her royal-blue windbreaker.

His lips twitched again and she gritted her teeth.

"I need to go too. Ms. Williams." He dipped his chin toward Kate, who smiled at him. He turned to Meryn. "Ms. O'Reilly. As I said before, be careful, please. And call me if there's anything you need." He walked back to his jeep and climbed inside.

Neither she nor Kate spoke until the vehicle had pulled back onto the pavement and disappeared down the road.

Then Kate spun toward her, eyes wide. "Meryn."

"Don't, Kate. Just don't." Meryn picked up both pails of berries and started down the shoulder of the road.

After a few steps, Kate caught up to her and grabbed her arm. "That was … that was …" She stopped, at a rare loss for words. "What was that?"

"That was the end of that."

"He couldn't take his eyes off you."

"Exactly. May I remind you that's his *job*, Kate? He's here to keep an eye on us. To make sure we stay in line. And if we don't, he'll arrest us. He's a soldier. The less we have to do with them, the better."

"I know. But—"

"No. No buts. He is here to keep us under control and is very clearly not one of us, which are reasons enough to stay away from him. Besides, even if he wasn't a soldier, you know I can't get involved with anyone."

Kate let go of her arm and set Gracie down on the shoulder of the road. After reaching for her daughter's hand, she started walking toward Meryn's home, moving at the pace of the toddler's tiny steps. "Do you really still believe that?"

"Of course I do. How could you even ask?"

"Because I'm pretty sure that at some point that stopped being a valid reason and started being an excuse."

Meryn bit back an angry retort. If she was going to take better control of her tongue, now was as good a time as any. "It's still a valid reason."

"So you aren't planning to call him?"

Meryn gaped at her. "Who?"

"Captain Christensen. Which, by the way, is a very interesting name, don't you think? Kind of like a sign."

"I believe that would be called ironic. And, no, of course I'm not going to call him. Why would I?"

"He did give you his card."

"For emergencies. There are plenty of other people I would call first if I needed something." She shook her head when Kate started to answer. "End of discussion, Kate. Things are what they are, and nothing is going to change that. And we better walk faster. It's almost dark. Here." She set down the pails and swung Gracie up over her head, settling her onto her shoulders.

Kate grabbed the pails. "Okay, fine. I'll drop it. For now."

"Thank you."

The three of them trudged toward her house in the waning daylight, their sneakers kicking up small clouds of dust as they walked. Meryn's gaze strayed down the road behind them where Captain Jesse Christensen's vehicle had disappeared.

It was an interesting last name, she had to admit. And it likely was some kind of a sign. A sign that there was trouble ahead, and not just the kind the soldier continued to warn her about.

Meryn quickened her pace. Thankfully, that was one kind of trouble, at least, that she *could* avoid.

Chapter Four

Jesse drove back toward the camp, fingers clenching the steering wheel of the jeep. He'd never in his life met anyone like Meryn O'Reilly. She had challenged every preconceived notion of what Christians were like from the moment he'd come face to face with her in the church basement. She was beautiful, sure, but it was more than that. Her spirit and fiery temper intrigued, amused, and terrified him in equal parts. If it flared up in an encounter with any of the other soldiers, especially Gallagher or one of his cronies ... well, Jesse didn't even want to contemplate what could happen.

He liked her friend also. It was entirely possible that Kate Williams did speak a little too freely, something she would have to learn to rein in if things got any tenser around here. *Still, I kind of like the openness and honesty.* Her daughter was adorable and had somehow risen in his estimation since he'd found out she didn't actually belong to Meryn.

He was going to have to keep an eye on her. Caleb would throttle him if he found out, and Meryn wouldn't exactly appreciate his attempts to protect her. Otherwise, it was a perfect plan.

His first step would be trying to convince her to move from that remote location closer to friends or family. Now that he knew she lived alone ...

He drummed his fingers on the steering wheel. His interest in that fact was simply concern for her safety, nothing more.

Yeah right, Christensen.

Jesse straightened in his seat. He really couldn't have any interest in the woman beyond that. He was here to do a job and, as she was very fond of pointing out, that job had to do with making sure that none of her people got out of line or were in any way living or acting outside of the constraints of the law. Developing a personal relationship with any of them, on any level, would only make his job that much harder.

Not that any of that matters. Given the way she looks at me, I'm pretty sure I'm the last man on earth she would ever voluntarily spend time with. He'd still be wondering what her name was if her friend hadn't spoken up and given it to him. Jesse laughed out loud at the memory of the look on Meryn's face when Kate had thrown that information out. Then he sobered. Meryn's comment about the family Bible had been funny, to him at least, but it also reminded him of the topic under discussion at Headquarters: the possibility of having the Christian Bible declared hate literature and the order given to confiscate and destroy all copies. Of all the distasteful things they'd had to do since arriving in the area, that would be by far the worst, and Jesse was keeping his fingers crossed that the motion would not pass.

She really does need to move somewhere safer, though.

Most of the soldiers were decent men and women who didn't particularly like this assignment any more than he or Caleb did. Some, though—namely Lieutenant Thomas Gallagher and his puppet followers—could get heady with power really fast, especially if alcohol was thrown into the mix, which it often was.

If they find out there's a beautiful woman living alone out in the middle of nowhere ... Jesse tightened his hold on the steering wheel as he drove through the gates of the temporary base camp the military had set up in a former psychiatric hospital and pulled into his parking spot. They would use the fact that she was a Christian to justify any acts that, in their little minds, would be teaching Meryn her place or showing her who was in charge.

Jesse sat for a couple of minutes, drawing in a few deep breaths, before he climbed out of the jeep. He started toward Caleb's room but stopped abruptly when he reached the door of the mess hall. Something stronger than the unappealing smell of over-cooked military food hung in the air. Whatever was going on, it wasn't good. All the wrong people were looking happy. Lieutenant Gallagher stood in line at the food counter, clutching an orange plastic tray. His two faithful lapdogs—Private Whittaker, known commonly as Whit or, to Jesse and Caleb, Half-Whit; and

Private Smallman, whose name they hadn't bothered to fool around with since it already suited him perfectly—tagged along behind. Gallagher said something to the other two over his shoulder, and the three of them burst out laughing.

Jesse scanned the room. In contrast to the lieutenant, most of the faces looked somber. Something was seriously wrong. He stalked past the entrance and headed for Caleb's quarters.

———•———

"Come in."

Jesse opened the door to Caleb's room and stepped inside. When the military had moved into this building a week ago, he and Caleb were given quarters that had previously been lounges for the psychiatric patients. The rooms were considerably more luxurious than either of them was used to, each having a floor-to-ceiling stone fireplace and a large window overlooking rolling, green hills. They were in the process of having the bars removed, but even through those, the view was pretty spectacular.

None of them knew how long they would be stationed there, but, as long as they were, he was going to enjoy the living arrangements.

Flames danced in Caleb's fireplace, but a chill hung in the air that had nothing to do with the fall weather.

The major stood in front of the window on the far side of the room. He glared at Jesse. "Where have you been?"

Jesse rubbed his palms along the sides of his camouflage pants. Something was definitely going on. "I was out patrolling. I told you I was going."

"Is your i-com off?" Caleb rounded the bed and stalked across the room to stand in front of him, planting both fists firmly on his hips.

Jesse pulled the unit out of the holder on his belt and peered down at it. "It's on vibrate. I guess I didn't feel it."

"Get it off that setting. When I need you, I expect to be able to get hold of you."

"What's going on here, Cale? Am I in trouble?"

Caleb exhaled loudly and ran a hand over his blond crew cut. "No. Sorry. For once it's not you." He waved a hand toward the two leather chairs in front of the fireplace.

Jesse reset his i-com to normal volume and shoved the unit, not much bigger than a credit card, back into the holder before taking one of the chairs.

Caleb dropped onto the other one. "The ruling went through."

"Which one?"

"About the Bibles. We're supposed to round up every copy we can find and dispose of them."

Heat roared through Jesse's chest. "You've got to be kidding me. These people have been nothing but cooperative since we arrived. No one we detained at the church knew anything about the bombings. In fact, there seems to be universal condemnation against the attacks. And they haven't complained too much about the curfew. Why is Command making us come down on them even harder than we already have?"

Caleb leaned back in his seat. "General Burns lost a nephew in the Montreal bombing. Apparently he's been on a rampage ever since, submitting proposal after proposal to the government on various ways to control the Christians and hopefully track down anyone who does know something about the bombings. This is the first one that has passed. So far. I guess the politicians felt like it might be the one that will cause the least outcry. I'm not entirely sure they're correct. Either way, we have to do it."

"When?"

"Twenty-one hundred hours."

Jesse's head shot up. "Tonight?"

"They want us to get to people before they hear about it and hide their Bibles." Caleb crossed an ankle over one knee. "It could have been worse. There was talk about taking all Internet-capable units too, but I think, for a change, reason actually prevailed there. The logistics of dealing with all those electronics are mind-boggling. It's a lot easier to implement the website-monitoring system and charge people who attempt to access what are, as of today, illegal faith-based sites. I.T. is already red-flagging anyone in this area who has visited a banned website, and we'll be sending someone out in the next few days to confiscate those units. People will learn pretty quickly that seeking out that kind of information online is not worth the risk."

"I don't like where this is going, Cale."

"I don't either, but don't tell anyone I said that. And do not repeat your concerns to anyone else. There are plenty around here that don't agree with us and would happily pass along our sentiments to Headquarters."

"Yeah. Gallagher and his buddies looked positively giddy in the mess hall tonight."

"No doubt. This sort of thing is right up their alley."

"Tell me more about these Horsemen. All I know is what I've heard on the news. Are they really a radical Christian group?"

Caleb ran the back of his fingers along his jaw. "New group we've never heard of. They claim to be Christian, although anybody can claim to be anything, of course."

"So you don't believe they are?"

Caleb dropped his hand. "You have more experience with those people than I do. What do you think? Is it feasible?"

"It doesn't seem that likely to me, but who knows? As a society, we've been pushing and pushing the Christians for years. Maybe a few of them decided it was time to push back."

"Well, they may regret it. Of course, it's unlikely to be the extremists who suffer, unfortunately, but the common people of faith. The Green Party is furious that all this has happened on their watch. Taking the Bibles is the first step. There are plenty more motions in the queue. The big one everyone's talking about is this Bill 1071, which sounds pretty ominous."

"In what way?"

"I don't know all the details yet, but it has to do with redefining what will now be considered hate crimes, and reclassifying them so they fall under the Terrorism Act. The bill apparently prescribes harsh new punishments for anyone charged under the act too."

"What, longer prison terms? The jails are already overcrowded and underfunded. How are they going to deal with that?"

A shadow passed over Caleb's face. "I haven't heard specifics, but I get the impression the new punishments may not involve prison sentences."

Jesse's stomach had been unsettled since he'd heard about the Bibles, but Caleb's words—and more than that, his delivery—stirred Jesse's uneasiness into a churning nausea. "What do you mean?"

His friend exhaled loudly. "I really don't know. I'm not even sure I want to know. But I'll tell you as soon as anyone passes along more information to me."

Jesse nodded. "So what's the plan for tonight?"

Caleb grabbed a file folder from the table between them and flipped it open. "There's been a steady decline in the number of churches in Kingston over the past twenty years or so. In 2010 there were more than forty. Now there are seventeen, mostly small to medium ones. Not sure why."

"Same as all over. My dad believed the church was dying out because the teaching had become so watered down it was pretty much useless. Personally, I think it had more to do with the huge drop-off in giving when the government revoked the Christian churches' charitable status thirty years ago."

"That'll do it." Caleb's smile was cynical as he ran a finger over the city map. "As you know, we've requisitioned membership lists from each of the churches. Based on that information, we've marked every home on these maps where church members live, and we'll need to get to every one between twenty-one hundred and twenty-four hundred hours."

"A three-hour plan? Are we going through the houses or letting them bring the Bibles out themselves?"

"Given the time constraints, I'm ordering the residents bring them out."

"Good. I'm much more comfortable with letting them come to us. What do we do if we suspect they haven't brought them all or if they won't do what we ask?"

Caleb shifted in his seat. "Then we do the search ourselves. If we find any Bibles they haven't given us, we arrest them and bring them in. We have to set a precedent now that we expect full compliance, or there will be serious repercussions."

Jesse nodded. *Meryn.* She was not going to be happy about soldiers showing up at her door. *And I doubt she'll have a problem letting whoever is demanding she give them her Bible know it.* "Can I see the map?"

Caleb shrugged and handed him the folder.

Jesse scanned the sheet of paper, feeling his friend's eyes on him as he did. He'd been hoping to be assigned her house, but two other soldiers, both decent guys, had her area.

At least Gallagher wouldn't be going to her place. Not tonight, anyway.

He set the folder back on the table and stood up. "Looks like you have everything organized. I'm going to get some dinner. You coming?"

Caleb crossed his arms. Even sitting, his large chest and six-foot-four-inch frame were imposing. "Where did you say you were this afternoon?"

"Out patrolling. Checking to make sure everything looked okay."

"And did she?"

He blinked. "Did who what?"

"The girl you're not supposed to be going anywhere near. Did she look okay?"

Jesse sighed and sat back down, submitting to the inevitable. "Seriously, how do you do that?"

"It's a gift," Caleb said dryly. "So?"

"So, yeah, she looked okay. I didn't go searching for her, by the way. I was driving on one of the back roads and came across her and her friend."

"Was her daughter with her?"

Jesse straightened in his chair. "You know, we could talk about girls later tonight at the slumber party. It might be a better use of our time to grab something to eat now and get ready to head out."

Caleb didn't answer.

Jesse held out as long as possible under his penetrating stare. "The same little girl was with her, yes, but it turns out she's the friend's daughter, not hers."

"Interesting. And what were they doing out in the middle of nowhere that close to dusk?"

"She lives out there."

Caleb raised an eyebrow. "With this friend?"

"No, she lives alone."

He dropped his arms and reached for the folder. "Show me."

Jesse found the place on the map and pointed to it. "She's got a bit of a temper, and she's not particularly fond of soldiers."

Caleb let out a short laugh. "Shocker. Will she give them trouble tonight?"

"I hope not. I checked to make sure it wasn't Gallagher or any of his buddies going out there, but Carson and Dettmer are okay."

"Well, if they do bring her in, at least I won't have to sit here wondering where you are while you're out scouring the countryside looking for her."

"I wasn't ..." Jesse's indignant reply died when he saw the grin on Caleb's face. "I know nothing can happen between us, not just because you've forbidden it, *Dad*, but because a military guy is the last person on earth she would want to get involved with. That's fine. But I'm still worried about her living way out there by herself. If things get any worse and the wrong people find out, really bad things could happen."

Caleb cocked his head, appraising him, before blowing out his breath. "Fine. Drive by there once in a while. Keep an eye on the place. But I want your word you won't do anything more than that or go out of your way to make contact with her. If you get caught, there will be serious consequences. And not just from me. I need you by my side here, Jess, and I need you to be one-hundred-percent focused. Understood?"

"Understood. Thanks, Cale."

"Don't make me regret it."

"I won't. Now, can we go get this debacle over with?"

"Take it easy. We're both going to have to quit talking like that. Until the government finds whoever carried out the bombings and shuts them down, things are going to get worse before they get better." Caleb tossed the folder onto the table and stood up. "A lot of people could go down. And if we don't want to go down with them, we're going to have to keep our mouths closed and do our jobs." Caleb held out his hand and pulled Jesse to his feet, then clapped him on the back a couple of times. "We can do this, Jess. Together."

Jesse had lost track of the number of times Caleb had said those words to him over the years. A slow ache spread through his chest. The difference in this case was that, for the first time ever, he couldn't help wondering if they really were true.

CHAPTER FIVE

"Wow." Meryn stood back to survey the half dozen jars of jam lined up on her counter, deep purple against the blue-and-white-striped wallpaper of the big farmhouse kitchen. "I had no idea such a thing was even possible."

Kate held her jam-covered fingers under the tap. "You did know that someone somewhere had to make the jam that's sitting on the store shelves, didn't you?"

"I assumed it was robots working in a factory somewhere in Mexico."

Kate shook the water off her fingers and reached for the towel hanging over the handle of the stove. "How could you have lived on the planet this long and still not have learned—"

A pounding on the front door cut her off.

Both women stared at the entranceway off the kitchen.

Darkness had fallen soon after they had returned from picking berries, but they'd been hard at work the last couple of hours, and Meryn hadn't had a chance to flip on the porch light yet. She peered through the glass in the door but couldn't make out who it was.

"Army! Open up!" The sharp command carried through the open kitchen window.

A knot formed in her stomach. "What do they want now?"

Kate replaced the towel. "There's only one way to find out. Open the door before they kick it down."

Meryn drew in a calming breath. She pulled the door open as the soldier on the other side, dressed in camouflage from head to foot, with a rifle slung over his shoulder, raised a fist to pound on it again. Behind him, a second soldier, face hard and cold, held open the screen door.

Clearly this was not a social call.

"Meryn O'Reilly?"

"Yes."

The first man held out an i-com. The symbol for the Department of National Defence dominated the top third of the screen.

Meryn bit her lip as she studied the warrant and the logo above it. A golden circle surrounded a red maple leaf with two crossed swords behind it. A large red-and-gold crown sat on top of the circle, and beneath it, five golden maple leaves climbed each of the sides, the words *Vigilamus pro Te*—we stand on guard for thee—written across them. The logo was impressive and as intimidating as it was no doubt intended to be.

The soldier pulled back the i-com. "We have orders to confiscate all Bibles from this residence."

Kate gasped, an echo of Meryn's own shock and horror at the soldier's pronouncement.

Please, God, not my Bible. Meryn glared at him. "If I refuse?"

"Then we will search the residence and seize the items, and you will be arrested, taken to jail, and held indefinitely. To comply fully is mandatory, and failure to do so will place you in breach of the law."

A few choice words about a law that stripped citizens of their rights and freedoms sprang to Meryn's lips. She took a step forward.

Kate came up beside her and laid a hand on her arm. "Why don't you gentlemen come in?" She pulled the door open wider.

Meryn moved back when the man stepped into the doorway.

He looked at Kate. "And you are?"

"Kate Williams."

"Do you live here as well?"

"No. I live in town with my husband and children."

"Address?"

When Kate gave it to him, he typed it into his i-com and scanned the screen before shoving the unit into the holder. "Is your husband at home?"

"Yes."

"All right, then." His attention shifted back to Meryn. "Your Bibles?"

"Let's go, Meryn. I'll help you." Kate turned to the men and waved a hand toward the kitchen chairs. "Do you want to make yourselves comfortable?"

"Thank you, ma'am, we're fine here."

The second soldier pulled the screen door closed, and the two of them stood just inside the kitchen, hands clasped behind their backs.

Shaking her head, Meryn followed Kate out of the room and up the stairs. She waited until they were in her bedroom before she grabbed her friend's arm and hissed, "What are you doing?"

Kate's eyes were filled with sadness. "I'm trying to keep us out of jail, Meryn. What good would it do to resist and be arrested? They'll still take our Bibles, and we'll be locked up. I can't do that to Ethan and Gracie and Matthew. Maybe we can lodge a protest or file some kind of complaint, find a way to get our Bibles back, but for now we have to do what they say."

Meryn clenched her fists. Kate was right, but it galled her to give in so easily to demands that clearly denied them their rights to their own property.

"We're not called to insist on our rights, Mer," Kate said, as though she'd read Meryn's thoughts, "but to submit to authority and trust that God will ultimately put things right."

The calm strength in the words, and the truth she couldn't deny in them, unclenched Meryn's fists, and she stumbled toward the table next to her four-poster bed. She blinked back tears of grief as she picked up her Bible and reverently ran a hand over the worn cover. "I can't do it, Kate. I can't give it up." Meryn clutched the book to her chest.

"Then I will."

For a few seconds Meryn didn't move, then she reluctantly held out the Bible.

Kate took it and walked back out of the room.

Meryn started down the stairs behind her friend. Her Bible. That was a loss beyond measuring. She only wished she had studied more, learned more, committed more of it to memory before it was taken from her.

Without a word, Kate walked over to the soldiers and held out the Bible.

The one who had knocked on the door reached for it, then handed it to the man beside him. "Are there any others in the house?"

"No. I only have ... *had* one." When their eyes met, Meryn held his gaze, willing him to believe her so she could avoid an invasive search of her home. Gracie was asleep in a bedroom upstairs, and the last thing Meryn wanted was for her to be woken up by soldiers barging into the room.

He tapped a finger on the rifle.

The sudden realization that, despite the gruffness of his manner, he was not entirely comfortable with what was going on gave her a little comfort.

Finally, he nodded curtly. "Then we're done here."

Kate nudged her in the ribs. When Meryn looked at her, she jerked her head in the direction of the jars of jam.

"You've got to be kidding me." She could feel the soldiers' eyes on her as Kate raised her eyebrows, refusing to look away from her heated stare. Meryn exhaled loudly. "Fine." She turned back to the soldiers. "We've been carrying out the extremely subversive act of making jam." When Kate jabbed her in the side again, she winced and forced a sweetness she didn't feel into her voice. "Could we offer you a jar to take with you?"

Both the men looked surprised and a little uncertain about whether they should accept her offering.

Meryn stomped to the counter. She grabbed a jar of the jam, returned to the door, and thrust it into the hand of the soldier who had handed off her Bible. "Here you go. Enjoy."

He still looked unsure but did take the jar. "Thank you. We will. We don't get this type of thing in the mess hall, that's for sure."

"Here. Take one for Captain Christensen too." Kate walked up beside her and held out a jar toward the other man.

"Kate!" Horrified, Meryn practically spat out the word.

Her friend smiled and kept her gaze on the soldier.

He took the jar from her, dipping his head in her direction. "Thank you. I'm sure he'll appreciate it."

Both soldiers left without another word.

Meryn waited until they pulled out of her driveway before shutting the door and leaning against the back of it. "Really? Jam?"

"It's called heaping coals, Meryn. I'm hoping every bite they take makes them feel guiltier and guiltier about what they're doing to us." Kate flounced over to the table and settled her slender body onto a kitchen chair.

"Kate!" Meryn pressed her lips together to hold back a laugh.

"What?" Her friend's hazel eyes widened in feigned innocence. "It's biblical."

"The sentiment might be, but I seriously doubt the smugness is." She flipped the lock on the door. "Honestly, only you could make me laugh at a time like this. What would I do without you?"

"Go to jail, I'm sure. You looked like you were about to tell those men where they could put that i-com they were shoving in your face."

"That's exactly what I was going to do." Meryn rubbed a hand across her forehead and groaned. "I guess it wouldn't have been the smartest move, but it would have made me feel a whole lot better. Temporarily, at least." She walked over to the table and sat down on a chair beside Kate. "But why on earth did you have to give them a jar for Captain Christensen? He'll get the entirely wrong idea if he thinks it was me that sent it to him."

"It's jam, Mer." Kate reached over and squeezed her hand. "He was kind to us and we're thanking him, that's all."

Meryn exhaled. "I hope that's all he thinks."

"It's too late to change anything now, so don't waste time worrying about it."

Meryn steadied herself on the back of a chair as a new thought occurred to her. "The store. Do you think they'll take all the Bibles from there too?" She always stocked quite a few Bibles of various versions and a lot of other books on the Christian faith, which she suspected would no longer be allowed either.

Kate gazed at her. "Probably, Mer. I don't see them taking our personal Bibles away but leaving more in the store for us to replace them with."

"I could go in early and hide them. Or some of them, at least."

"You could try. As long as you understand the risk you're taking."

Kate's i-com vibrated on the kitchen table and she picked it up and looked at the screen. "It's Ethan. He's checking to make sure we're all right. Soldiers came by our house too. I should call him."

"Of course."

Kate stood up. "After I talk to him, I'll check on Gracie. Then maybe we can watch a movie. At least they left us the TV."

"So far." Meryn gave her a wry smile. After Kate left the room, Meryn sat staring at the door the soldiers had gone out, taking her most valuable possession with them. *What will they do with my Bible, with all the Bibles—burn them?* Meryn pressed a fist to her mouth. She didn't want to know about it if they did.

The idea was too horrifying. Such an act would have to signal an irreversible downslide of their lives, and of their country, wouldn't it?

Meryn dropped her face into her hands.

Of course the downslide would be irreversible. She'd read the whole book before they'd taken it away from her. She knew how it ended, with all things restored and, as Kate had reminded her, put right again.

But she also knew—and the thought contracted the muscles in her stomach until she almost gasped from the pain—that before that end came, things were going to get very, very bad.

And losing her Bible was just the start.

CHAPTER SIX

Jesse nudged his tray through the breakfast lineup. Nothing looked appealing. His stomach still hadn't settled from a night of pounding on people's doors and demanding they hand over the item that meant the most to them in the world. Sometimes he really hated his job, and never more so than last night.

When he had finally crawled into bed, well after midnight, he'd tossed and turned for hours, trying to wipe the image of sad, accusing eyes out of his mind.

Now he surveyed the various food offerings and moved past sausages lying in grease and undercooked eggs to grab a couple of pieces of dry toast. At least the coffee smelled strong. He filled a mug nearly to the brim and carried his tray around the crowded tables, nodding in response to several greetings as he passed by.

As he'd suspected it would be, the mood in the room was mostly subdued. Normally Jesse ate in the officers' dining hall, but today he felt the need to be with others who felt the way he did.

Dettmer and Carson, the men who had been assigned the territory that included Meryn's house, sat at a table on the far side of the room. He made his way toward them, his heart rate picking up.

Raids had taken place across the country, and, according to this morning's report, the national arrest total was a little over nine hundred. Thankfully, in this area, only six people had been brought in, all of them men. Jesse had scanned the list for Meryn's name and didn't see it. Still, he was dying to know how things had gone at her place.

"Captain." Private Dettmer dipped his chin toward his chest.

Private Carson gestured toward an empty seat. "Want to join us, sir?"

"Thanks." Jesse set down his tray and settled onto the chair. His eyes narrowed at the sight of two jars of jam on the table. Definitely not army issue. "So, gentlemen, how did it go last night?" He took a sip of the hot, black coffee.

Carson and Dettmer shared a glance.

"What is it? Did you run into problems?"

"No, sir." Dettmer picked up a piece of toast he'd smeared with the blackberry jam and looked at it, then set it back down on his plate.

"It's all right, you can speak freely."

Dettmer grimaced. "It didn't seem right somehow, taking things from those people. Most of them looked so upset. Some of them even cried. It ... didn't feel right."

Jesse set down his coffee. "I understand. I didn't enjoy it either. But we had our orders, and we had to follow them. We were doing our jobs. And you should know now that it's only likely to get harder, so you're going to have to find a way to deal with that."

"Yes, sir," Dettmer mumbled. "Oh, and we got in pretty late last night, and the storage room door was locked. We'll transfer the boxes of Bibles there right after breakfast."

Jesse tapped his fingers on the table. "I'm sure that's a lot of boxes. I'll come by and help you." He looked across the table at Carson. "Did anyone give you a hard time?"

"Not really. Like Dettmer said, they were all pretty unhappy about us showing up at their doors. A few got mad, but no one was aggressive or anything. One of them even gave us this jam." Carson pointed at the jars on the table.

"Really? Who was that?" Jesse sipped from his mug.

"I don't remember her name. Something different. She lives in a big, old farmhouse in the country by herself, although there was another woman there with her last night."

His stomach muscles tightened. Meryn? She and Kate had been picking blackberries when he ran into them ... "And she wasn't upset when you took her Bible?"

Another look passed between the two men before Carson grinned. "Oh yeah, she was upset. I thought for sure she was going to lose it, because she was so mad when we told her what we were doing there. Lucky for her, the other woman came over and calmed her down. She's the one who invited us in, convinced the one who lived there to give us what we asked for, then made her give us the jam."

"Made her?"

"Yeah, it was her friend's idea. She didn't want to do it, but then she marched over and grabbed a jar, shoved it in my hand, and told me to enjoy it. Although I don't think that's what she wanted to tell me to do with it."

Jesse repressed a grin of his own. *That all sounds about right.*

"She was pretty funny. The window was open when we walked up, and the two of them were talking about how they'd made the jam themselves. She said she didn't even know such a thing was possible; she'd always thought it was made by robots somewhere in Mexico or something."

Jesse chuckled.

"Oh hey," Carson palmed the unopened jar and held it toward him. "This one's for you, actually."

Jesse blinked. "Me?"

"Yeah, the friend, the redhead, asked us to give it to you."

Ah. Kate. Jesse fought off a twinge of disappointment and took the jar. "Thanks."

Dettmer picked up his fork. "You know the ones we're talking about, then?"

"I've run into them a couple of times, yes."

"So you know their ... situation?"

"Their situation?"

"Yeah, I mean, are they available? The redhead mentioned a husband, but we were thinking the one with the dark hair must be single, since she lives out there alone."

Jesse set the jar down on the table with a thud. "Do I need to remind you both that we are here to keep an eye on the Christians, to ensure that they are not involved in subversive activities that threaten national security? We are not here to fraternize with them, and we're certainly not here to harass them with unwanted attention. Do I make myself clear?"

"Excellent advice."

Carson and Dettmer scrambled to their feet.

Jesse's face warmed. Behind him, someone called out, "Room, attention!"

Chairs scraped across the floor as everyone stood. Jesse mentally kicked himself for sitting with his back to the door and not seeing Caleb come in.

"Gentlemen, if you've finished your breakfast, I'd like to see you in my office. And bring the jam." Caleb clapped a hand on Jesse's shoulder. "Join us, Captain."

"Yes, sir." He picked up his tray and went out the mess hall door behind Caleb.

The major unlocked his office door.

Jesse waved the other two in ahead of him, then shut the door with his free hand. He set his tray down on a small table between two leather chairs.

Caleb walked around to the far side of his desk and planted both palms on the surface. "Did I hear you say that someone gave you that jam last night?"

Jesse's eyes narrowed at the sternness in his voice.

Carson and Dettmer looked suddenly nervous as well.

Dettmer spoke up first. "Yes, sir. Two women in a house out in the country. They offered us a jar and sent one back for Captain Christensen."

Caleb's mouth tightened. "I realize it seems like a small thing, but accepting gifts of any kind from people we are here to control sets an extremely dangerous precedent. If word were to get back to Headquarters, you could be charged with accepting a bribe, which, regardless of the value of the item, is a serious offence that could result in a court-martial. And I would really hate to see that happen to either of you."

Jesse focused on the two men, whose faces paled.

"We're sorry, sir," Dettmer said. "It won't happen again."

"See that it doesn't. Have you mentioned this to anyone else?"

"No, sir."

"Good." Caleb pushed himself away from the desk. "Leave the jars here so no one asks you any questions. As long as the two of you promise not to let this get around, I think we can let it rest."

"Thank you, sir." Carson sounded so relieved Jesse almost smiled.

"You're welcome. The two of you are dismissed. Captain, a word, please."

Dettmer set his jar of jam on Caleb's desk, then strode out of the office behind Carson.

Jesse shut the door behind them and walked back to the desk. Both eyebrows rose as he set his jar down beside the other one. "Bribery? Really? It was a jar of jam."

Caleb dropped onto his chair. "I don't care about the jam. What I do care about is not letting it get around that two of the Christians sent a gift here specifically for you."

Jesse lowered himself onto the leather chair behind him. "Ah. That's what that was about."

"What, you're surprised that I was cleaning up after you? That is what I spend ninety percent of my time doing, you know."

Jesse grinned. "I know. And I appreciate it."

"You'd better. I just hope I made those two nervous enough about the possible consequences of their actions that they'll keep their mouths shut."

"Oh, I'm pretty sure you did that. They both went as white as fresh snow when you mentioned the word 'court-martial.'"

"Good."

"You know ..." Jesse pointed at the jars on the desk. "That does look like good jam. Seems a shame to waste it."

"I suppose so. I thought about making you return it, but I didn't really want to hand you the opportunity to—how did you put it?—fraternize or harass the Christians with unwanted attention."

"What makes you think it would be unwanted?"

Caleb gave him a dark look. "Not helping yourself, smart mouth."

"I rarely do. Here." Jesse moved his tray onto Caleb's desk so they could share the food he'd brought.

Caleb reached for the jar that had been opened. He spread some on a piece of toast, and they both ate in silence until Caleb looked up. "This is really good. Glad something positive has finally come out of your insubordination."

"Hey," Jesse protested. "Other than letting them go at the church, I've done what you told me to. I haven't made any attempts to see her. It wasn't my fault I ran into her yesterday. And incidentally, I prefer the term 'creatively subordinate' to 'insubordinate.' It sounds so much better."

Caleb snorted. "'Creatively subordinate.' Someday, when you're facing a court-martial—and I'm convinced it's only a matter of time—I can't wait to hear you make that argument to the committee. There's nothing the army loves more than a defence that uses the word 'creative' in reference to the ability to follow orders. You'll be in jail before the words are out of your mouth."

Jesse shoved the last corner of toast into his mouth. "I'll leave you to dream about that day. Some of us have work to do."

Caleb cocked his head. "Does this *work* involve your sudden penchant for patrolling the outskirts of the town?"

"No. I'm helping Dettmer and Carson move boxes of Bibles into the storage room. Then mostly desk work today. Feel free to check my office any time to make sure I'm not violating the conditions of my parole or anything."

"Technically, you're not on parole, but I'm sure that's just a matter of time too."

Shaking his head, Jesse moved toward the door. Halfway across the room he stopped, spun around, and tromped back to the desk. He snatched up the unopened jar of jam, then left the room without another word, Caleb's laughter echoing behind him.

CHAPTER SEVEN

A fresh loaf was baking in the bread maker. Meryn tilted back her head and inhaled deeply, letting the warm, fragrant aroma waft over her. "Mmm, Kate. I love when you come to visit. All the appliances I own and have no idea what to do with finally get used."

"I know. For a non-cook, you have the best-stocked kitchen I've ever seen. It's maddening. Where did all this stuff come from?"

"My parents, mostly. Mom's such a good cook, I think she's still hoping her genes will surface in me one of these days."

"We're all hoping that." Kate set a sippy cup in front of Gracie. "So what are you going to do about the Bibles in the store?"

"I'll try to get some out." Meryn poured cream into her coffee and stirred it absently. She'd tried in vain to stem the frenetic flow of her thoughts so she could fall asleep the night before. Finally, she'd given up and flopped onto her back with a heavy sigh. Hiding the Bibles was a huge risk. Rumours had been flying about a new bill before Parliament that included a long list of mainly faith-based activities. If it passed, those activities would be considered hate crimes.

Taking the Bibles out of the store and attempting to smuggle them to believers would likely be classified as such a crime. Still, some time before dawn she'd decided she couldn't stand by and do nothing.

"Really? Even though you could be arrested?" The gold flecks in Kate's hazel eyes shimmered with concern as she contemplated Meryn.

"I know. I thought about that." She outlined a blue flower on the plastic tablecloth with one finger. "But, Kate, we are in desperate need of Bibles, and I'm the only one with access to the ones in the store, which might be the last ones in town. I know it's risky, but I can't let them come and take them away. Not if there's anything I can do to save at least some of them."

"What will you do with them?"

"I'm not sure. I'll bring them back here and hide them for now, I guess, but we'll have to pass them out as soon as possible."

Bright sunlight streamed past the lace curtains hanging on the window above the sink.

How was it possible they were having this conversation?

"Ethan and I will help."

"I don't know if you should. What about Gracie and Matthew?"

"We can't stand by and do nothing. God will protect us, and if we are arrested, the kids can go to Ethan's parents. God will take care of them too."

Meryn swallowed the last of her coffee and stood. "Let's not worry about it until I find out if I can get in there and get the Bibles out before any of the soldiers show up."

Kate gave her a quick hug. "Gracie and I are going to head back home. Call me and let me know what happens."

"I will. Thanks for breakfast."

———•———

Meryn turned onto the main street of town and drove toward her store. She needed a plan and a quick, efficient way of distributing the Bibles. They couldn't be in her house for long, and even if she—

Four soldiers leaned against the wall outside the store, all dressed in full camouflage gear, green berets on their heads.

Her foot eased off the gas pedal. What should she do? If she didn't show up today, maybe they would give up and head back to their base, and she could go in later and get the Bibles.

Meryn sighed. Somehow she doubted the soldiers would give up entirely. If they did go, they would probably leave one person behind to keep an eye on the store. Either that or they would smash the lock on the door and go in and help themselves to whatever they wanted. Under the current martial law, rights she'd always taken for granted appeared to have been set aside in the interests of "the greater good." Gritting her teeth,

Meryn pulled up to the curb and put the car into park. Maybe if she kept her mouth shut and cooperated, they'd let her keep some of the books.

When she got out and slammed the door a little harder than necessary, all four soldiers straightened and watched her approach. She stopped a few feet in front of them. "Can I help you?"

A female soldier stepped forward. "I'm Second Lieutenant Bronson, ma'am. Are you the owner of this store?"

"Yes."

The soldier pulled out her i-com and flashed the warrant with the Department of National Defence logo printed across the top at her.

I am really starting to hate that gold crown and circle.

"We have orders to search the premises and confiscate any contraband materials."

"Contraband?"

"Yes, ma'am. Bibles, religious books, that sort of thing. As I'm sure you are aware, those types of materials are no longer permitted."

"Yes, I am aware. I became aware when some of your colleagues pounded on my door last night and *confiscated* my personal property."

The woman shifted from one foot to the other but didn't drop her gaze.

Meryn grudgingly admired that, even as she took it as a bad sign.

"Would you open the door, please?"

For a few seconds Meryn didn't move, then she pulled a set of keys from her pocket and walked toward the entry. The sound of bells jingling softly didn't bring her pleasure like it usually did.

The four soldiers followed her inside.

So much for trying to sneak any of the Bibles out. Meryn waited until the last person had come inside before shoving the door shut behind them, the bells jangling out a discordant tune at the abrupt movement.

The woman gestured toward the shelves. "It would minimize the intrusion to your business if you showed us the books we're looking for. Otherwise, we will be forced to go through the store and search through all the shelves ourselves, which will result in a greater disruption to the system you have in place."

So either she took them to the Christian book section, or they would tear the place apart. Meryn stormed over to the set of shelves in front of the large picture window, the wood flooring creaking beneath her feet. "I believe these four shelves here"—she waved a hand through the air—"contain the *contraband* materials you're looking for."

"Do you have any boxes?"

She whirled to face the female officer, who had come up behind her. "Should I pack them up and deliver them to you as well?"

One of the soldiers behind her snickered, but the woman shot him a look that silenced him, before turning back to Meryn. "That won't be necessary. We brought some boxes with us, but you have more items than we had anticipated. If you don't have any we can use, or if you refuse to get them for us, one of the men will go back to the base and get some, but that will mean we are here that much longer."

Meryn spoke through clenched teeth. "I have some in the back."

The woman jerked her head, and two of the men fell into step behind Meryn as she walked toward the rear of the store.

The soft, plush armchairs hidden in out-of-the-way corners and the musty smell of old books neatly lining antique shelves had always filled her with peace. Today, though, that peace lay shattered in the pit of her stomach.

When the soldiers returned, arms filled with empty boxes, Meryn left them to their work and moved behind the counter. She thrust her hands into the pockets of her windbreaker, and her fingers closed around a small piece of paper.

Captain Christensen's business card. Meryn pursed her lips as she tapped the card against the counter. *Should I call him?* She shook her head. The last thing she wanted was to owe the captain anything.

Besides, what would he be able to do? There was no way he could come in and countermand a government order, one that he may even have given to his subordinates.

Meryn shoved the card back into her pocket.

The second lieutenant came and stood on the other side of the counter. "You've been very cooperative. Thank you."

Meryn bit back a sharp retort. "You are taking a sizeable amount of my inventory, which represents a large percentage of my annual budget. Will the army be compensating me for my losses?"

The woman met her gaze, appraising her. When she spoke, her voice carried a hint of steel. "As your *losses* are comprised of what are now illegal and banned items, compensating you for them would be equivalent to us offering to purchase the drugs we've confiscated from a dealer."

"Do you honestly believe those scenarios to be equivalent?" Meryn forced calm into her voice.

The soldier responded with matching control. "According to the new law, yes. The only difference is that, because you have not resisted, we will not be forced to take you in, which is going to have to be compensation enough. You should know, though, that if you attempt to replace the materials we have removed, you will be arrested and prosecuted to the fullest extent of the law, and your store will be permanently shut down. Do you understand?"

"Yes."

"Then we will get out of your way." The soldier offered her a curt nod before following the other three out the door with the last of the boxes. Meryn hadn't seen any jeeps on the main street. They must have parked on a side street, out of sight, which didn't seem entirely fair to her.

Of course, nothing about what had happened the last few days seemed fair, but no one—especially not the Canadian Army—appeared to care about that in the slightest.

Well, maybe Captain Christensen does, but there's really nothing he can do about it either. Meryn sighed. *All of this is bigger than any of us.*

She did need to remember that. And it wouldn't hurt to keep Kate's admonition in mind either, that they weren't called to insist on their rights, but rather to submit to authority and trust that God would take care of the rest. *Maybe I should have that stitched onto a wall hanging to stick up by the cash register.* Meryn grinned wryly. *Would the next soldier through the door consider that a contraband item now too?*

Her gaze lingered on the solid oak entrance to the store. *Is there any chance the next soldier through the door could be Captain Christensen?* With a small shake of her head, Meryn shoved that thought away.

The soldiers were here to control and contain them, not to be their friends. Any further interaction with the captain could only cause problems, for her and for him.

And since he was the one who had told her to do everything she could to avoid trouble, it was time to take his advice and put him out of her mind for good.

CHAPTER EIGHT

Jesse hadn't had a day off in almost two weeks. After a quick breakfast in the officers' hall, he headed out for a run. It was a beautiful November day, and he pushed himself hard, trying to clear his mind of everything that had happened in the weeks they had been stationed here. Jesse ran until his navy T-shirt clung to his back and his breath grew ragged.

Unfortunately for him, the memories he was working the hardest to get out of his mind were the ones that only seemed to grow larger and more prominent with every slap of his running shoes against the hard dirt shoulder of the road. Finally, he slowed to a jog and then to a walk, hands resting on his hips as he waited for his heart rate to lower. The problem was the thoughts that overwhelmed him—of Meryn O'Reilly and her flashing blue eyes—elevated that rate again every time it started to approach resting speed.

What is wrong with me? I barely know the woman. He hadn't seen her in over a month, but he still couldn't seem to get her out of his mind. And he needed to. Her faith was not only a barrier between them, but set him up as an opponent to everything she believed and the way she lived her life. His course seemed obvious. Clearly he should stay as far away from her as he possibly could.

There were plenty of other soldiers who could deal with her if she got herself into trouble. He rolled one shoulder and then the other, loosening them up.

A cool breeze whispered across his damp skin. As he started back toward the base at a jog, he drank in the sight of the maple trees lining both sides of the road, their red, yellow, and orange leaves rustling in the wind.

The sound of gravel crunching beneath shoes up ahead brought his gaze back down to the road. His chest tightened as he recognized the soldier jogging toward him: Lieutenant Gallagher. So much for a relaxing run in the country. He slowed his pace to a walk again as the lieutenant drew close, and Gallagher did the same.

"Captain." The nod and the title were protocol, but the smirk that seemed a permanent feature on Gallagher's face undermined any hint of respect.

"Lieutenant." Jesse stopped and swiped his arm across his forehead.

"Things seem to be going well here, don't you think?"

Jesse shrugged. "As well as can be expected, I guess."

"What do you mean?"

"Any time you start imposing new rules on people, there's going to be some resistance."

"We may need to bear down and deal with that resistance. Make it clear it won't be tolerated."

Jesse's eyes narrowed. Maybe he should suggest to Caleb that they build a boxing ring on the base. Nothing would give him more pleasure than going a few rounds with Gallagher and relieving the festering irritation that tunneled holes in his stomach lining whenever he was forced to deal with the man. "Meaning?"

"It's essential these Christians understand right from the start who's in charge here, whatever that takes."

"I think the people understand that. The resistance I mentioned has been the odd rumbling here and there, nothing serious."

Gallagher grasped an elbow and stretched his arm over his head. "That's where you and I differ, Captain. I look down the road and see where those odd rumblings will lead to full-blown rebellion if they're allowed to percolate. Stamping out minor resistance immediately and decisively leads to complete submission and has things running smoothly that much faster and more long-term. That's just good leadership, as far as I'm concerned."

Jesse counted to ten in his head to keep from reaching out and smacking the smug look off the lieutenant's face. "I'll take your suggestion to the major and see what he thinks."

"I'm sure you will." Gallagher stretched his other arm over his head. "In the meantime, we can pass the time enjoying the view around here, can't we?"

"The view?"

"Yeah. Some of these women are quite attractive. Not a good idea to get involved, I know, but it doesn't hurt to look, does it?"

Jesse drew in a long breath. There were lots of women in town. Chances of him referring to either Meryn or Kate were slim, but he still didn't like the insinuation. "That's where you and I differ again, Lieutenant. I look down the road and see where seemingly harmless looking leads inevitably to full-blown trouble. Stamping out that kind of behaviour immediately and decisively leads to long-term mutual respect. That's just common decency, as far as I'm concerned."

The smirk on Gallagher's face intensified to something darker. "Of course, Captain. Enjoy the rest of your run." The lieutenant took off down the road.

Jesse mentally kicked himself. As low a life as the man was, they did have to work together. He really had to stop taking the bait every time Gallagher dangled it.

Jesse covered the rest of the distance back to the base at a slow jog.

———•———

After showering and changing, Jesse straightened up his quarters and did some of the paperwork he'd been putting off until he had a bit of free time. It was supposed be a relaxing catch-up day, but he found himself pacing the room or standing and staring out the window often, his thoughts restless.

Finally, he gave up. He strode down the hall to the library and scanned the shelves. Most of the books there were ones he had donated from his own collection, and he couldn't find a single title to capture his attention. Jesse ran a hand over his head in frustration. What he needed was a new book, or maybe an old favourite, something to take his mind off everything—and everyone—he didn't want to be thinking about.

"Hungry?"

He spun around.

Caleb stood behind him, a tray in each hand.

The aroma wafting from the steaming plates reminded Jesse that he hadn't bothered with lunch, and his stomach rumbled. "I am, actually."

Caleb jerked his head in the direction of the two dark-blue armchairs in front of the window. Jesse made himself comfortable as his friend set the trays down on the coffee table in front of them.

"Thanks." Jesse reached over and grabbed a plate that was loaded with roast chicken, mashed potatoes, and mixed vegetables. For a moment he looked down at it, a sudden urge to say grace flooding through him. His head jerked. *Where did that come from?* He hadn't prayed over a meal since he was a kid.

A vivid picture of his father, head bowed over his dinner, flashed through his mind.

Jesse leaned back in his seat with a sigh. The decision to turn his back on the faith he'd been raised with had hurt his parents, but he couldn't buy into what they believed. And he couldn't pretend that he had, not even for them.

"I thought you were hungry."

He looked over at Caleb, who was studying him, a quizzical look on his face. "I am." Jesse lifted a fork halfway to his mouth, then set it down again. "I was."

"What's up, Jess? You haven't been yourself for days."

"I don't know. I'm not sure what's bothering me."

"Aren't you?"

Jesse shifted in his seat. "Okay, I am. I need a good book to read, and there's nothing around here I haven't already read a dozen times."

Caleb let out a short laugh. "Yeah, I'm sure that's it."

"I think I'll head into town after dinner and check out that bookstore on the main street. It might be open later tonight since it's Friday."

"Okay, I get it. You don't want to talk about it. But I'm here when you do, okay?"

"I know. Thanks." Jesse was able to get down a few bites before leaning back in his chair. "I ran into Gallagher today."

Caleb grimaced. "Please, make my day and tell me you were driving one of the tanks at the time."

Jesse laughed, something he hadn't done for a while. "Unfortunately not. I saw him while I was out for my run."

"That does at least partly explain the mood you're in."

He frowned. "I'm not in a mood."

"Yeah, okay. So what did the good lieutenant have to say?"

"He thinks we should be coming down harder on these people, stamping out any rumblings immediately and decisively in order to avoid full-blown rebellion down the road. 'Make sure they know who's in charge here,' as he put it."

Caleb stabbed a piece of chicken with his fork. "I have a pretty good idea what he means by that, and I'm positive the raping-and-pillaging type of domination he favours would only bring about full-blown rebellion that much faster."

"I totally agree. And speaking of which, he also mentioned the fact that there are quite a few attractive women in town, and he's been enjoying the view so far."

Caleb's fork clattered onto his plate. "Did you set him straight on that front?"

"I gave him my opinion on what I thought about that kind of behaviour, yes."

"And what did he say?"

"That he completely saw my point and that, as usual, I was right, and he appreciated me taking the time to enlighten him. Oh, and he thinks we should be best friends and can't figure out why we haven't been up until now. Basically, we bonded. It was a beautiful moment."

Caleb snorted. "Any time he wants to take you off my hands, I'll gladly give over the responsibility. Might free up some time for me to actually get some work done around here."

"I'll let him know that the next time the two of us are hanging out, shooting the breeze."

"You do that." Caleb took Jesse's plate from him. "I'll take these back to the mess hall and then I have an exciting evening of paperwork planned." He stood up and clapped a hand on Jesse's shoulder. "Have fun in town. I hope you find what you're looking for."

For a few more minutes, Jesse sat, staring at the shelves of books without really seeing any of them. Then he pushed to his feet with a heavy sigh.

As he walked back to his quarters to grab his keys and wallet, Jesse ran over the list of classic books he'd read over the years. *A Tale of Two Cities,* one of his favourites. He'd had a copy of it once, but things had a tendency to disappear around here, and he hadn't spotted it on the shelf. He pulled the door to his quarters shut behind him.

That's what he wanted. If Charles Dickens couldn't lift his spirits, nothing could.

CHAPTER NINE

Bells jangled above the door of the store, and Meryn looked up from counting receipts. The breath she'd been about to take got tangled in her throat, and she closed the drawer of the till with a loud clang.

Captain Christensen looked as surprised to see her as she was to see him. "Ms. O'Reilly." He closed the door and walked over to the counter. "I didn't know you worked here."

"Yes." Her voice was hoarse. She cleared her throat. "This is my store, actually. At least, what's left of it."

His brow furrowed. "What's left of it?"

She waved a hand toward the empty shelves. Filling them with inventory from other parts of the store had been on her list of things to do for a month, but every time she started to do it, the capitulation stopped her. Maybe it would be good to leave the soldiers' handiwork on display for a while longer. "Some of your professional thugs were here a few weeks ago, helping themselves to my assortment of Bibles and anything else they considered *subversive*. Of course, the books on every other faith and religion are here and perfectly fine." She didn't bother to try and keep the bitterness out of her voice as she turned back to him and cocked her head. "Does that seem right to you, Captain?"

"It's not my place to decide whether orders that come down from my superiors are right or wrong."

"As a soldier, maybe not. But what about as a human being?"

He didn't answer, but something in his eyes, guilt maybe, or regret, tugged at her conscience.

"Were you looking for something in particular?"

The captain studied her for a few seconds, as if he couldn't remember. Then he planted his palms on the counter. "I was wondering if you had *A Tale of Two Cities.*"

She worked to keep her features even. "Dickens? Really?"

He let out a short laugh. "Yes, really. We soldiers may be professional thugs, but we aren't all illiterate."

"I wasn't suggesting you were, only that almost no one asks for Dickens anymore."

"Well, he's one of my favourites, and I've been feeling the need lately to remind myself that the worst of times can also be—"

"The best of times," she recited with him. "I guess that's a good thing for all of us to keep in mind." She came around the counter. "I'm pretty sure I have a copy in the classics section."

His footsteps thudded on the wood flooring behind her.

At the end of the first aisle, she turned and followed the shelves that lined the far wall of the store until she reached the section she was searching for. The books were filed alphabetically, with Dickens near the top of the wall, so she pulled the ladder over and started up, keenly aware of his eyes on her.

The Charles Dickens books took up most of the second shelf. She ran her fingers along the titles until she found the right one and pulled it out. Clutching the side rail in her free hand, she made her way carefully back down the rungs. She would not become a cliché and stumble into his arms. The heat in her cheeks deepened at the thought. Meryn reached the bottom of the ladder and turned abruptly.

As though a similar thought had entered his mind, the captain had waited close to the bottom of the ladder, and her sudden movement brought her almost into contact with him. Infuriating amusement danced across his face when he looked at her.

"Here." She thrust the novel toward him, so he would have to step back or be hit in the chest.

He stepped back. "Thank you." The captain brushed a thin layer of dust off the top of the book. He handled the book almost reverently. Not as a casual reader, but an avid booklover.

"Sorry. This section's a little dusty. Like I said, not a lot of people buy the classics anymore."

He ran his fingers over the cover. "I'm happy they're buying books at all. There was a time when I thought these little independent bookstores were about to become a thing of the past."

"They were. That's one good thing about the cost of firewalls sky-rocketing and fewer people using the Internet. They actually had to go back to shopping in real brick-and-mortar stores."

"This one's a beauty. I love the wood floor and all the armchairs in the corners and the couch in front of the woodstove. This place begs you to sit down and read for a while."

In spite of herself, Meryn smiled. "That's the idea. Well, reading and hopefully buying something." She skirted around him and went back to the counter to ring up his purchase.

The captain trailed after her, flipping through the pages as he walked. When he reached the counter, he leaned a hip against it and opened the book to a page he'd marked with his finger. "What a writer he was. 'Sadly, sadly, the sun rose; it rose upon no sadder sight than the man of good abilities and good emotions, incapable of their directed exercise, incapable of his own help and his own happiness, sensible of the blight on him, and resigning himself to let it eat him away.'" The captain glanced over at the empty shelves before turning back to her. "And what incredible insight he had into the human condition. Feels like he's talking about me, even though he wrote the words a couple of hundred years ago."

"I guess all of this"—Meryn waved a hand toward the shelf he'd indicated and at the darkness pressing up against the glass of the front window just beyond it—"is the changing background against which we humans have lived and relived the same mistakes over and over since the dawn of time."

"So then the pain we all feel, that we're causing each other, is nothing new either."

"I suppose not, but it feels sometimes like we're coming up with original ways to inflict torment on each other daily."

"If Dickens is right"—the captain turned back to the first page—"for every dark element, there has to exist a counteracting ray of light. Best and worst, wisdom and foolishness, belief and incredulity. If the pain is real and strong, so must be ... what, joy? Hope? Love?"

Meryn played with the silver ring on her right hand. "It's just a book."

"Yes, but great books must, by definition, accurately reflect reality. And you're not going to argue that this isn't a great book, are you? I saw you carrying it down the ladder like it was a priceless treasure." His forehead wrinkled. "Which actually concerned me a little. How much is it?"

She laughed as she took it from him. "It's sixteen fifty with the tax. An incredible bargain, really, for the magic mirror reflecting back the depths of the human heart and condition."

He grinned as he pulled his wallet out of his back pocket. "Spoken like a true salesperson." The captain pulled out a twenty amero note and handed it to her.

Meryn rang the purchase through the antique cash register and scooped the change out of the holder. By the time she held out a fist with the coins, his face had grown serious again.

He reached out and closed his fingers over her hand. "I'm sorry, Meryn."

At the feel of his skin against hers and the sound of her name on his lips, she struggled to draw in a breath. "For what?"

"For all of it, really. But specifically for this ..." He waved his free hand in the direction of the empty shelves. "And for taking all the Bibles. Right or wrong—and I could be court-martialled for saying this, but I'm going to say it anyway—that order didn't sit well with me."

"Thank you. That helps, actually."

"I hope so. I really do want to help you."

Her forehead wrinkled. "Why? Why do you want to help me?"

"Because I—"

The world suddenly exploded around them with a deafening crash and a shower of broken shards of glass.

Meryn gasped.

Jesse dropped her hand, pulled the pistol from the back of his jeans, cocked it, and gripped it in both hands, arms outstretched, before he even fully whirled around to face the window.

She followed his gaze.

No one was there.

He turned his head slightly toward her, his eyes still on the window. "Are you okay?"

Stunned, Meryn could only manage a whispered, "Yes."

"I'll be right back." He pointed the weapon toward the floor as he stalked to the door, flung it open, and disappeared outside.

Meryn slumped against the counter, trying to take in the jagged hole in the centre of the large pane of glass at the front of the store. For several seconds she contemplated the destruction, one hand pressed to her mouth, then a wave of white-hot rage slashed through her muddled thoughts. She strode down the aisle to the small closet at the back and grabbed a broom and dustpan. Weaving around racks of books, she made her way to the front of the store. She tossed the dustpan to one side and jabbed furiously with the broom at the pieces of glass scattered around the floor.

A red brick had settled near the end of a shelf of books, a piece of white paper folded and taped to it with silver duct tape.

The broom clattered onto the floor.

Fingers quivering, Meryn reached for the brick. After carrying it back to the counter, she brushed small slivers of glass from the paper, ignoring the sharp pricks digging into her fingers, and tore it carefully from the brick. When the paper came loose, she bit her lip and pulled it open. The words typed in thick, black font screamed at her from the page.

We Can Get to You Anytime, Jesus-Lover
There is No Safe Place

The words hit her like a punch to the stomach, leaving a dull, throbbing pain. She closed her eyes. *This is never going to end, is it?* She dropped the paper onto the counter before making her way back to the broom and picking it up. She swiped at the pieces of glass, directing them into a pile in the centre of the room. Through a thick haze of fury, she heard her name, but she ignored it and continued to work.

Two strong hands closed over the ones she had clenched around the broomstick. "Meryn, stop."

She didn't want to concede the broom, but when he didn't let go, her shoulders slumped and she stepped back.

The captain propped the broom up against the nearest shelf and turned to her, cupping her shoulders as he searched her face. "You're bleeding." The concern in his voice nearly cut through the tenuous grasp she had on her composure.

"I'm fine."

"No, you're not. Let me help you. Do you have a first-aid kit?"

For a moment she didn't answer, wouldn't even meet the eyes that watched her closely. Then she gestured toward a doorway off to the side of the store area. "In the break room."

"Okay. Come on." He waited until she started across the room, then followed her. "Whoever it was, they were gone by the time I got out there. I've messaged my superior, Major Donevan. He's sending a team over to board up the window and clean up the debris."

Meryn nodded as she entered the break room and crossed over to the cupboard above the sink. After yanking open the door, she pulled out the first-aid kit and carried it over to the table.

The captain touched her arm. "Why don't you sit?"

She pulled a chair out from the little metal-framed Formica table. "I really can do this myself. You should go out and wait for your people to arrive."

"They won't be here for a while." He turned on the tap at the sink. He wore civilian clothes today: a pair of jeans and a long-sleeved, white T-shirt that stretched across the muscles of his back as he leaned in to rinse his hands under the water.

Meryn pressed her lips together and looked away.

After drying his hands on a paper towel and tossing it into the waste basket at the end of the counter, the captain pulled the chair from the other end of the table over and sat down in front of her. He lifted her chin with two fingers and examined her. Meryn hadn't realized she'd been cut by the flying glass, but now the stinging in several places on her face—most intensely on her right temple—tingled through her.

The captain ran his thumb below the tender area. "This one's the worst. You might need stitches, but I'll see what I can do." He let go of her chin.

Her skin suddenly felt cold where his fingers had been. She suppressed a shiver.

Captain Christensen unzipped the little case and withdrew a box of Band-Aids, a small jug of rubbing alcohol, and a bag of cotton balls. He unscrewed the lid from the jug and poured some of the clear liquid onto one of the cotton balls. He brought it up to the side of her head, then stopped and looked at her. "This is going to hurt."

Meryn smiled faintly. "I know."

He wiped the cut gently. Meryn jerked and he paused. "Sorry."

"It's okay."

The captain finished cleaning the small wound and threw the cotton into the garbage. After tearing the paper off one of the Band-Aids, he pressed it over the cut. "It's not bleeding much anymore. It should be okay. You likely don't want to spend hours in Emergency if you can help it."

"No, I really don't."

"The rest of the scratches are small. I'll clean them, but it's probably best to leave them open for the air to get at."

Meryn couldn't figure this man out. By committing himself to a career as a soldier, he had become a professional killer, a man dedicated to following orders—even those he may not agree with—without dissension or hesitation. She wanted to see him in that light, as two-dimensional. All of this would be so much easier if she could use him as a target for the anger that flooded through her at everything that had happened.

He wasn't allowing her to do that. His kindness, his concern for her safety, his love for literature, and his sense of humour made it impossible for her to dismiss him as the thug she had accused the soldiers of being.

Most damaging to her ability to detest him and everything he stood for was the tenderness in the fingers that dabbed at the cuts on her skin. As capable as his hands were of handling a deadly weapon, they were equally adept at easing pain and giving comfort.

"Are you done?"

His hand stopped its ministrations and he looked at her, the amusement back in his eyes. "Just about."

"What made you decide to become a soldier?"

"I wanted to be like my big brother and his best friend, Caleb, the major I mentioned before." He resumed his work. "The major and I grew up together. He and my brother, Rory, were a couple of years older, and I was pretty sure there was nothing the two of them couldn't do. They were inseparable, and I tagged along wherever they went, like the pesky little brother I was. The thing is, neither of them made me feel like a pesky little brother. They included me in whatever they were doing, and taught me everything I know about ... well, just about everything."

Meryn drew in a long, slow breath. Big mistake. The faint smell of musky aftershave drifted in the air between them. He was too close. His eyes, the smile that flashed without warning, the broad shoulders ... She had nowhere to look. *What would it be like to feel those arms around me?* She frowned. *Pull yourself together. He is a stranger. And the enemy ...*

He tossed another cotton ball into the garbage. "How about your hands?"

Meryn pulled them off the table and into her lap. "They're fine. Just a few tiny scrapes."

"All right, then. I think that should do it." He replaced the items he had taken out of the first-aid kit and zipped it shut. "Remember when the American economy tanked in the late twenties, and the U.S. pulled most of their troops back to focus on homeland security? After that, the Canadian government launched a huge campaign to recruit soldiers. When Rory and Caleb finished high school, they joined up. I graduated a couple of years later and signed up too. I did tours in a few different countries, then Caleb and I were both assigned back to Canada about three years ago."

"Where is Rory now?"

The captain pushed back his chair and stood. He picked up the first-aid kit and carried it to the cupboard above the stove, then turned around and leaned against the counter.

She rocked back in her chair at the look of grief entrenched on his face.

"He was killed. Five years ago, in Somalia."

"I'm sorry."

He nodded. "Caleb was with him and risked his life trying to drag him to safety, but it was too late. Rory had been injured too badly. It wasn't Caleb's fault, but I don't think he's ever forgiven himself for what happened. He got himself assigned to my unit shortly afterward. He's never come right out and said it, but I gather he made some sort of promise to my brother that he would take care of me, so we've worked together ever since."

"You must be pretty close."

The grief that had churned in his eyes cleared when his mouth turned up in a half smile. "At the risk of sounding like a twelve-year-old girl, he's my best friend in the world. And he's as much of a brother to me as Rory was, including giving me a hard time at every possible opportunity."

"And your parents?"

A shadow crossed his face. "They're both gone. They died before Rory, which was a blessing in a way. He was their golden child. I doubt they would have survived the news that he had been killed."

"And neither you nor Caleb are married?" Meryn gulped in air, trying to take back the words. Why had she asked that? She had no desire to have such a personal conversation with this man. His openness and honesty swept her along like a tidal wave, though, and she felt helpless to fight against the current.

"No. I've never been. Caleb was for about five years, to a girl named Natalie. She was amazing, but she was diagnosed with breast cancer a year after they were married and died a couple of years ago."

Her chest ached. Both of them had suffered so much loss. "So you're ..."

"Alone in the world? Pretty much, except for Caleb. Probably why the two of us are so close. He has a sister, but she moved to the States a few years ago and he doesn't see her much. We've had to be each other's family. I've been through a few rough times in my life I'm not sure I would have survived without him."

"Did you ever wish you had some sort of faith to help you through?"

He shot her a look. "No."

She waited, but he didn't elaborate.

He crossed the room to stand behind the chair across from her. "What about you, any brothers or sisters?"

"Two brothers, one sister, all older."

"Are you close?"

"Not to my sister, but to my brothers, yes."

"Where are they?"

"They both answered the siren call of the west. Brendan's in Calgary, working for an oil company, and Shane's a forest ranger in B.C."

The captain flipped the chair around, settling onto it backwards and resting his arms on the back of it. "What happened between you and your sister?"

Meryn shrugged. "We're very different. We've never gotten along."

"Do your parents live around here?"

"No, they're in Ottawa, where I grew up."

"How did you end up here?"

She hesitated. "Kate and I went to Queen's together. After we graduated and she married Ethan and decided to stay here, I stayed too."

"Is there an apartment above the store?"

Her eyes narrowed. "Yes. But I've rented it out. Why?"

His lips twitched. "I wasn't suggesting we go up there, don't worry. It's just ..." He paused as though measuring his next words. "I hate to see you living way out in the country. It's not safe, especially after what happened to the store tonight. If that wasn't some random act of vandalism but a personal attack ..."

Her fingers fluttered to her throat.

He searched her face. "What is it?"

"I don't think it was random."

"Why not?"

"Here." Meryn rose and crossed the break room to the store. Behind her, the front legs of the chair thudded to the floor as the captain stood up to follow her.

The brick still lay on the counter, the folded piece of paper beside it.

She picked up the note and handed it to him.

The captain unfolded it, his jaw tightening as he scanned the words.

Meryn steadied herself with a hand on the counter. "People always consider that such an insult. It's quite funny really, when it's ..."

He looked up, eyes hard. "None of this is funny, Meryn."

She swallowed. "I know."

"Now I really hate to see you out there alone. Is there somewhere else you can go? Someone you could stay with for a while?"

She shook her head. "I appreciate your concern, Captain. I don't fully understand it, but I appreciate it. Still, I'm not going to let whomever did this drive me out of my home. That's crazy."

"The whole world's gone crazy. We can't ignore that. We have to do whatever we can to keep our own lives as sane as possible. And you staying out there in the country by yourself is not sane. It's asking for trouble."

"I don't really see how it's any of your business where I stay or how I live my life."

"Maybe I'm making it my business."

She shook her head. "Listen, I know I've made a couple of stupid comments about being a threat to national security, but only because I was angry. I didn't mean anything by them. You really don't have to keep an eye on me when there are actual terrorists out there somewhere you could be investigating."

A funny look contorted his face, as if he wasn't sure whether to strangle her or burst out laughing. "I never thought you were a terrorist. And if I've been keeping an eye on you, it's not for the sake of ensuring national security, although I have no doubt that, if you wished to threaten that security, you could."

"Then why?" She threw both hands in the air.

The captain didn't answer, but the eyes that locked on hers said more than words.

She lowered her hands. "Captain, I—"

"You don't have to say it. I know it's way too complicated." He exhaled and ran a hand over his face. "Believe me, I know. That doesn't mean I can't be worried about you and want to do everything I can to make sure you're safe. Especially now." He crumpled the piece of paper in his hand. "Whoever did this wanted to scare you. And if you're not scared about what they could be planning to do next, I am. So could you promise me one thing?"

"What?" Her throat tightened and she had to push out the word.

"That you'll think about moving somewhere safer. And that you'll consider staying somewhere else for a couple of days, maybe Kate's, until we have a chance to investigate. And that you'll call me if you notice anything odd or anyone strange around or something doesn't feel right to you. Or if you're thinking about me and you want to talk."

A small smile played at the corners of her mouth. "That's—"

"Three things, I know."

"At least. But okay, I will."

"Which one?"

"All of the above. I owe you that much."

"At least."

Bells jangled again, and a tall, broad-shouldered man in military khakis and a blond crew cut stuck his head into the store. "Jess?"

"Here."

The man nodded and covered the distance from the door to the counter in three strides. Glass crunched beneath his boots, and he winced as he glanced over at the front window. "They did a number on it all right." He looked at Meryn and his eyes narrowed. "And on you too, it looks like. Are you okay?"

"I'm fine."

"Meryn O'Reilly, I presume?" He held a large hand over the counter.

She slid hers into his solid grip. "Yes. And you must be Major Donevan. Captain Christensen's been telling me good things about you."

"Of course he has." The major nudged Jesse's shoulder. "He's been telling me good things about you too. And he was right."

The captain cleared his throat. "Did you come to chat, or could we maybe talk about the *crime* that just took place?"

Major Donevan held up both hands. "Easy. I'm only saying you weren't exaggerating." He winked at her.

Meryn suppressed a grin. Her resolve to strenuously dislike every soldier that had invaded her city, on principle, weakened further.

Captain Christensen lifted a hand in the air and glared at his superior. "Really?"

"Sorry." Major Donevan pressed his lips together and pointed at the paper. "What's that?"

The captain showed him the note. Good-natured sparring aside, the strong bond between the two of them was almost palpable. They were both clearly good men, who cared about each other and their country and who were trying to do the right thing.

So how could they do what they had come here to do—harass and oppress innocent people?

She sighed. Life had been so much simpler when she could despise the soldiers in one big nameless, faceless mass. *He's right. This has all become far too complicated.* She grabbed her purse from behind the counter. "Do you need me to be here?"

Both men looked over at her.

The major shot a glance at the captain before turning back to her. "I suppose not. We'll be here for a while, investigating and cleaning up, so it's probably not a bad idea for you to go home and get some rest. Is there a way for us to lock up when we leave?"

"Push the handle in on the inside and pull the door shut."

"Can I get your number, in case we have any questions for you?"

Meryn scribbled her i-com number on a scrap of paper beside the till and handed it to him.

The major hesitated, as if he knew she wouldn't like what he was about to say. "Do you need a pass to be out after dark?"

She tightened her hold on the bag, the restriction still galling her. "No, I have one scanned to my i-com that allows me to be out Friday nights, when the store is open later."

"Good."

The captain rubbed his forehead with the side of his hand. "Do you want me to drive you?"

"No, that's okay. My car's just down the street."

"I'll walk you out."

Meryn nodded. He pulled the door open and she stepped outside, tilting back her head to let the cool evening breeze brush past her face.

A green army jeep pulled up to the curb. Meryn moved back against the outside wall as four soldiers jumped out and passed by them, nodding to the captain before they disappeared into her store.

She started down the sidewalk toward her little white solar/electric hybrid Ford Kev, parked under a streetlight a block away from her store. When she reached it, she rounded the front of the car and entered the code into the pad beneath the window.

The locks clicked.

The captain reached for the door handle and pulled it open. "Meryn."

She turned toward him, her hand clutching the top of the door. He stood on the other side of it, close enough for her to see the tiny lines threading out from the corners of his eyes. It took everything she had not to lift her hand to his face and smooth them away.

"You'll go to Kate's for the night? After the team investigates, we may be able to figure out who did this and bring them in, but until then I won't rest easy if I know you're out there alone."

She considered his request.

"Please."

Her shoulders slumped. "Okay. For tonight."

"Thank you."

Meryn glanced back at the store. Pain pricked her chest like the tiny slivers of glass that had dug into her fingers when she'd brushed them off the brick.

The captain must have seen it on her face, because he followed her gaze to the shattered window, pieces scattered all over the sidewalk. "I'm sorry, Meryn."

"No." She shook her head. "I'm the one who's sorry. When you first came in the store, I was angry and frustrated about losing my Bibles and all those books." Her voice broke and she drew in a quivering breath. "Once again I took it out on you, but it wasn't your fault. You didn't take them and, even if you had, you would have been following someone else's orders and doing your job, even if it wouldn't have been easy for you. I ... admire that."

When he smiled, the corners of his eyes crinkled. "We seem to always be apologizing to each other."

"Yes, we do."

He tilted his head. "Maybe that's it. Maybe we've found it."

"What?"

"The ray of light that counteracts the darkness of all this pain."

"What is it?" She held her breath.

"Forgiveness."

Meryn let the power and beauty of the word brush over her skin like the breeze had a few moments earlier. "I think you might be right."

He touched his hand to hers. "By the way, thank you for that jam. I've really been enjoying it."

"Kate sent it."

"Yes, my men did tell me that. And I have to admit I was a little disappointed to hear it."

Meryn dropped her gaze to the hand clutching the door. "I did make the jam. My first-ever attempt."

"Really? I always thought that sort of thing was done by robots in Mexico somewhere."

Her head shot up, and she stared at him. "I see I have to watch what I say from now on, even in my own home."

His face grew serious. "It's a good idea, actually, especially when you leave your window open. You can't be too careful these days." He took a deep breath. "Still, I did appreciate the gift, so ..." He leaned over the door and kissed her on the cheek. "Pass along my thanks to Kate, will you? And make sure she knows it's from me. I wouldn't want her to get the wrong idea."

"That's not why I didn't send it."

"No? Then why didn't you?"

He was dancing pretty close to the flames. Meryn bit her lip. Two could play at that game. "All right, maybe that is why. But out of curiosity, if I had sent it, would you have thanked me the same way?"

"Actually, no."

"No?"

"Based on what my men told me, it wasn't easy for you to give them that jar of jam. So I think I would have had to find a better way to thank you. Something like ..." Both his hands slid along her jaw until they framed her face. Meryn's breathing grew shallow as he leaned in close and stopped an inch before his mouth touched hers. "And then I would have kissed you. If you had sent it, I mean."

Meryn swallowed. "Did I mention I *made* the jam?"

He grinned. "That's true. And I guess that's a lot more work than just handing someone a jar, physically at least, if not psychologically. I *do* owe you a proper thank-you." He closed the distance between them and touched his lips to hers, so lightly he barely brushed them.

Still, the kiss was unbearably sweet and so powerful Meryn had to brace herself against the car door so her knees wouldn't buckle beneath her.

The captain pulled back and gazed at her. "I have to say, I'm very glad your theory was wrong. That was much better than kissing a robot."

Meryn's smile was shaky. "I'm glad to hear it."

He cupped his hand around hers for a few seconds before pulling it away and stepping back. "Be careful, Meryn."

She slid behind the wheel of the car.

The captain waited until she was in, then closed the door and walked around the hood to step up on the curb.

Meryn pressed the button to start the car and pulled out onto the street. For several blocks she could still see him in the rearview mirror, standing in the warm glow of the streetlight, watching her go. She pressed a finger to her lips and smiled.

Suddenly, she dropped her hand. What was she doing? A stab of guilt shot through her. She had no right ... She lifted her chin.

Well, he started it.

That's great, Meryn. Act like a five-year-old. That will really help the situation.

Not that this was a situation. They'd both gotten caught up in the moment, that was all. There was nothing more to it. There couldn't be anything more. And when—if—she saw him again she would tell him that and make sure he understood it.

Even so, what he had said about forgiveness was interesting. The truth of it reverberated through her, and, for the first time since the soldiers had burst into church that Sunday morning, she knew what she had to do. She had to let go of her anger and forgive. Not only those high up in power whose new laws were wreaking havoc on their lives, or the special-interest, agenda-driven groups pressuring them to make those laws, but also the ones whose dedication to service demanded that they enforce them.

And—she screwed up her face—even whomever it was that had thrown a brick through the window of her beloved store.

The heaviness that had pressed down around her for weeks lessened slightly. In spite of everything that had happened that evening, Meryn laughed out loud as a revelation struck her.

An unbeliever had just preached the best sermon she had ever heard.

CHAPTER TEN

When Jesse came back into the store, Caleb was leaning against the counter, speaking in a low voice into an i-com. He looked up when Jesse approached, his gaze narrowing to laser-intensity as he lowered the unit. "I have a couple of questions for you for the incident report." He pointed at the screen.

"Shoot."

"What time did the brick come through the window?"

Jesse pressed a button to illuminate his watch. It seemed like a lot longer, but it had probably only been about forty-five minutes. "Nineteen fifteen-ish."

Caleb typed something into the unit. "Did you see anyone?"

"No. There was no one at the window when I turned around, and by the time I got outside they were gone."

"And what were you doing when it happened?"

"What difference does that—?"

"Just answer the question."

He blew out his breath. "We were standing at the counter talking."

"Talking."

"Yes." Jesse flicked a finger toward the device in Caleb's hand. "You're not inputting that response."

"That's because it's for my personal information."

His jaw tightened. "Anything else you need for your *personal* information?"

"Since you asked, what were you doing standing at the counter talking to someone I expressly told you to stay away from?"

"Cale." Jesse rammed his fingers through his hair. "I came in looking for a book, like I told you I was going to do. I had no idea this was Meryn's store until I saw her here."

Caleb set the i-com down on the counter. "Can I be honest with you?"

"Would it stop you if I said no?"

"Has it ever?"

"No."

"Then, no."

Jesse sighed. "So go for it, then."

"I don't see it."

"What?"

"You and her together."

"We're not together, so there's nothing to see."

"I mean, she is gorgeous. You were right about that," Caleb said, as if Jesse hadn't spoken. "But frankly, I didn't feel any sort of connection between the two of you. I actually thought there was more of a spark between her and me."

Heat rushed into Jesse's chest. He glanced at the soldiers sweeping the floor around the bookshelves and removing what was left of the glass in the front window, then jerked his head toward the small room off the store. "Could we move this conversation somewhere a little more private?"

Caleb shrugged and followed him into the break room.

Jesse waited until Caleb had come through the doorway, then he slid the pocket door across the opening and faced his superior. "Are you seriously suggesting that you and she should get together?"

"Hey, Natalie's been gone for two years now. I'm not going to stay a monk forever. Who better than the beautiful Meryn O'Reilly to help me get back—?"

"Caleb." Jesse ground out the word. "If you want to live to see another day, you will not finish that sentence." His fists clenched. Caleb had a couple of inches and about thirty pounds on him, but Jesse figured he had in his favour the fact that he was spitting mad at the moment.

His friend didn't finish the sentence, just looked at him and then exhaled loudly. "You'd really do it, wouldn't you?"

"What?"

"Take a swing at me."

"Say one more word about how beautiful she is or how good the two of you would be together and you'll find out."

"Jess. You know I would never, in a million years, go after a woman you were interested in, don't you?"

The muscles across his shoulders relaxed slightly. "So what, you were messing with me?"

"I'd never do that either."

Jesse cocked his head.

Caleb grinned. "Okay, I would do that. But that's not what I was doing now."

"Then what?"

"I was assessing the situation to see how much trouble you're in here."

"And?" Jesse's knees felt suddenly weak, and he walked over to the table and sank down onto one of the red, padded chairs.

Caleb's grin faded. "You're in a lot of trouble."

Jesse propped his elbows on the table and pressed his fingers into his forehead. "I know."

"The two of you haven't ...?"

He dropped his hands. "What?"

"You know, been together."

Jesse let out a short laugh. "With you watching me like a hawk? When would we have had a chance to do that? Besides, do you really have no idea what these people believe?"

"Oh yeah, there is some clause that says they can only sleep with the person they're married to or something, isn't there?"

"It's not a clause. People don't have to sign a legal contract to become a Christian. It's a moral code. And incidentally, I happen to follow one myself. I may not be a monk like you, but I don't hop into bed with every woman that comes along either, which I hope you know."

"So the thought hasn't crossed your mind?"

Jesse traced a pattern in the speckles on the Formica tabletop with one finger.

"That's what I thought." Caleb folded his arms over his chest. "What are you going to do?"

"Nothing. You don't want me to have anything to do with her, and she doesn't want to have anything to do with me. So it all works out nice and neat. We go our separate ways, and everybody's happy."

"Except you."

Jesse shrugged.

"And possibly her."

His head shot up. "What does that mean?"

"I wasn't completely honest with you earlier. I did sense a connection between the two of you, a pretty strong one. And whatever you might say, from the way she was looking at you, or trying not to, I think she feels it too. Of course, you already know that, since I'm pretty sure you kissed her outside. And from the look on your face when you came back into the store, I'm guessing it wasn't entirely one-sided."

"Cale ..."

"I'm not saying you should pursue it. In fact, I think it would be a huge mistake. But that's never kept you from doing something before, and I seriously doubt it's going to now. You had already decided you were going to do everything you could to keep her safe, even before that brick came through her window tonight, hadn't you?"

Jesse thought about denying it, but it would be a waste of time. "Yes."

"So, not going your separate ways."

"I didn't say that."

"You didn't have to." Caleb pulled out the chair beside Jesse and sat down. "Okay. So we keep an eye on her. Probably not a bad idea, anyway. From what you've told me, she's capable of causing trouble, and she's obviously also a target now. Whatever her beliefs, I don't want her being harassed, or worse, on our watch."

"Thanks, Cale."

"You're welcome."

Jesse drew on the adrenaline still coursing through his body to shoot out a fist and punch Caleb hard in the upper arm.

Caleb didn't even flinch. "Feel better?"

Given that punching his friend's arm was a little like driving his fist into a hydro pole, it probably hurt him more than Caleb, but still, it helped. "Actually, yes. Don't ever do that to me again."

Caleb laughed. "You're so easy. You should have seen your face when I said she and I had more of a spark than the two of you."

"So you think she feels a connection too?"

Caleb shoved back his chair and stood up. "Don't push it, my friend. I'm not going to say it again. I have no desire whatsoever to encourage whatever this thing is between you. In fact, if I wasn't so soft, I would order you to stay away from her, for all the good it would do me. Now, let's go get some work done, or we'll be here all night."

Jesse rose. "But you did say that we have a connection."

"You're pathetic, you know that?"

"I know. Almost as pathetic as you were when you first met Natalie."

Caleb slung an arm around Jesse's shoulders as they headed for the door. "It's sad, isn't it? We can face an entire platoon of enemy soldiers desperately trying to kill us, no problem. But a woman gives us a single glance, and we get messed up so fast we can barely remember our own names."

"It's true. If she's the right woman."

Caleb dropped his arm. "Are you saying she's the right woman? As in, 'the one'?"

"I don't know. Maybe."

"Wow. You're in worse trouble than I thought." Caleb slid the door back into the wall and stepped out into the store.

Jesse walked out behind him, head spinning. *Was* that what he was saying? Was Meryn O'Reilly the woman he'd been waiting for his whole life? He bent and straightened his fingers, trying to release some of the tension that had tightened his muscles when that brick had come through the window.

He had never felt this way about anyone before. And he'd never come as close to losing it with Caleb as he had when his friend hinted that he might go after Meryn himself.

Jesse made his way to the counter.

This was bad. This was very, very bad. Except ...

He rested his hand on the copy of *A Tale of Two Cities* still sitting beside the cash register, coins scattered around it. That conversation they'd had about Dickens, the look on her face when he'd suggested that forgiveness was the answer they'd been looking for—somehow it was also very, very good.

CHAPTER ELEVEN

Meryn filled two Styrofoam cups with steaming coffee, splashed in some cream, and carried them over to one of the folding tables set up in the church hall.

"Thanks, Mer." Kate looked up from wiping crumbs off Matthew's face. "Okay, son, go play for a bit." She gave him a gentle push, and he took off running toward his friends, who were tossing around a ball in the corner of the room. Kate watched him, smile faltering.

Meryn eyed the group of children. Christmas was approaching, but it was a beautiful, sunny day. Normally the kids would have fled the confines of this room filled with muted adult conversation as soon as they had grabbed their cookies and juice. Now, though, parents were keeping their kids close, never sure when the army might storm into the church again. As it was, three armed soldiers had stood at the back of the sanctuary the whole time the service was going on.

Making sure no Bibles appeared in anyone's hand, including the minister's, probably. Or maybe gathering ammunition to be used against them at some unknown time in the future.

Her hold on the Styrofoam strengthened until the cup started to crack beneath her fingers and she set it down abruptly.

She *was* grateful the soldiers had allowed everyone in and hadn't made any attempt to stop the pastor from speaking or even from quoting the Scripture passages that, thankfully, he had a vast store of memorized. *How long will they allow that?* She pushed the thought away. Worrying about what might come in the future was a highly unproductive activity. Appreciating the small blessings they enjoyed in the present was much more worthwhile.

And she was learning to let go and forgive.

A small smile played around Meryn's mouth. She'd even been able to greet the soldiers civilly, if not exactly warmly, that morning, something that had brought surprise flitting across all of their faces. And she'd prayed for them during the service, that they might hear the truth and that it would impact them in some way. As she prayed, she felt her lingering resentment slipping away. It was very difficult to bring someone before God and hold on to hatred at the same time. If Captain Christensen hadn't exactly been referring to the forgiveness that came only on one's knees, he had still directed her to that place, and for that she was incredibly grateful.

"What are you smiling about?" Kate was watching her, a bemused expression on her face, as she manoeuvred the plastic poinsettia away from the centre of the table with the edge of her hand.

"I was remembering something someone told me about forgiveness being the answer to all this pain and suffering. And it's true, Kate. Praying for those soldiers at the back of the church today really helped me let go of my anger. I feel like this huge weight has been taken off my shoulders."

"Glad to hear it. And who, may I ask, was this fount of wisdom and revelation for you, since I've been saying basically the same thing to you for years without the words sinking in?"

Meryn's cheeks warmed. "It doesn't really matter who, the point is that it sank in this time." She gulped a large mouthful of coffee. When she set it down, she met her friend's intense gaze. Kate Williams had never let anything go in her life, not when it came to Meryn.

"It was Captain Christensen," Meryn mumbled, etching a line with her fingernail across the red-and-green paper tablecloth.

Kate was uncharacteristically silent across the table.

Meryn held out as long as she could. "Like I said, it doesn't matter who, the point is—"

Kate flashed a palm in her direction. "Actually, the *who* is pretty relevant in this story. When exactly did you have this profound conversation with the man? I thought I was with you both times you saw him."

"You were with me the first couple of times, but I saw him again at the store last Friday."

"You mean he was one of the soldiers who came when the brick was thrown through your window? You didn't mention that."

"That's because I was hoping to avoid this interrogation."

"Well, that's not going to happen. So tell me. How did you have an opportunity for a conversation like that when the place was swarming with army guys?"

"It wasn't, not when he first arrived. He didn't come because the brick was thrown through the window. He happened to be there when it was."

"So he came into the store earlier? Was he looking for a book or for you?"

She blinked. "For a book, of course. He didn't even know it was my store until he came in. And why on earth would he come in looking for me?"

Kate sent Meryn a knowing look.

She lifted her chin. "What did you think of the sermon this morning?"

A smile played over Kate's lips. "Nice try. How about you tell me everything else that happened Friday night, so I don't have to keep pulling it from you piece by piece?"

Meryn sighed. "Fine. We were talking when the brick came through the window. The captain ran outside, but whoever had done it was gone. He called his commanding officer and asked him to send some soldiers over to investigate and clean up the place, and while we were waiting, he treated my cuts. Then the others arrived, and I left."

Kate let out a small laugh. "Okay, *Reader's Digest,* that was the most boring, abridged version of a story I've ever heard. He doctored you up? That must have been ... intense."

Meryn ran a finger absently over the Band-Aid on her temple and repressed a smile, not wanting to give her friend the satisfaction. "I guess it was. He did open up and tell me a little about himself. He and Major Donevan, his commanding officer, are best friends. The major was very close to Captain Christensen's older brother, who was killed in Somalia. Major Donevan and the captain have worked together ever since."

Kate's hazel eyes softened with compassion. "Everyone has a story, don't they? Some kind of suffering and loss they have experienced in their lives. That's a good thing to remember when these soldiers come along disrupting our lives."

"You're right. And some of them, at least, seem interested in our stories too. The captain asked about my family and how I ended up in this area."

Kate crossed her arms on the table. "Did you tell him … anything else?"

A picture flashed through Meryn's head, but she blocked it before it could come into focus. She swallowed. "Of course not. He didn't ask and I'm sure he couldn't care less. Besides, he already knows way more about me than he should and is far more worried than I want him to be." She bit her lip, realizing she'd said more than she had intended.

"He's worried about you?"

"He doesn't think it's a good idea for me to live way out in the country alone."

"Also something I've been telling you for years."

"Kate, you know why I can't leave."

"So what did you tell him?"

"That it wasn't any of his business where I lived."

Kate's eyes widened. "Meryn, you didn't. What did he say?"

Meryn drew in a long, slow breath, letting the familiar smells of brewing coffee and freshly baked fruit pies calm her. "He said he was making it his business."

"Wow. I don't even know how to respond to that."

"Good, because there is nothing to say. It's not his business. He did make me promise to stay with you while they investigated the incident at the store, which is why I ended up on your doorstep, but that is the only concession I plan to make to him."

"Why, did he ask you to make other ones?"

Meryn glared at her. "You can't let it rest, can you?"

"Not when we're finally getting to the good part."

Meryn took another sip of her coffee, but it was cold, and she almost spit it back out. "He also asked me to think about moving somewhere safer and to call him if I saw anyone strange or something didn't feel right to me. Or ..."

"Or?"

"If I was thinking about him and wanted to talk."

Kate rubbed her hands together. "That's the part I was waiting for."

Meryn looked around, but everyone near them was involved in their own conversations. "All right." She spoke just above a whisper. "I admit there's more to him than I was willing to see in the beginning. If things were different with me, or if he wasn't who he is, then maybe I could think of him that way. But, Kate, things aren't different, and he is who he is, so I can't. Even he admitted that the situation is far too complicated."

Kate didn't speak for a long moment, then sighed. "I'm really not trying to push you toward this man. In fact, as you have repeatedly said, there are lots of good reasons for you to avoid getting involved with him any further. Still, you deserve to be happy."

"I'm content, honestly, which is a lot for me."

"I know." Kate offered her a small smile.

"Mind if I join you?"

Both women looked up. "Hey, Drew." Kate pointed to the chair beside Meryn. "Make yourself comfortable."

Meryn shot her a look as the man set a paper plate holding a piece of apple pie down on the table and folded his tall, lean frame onto the metal folding chair. He was a couple of years older than she was, but the freckles sprinkled across his nose gave him a perpetually youthful look. "Hi, Drew. How are you doing?"

"Better now." He flashed her a smile. "I haven't seen you in a while. Where have you been hiding?"

"I haven't been hiding. I've been busy with the store. With Christmas coming in less than a month, business has really picked up."

"That's good news. Do you have plans for the holidays?"

"I'll probably go to Ottawa and spend a couple of days with my parents. To be honest, I'm having a hard time getting into the spirit this year."

Kate frowned. "You love Christmas. You always make a big deal of it."

"I know, but the highlight for me has always been the Christmas Eve service. With the army refusing to let us have one this year because of the curfew, all the other things like the tree and the food and the presents seem kind of pointless."

"We can still celebrate the birth of Christ, even if we have to do it at home."

"I know. And I will. It's just taking some time to get used to everything being so different."

Drew cut into his pie with the side of his fork. The aromas of cinnamon and nutmeg rose into the air on a cloud of steam. "So, what were the two of you talking about so intensely when I came in?"

Meryn glanced at Kate. "We were discussing this morning's sermon."

"Yes, right." Kate nodded. "The sermon. Very inspiring. I feel stronger now, more equipped to face whatever comes. I'm not sure everyone feels the same way, though."

"What do you mean?"

"A lot of people were missing today and have been since the soldiers arrived. And I've heard rumours about people pulling their memberships from the church. I hope and pray they find the people responsible for those bombings soon, so life can get back to normal."

Meryn's chest hurt, as if she'd just finished a long run and her lungs were fighting for air. "Do you really think life will ever be normal again?"

"I don't know. I keep hoping. If things are this bad now, what will they be like for the kids? How will they survive?"

"They will survive the same way we all will. The same way the church always has. By the grace of God and by helping each other through whatever lies ahead." Drew picked up his white plastic fork and waved it through the air. "Sure, some people have left. But more have come, searching for hope. That's what we have to offer. And no matter how bad things get, it's what we can never let go of."

The ache in Meryn's chest subsided. None of them knew what the future held, but God did. All they could know for sure was that they wouldn't have to face it alone. "You're right, Drew. We have to stand together."

"Yes, we do. If there's anything I can do, for either of you, please let me know." Drew covered Meryn's fingers with his.

She let them rest there for a few seconds before slowly pulling her hand away. She and Drew had been friends for years, but the last few times they'd met, he had acted differently toward her. Less simply friendly and more ... well, more than friends. She didn't want to encourage him in any way, especially now.

No, not especially now. She had never felt that way about Drew. Nothing that may or may not have happened recently had any bearing on that.

Kate smiled. "Thanks, Drew. I needed to hear that today."

Drew's gaze shifted from Meryn to Kate. "Meryn has a point. It's more likely that things will get worse, not better. But we don't have to live in fear. We just have to remember that we have each other." He gathered up his dishes and stood. "It was good to see you both."

Meryn looked up at him and forced a smile. "Thanks, Drew. You too."

He nodded and wended his way through the tables, stopping long enough to toss his uneaten pie into a garbage can before disappearing through the swinging doors.

When she looked over at her friend, Kate was studying her. Meryn shook her head. "Don't say it."

"Don't say what?"

"Whatever you were thinking."

"I was thinking that it never rains, but it pours. But okay, I won't say it."

"Thank you. I admire your incredible restraint."

"You know, there are some new people coming. I was talking to a couple of them before the service, and they are really interested in finding out more about Christianity. I wish we had Bibles to give them."

"Yeah." Meryn paused as an idea began to form in her head.

"Meryn." Kate reached across the table and gripped her arm. "What is that look on your face? You're not going to do anything crazy, are you?"

"Of course not."

"Good, because, as a wise man once said, this situation is already way too complicated. And he's right."

CHAPTER TWELVE

J ess?"

Jesse looked up from his computer as Caleb stuck his head around his office door. "Yeah?"

Caleb came into the room and shut the door behind him. "I need you to come to a meeting with me."

"Okay. Who with?"

"An informant."

Jesse scrunched up his face.

"I know. I'm not overly fond of those types either, but they can be useful, and I suspect this one might be different than most."

"How so?"

"It's a woman, for starters. Code name Scorcher."

Jesse laughed. "Scorcher? Seriously? Who came up with that?"

"Someone at Headquarters. From what I hear, though, the name fits. Apparently she's gorgeous but a bit of a handful, and since I'm guessing you're immune to any but the lovely book lady's charms at the moment, I thought it would be good to have you with me."

"So basically I'm the chaperone."

"Basically." Caleb propped an elbow on top of the filing cabinet by the door. "I'm hoping we can get in, get the information, and get out relatively unscorched."

"Sounds like you put a lot of thought and effort into coming up with that brilliant strategy. I can't believe the Chief of the Defence Staff hasn't snatched you up to work in his office yet."

"On second thought, maybe this is a bad idea." Caleb walked over and tapped the top of the computer. "You should probably stay here and review the document I sent you this morning on military protocol. You know, the one about showing respect for ranking officers?"

Jesse powered down his laptop and closed the lid. "And miss the opportunity to watch you stammer and stutter through a high-powered meeting with some man-eating source? No way. This is going to be the highlight of my month. Besides, you send me that same document every Monday morning. I'll read it next week."

"Sure you will." Caleb retraced his steps and pulled open Jesse's office door. "Hey, any news on the broken window at the store?"

Jesse grabbed his green beret from the hook by the door. He pulled the beret on as the two of them started down the corridor, side by side. "Unfortunately not. I was hoping there might be fingerprints on the brick or the letter, but the lab couldn't find anything. No witnesses have come forward, so unless some new evidence surfaces, I guess that's it."

"Too bad. Is Meryn still staying with friends?"

"I don't think so. She did for a couple of days, but I drove by her place last night and her car was in the driveway, so I'm assuming she's gone back home. I left a message on her i-com yesterday, saying that the investigation hadn't turned up anything. She probably figures there's no sense staying in town any longer since she does have to go home sooner or later."

"But you don't like it."

"No, of course not. She is way too vulnerable out there. But she knows how I feel, and she promised to think about moving somewhere safer. There's not much more I can do about it."

"Except keep an eye on her place."

Jesse glanced at his friend. "You did say it was okay, right? I won't go out there every day or anything, but if I'm out anyway, I will likely drive by."

"Yeah, it's okay. I'll drive by sometimes too."

"Thanks, Cale, I appreciate it. As long as you don't get any ideas about dropping in to see her or anything."

Caleb smirked. "Still smarting about that, aren't you?"

"No." Caleb shot him a look, and Jesse's shoulders slumped. "Not much." They reached the exit and Jesse followed him out to the jeep.

"You don't have anything to worry about, Jess. Like I told you, I would never go after a woman you were interested in. And in spite of what I said about not being a monk forever, the fact is, I might be. I know it's only been a couple of years, but I still can't even think about getting close to anyone again. I can't imagine that I ever will."

"I'm starting to get that."

"What, the monogamy thing? I guess the Christians do have some things right." Caleb stopped in front of the vehicle. "In any case, I think I might have a cure for our pining away for women we can't be with."

"What's that?"

"Scorcher. Based on some of the stories I've heard, if we survive this meeting, we'll likely be quite happy to retreat to our quarters and stay away from women for a while." Caleb rounded the jeep and opened the driver's side door.

Grasping the handle on the passenger side, Jesse met his friend's eyes over the top of the vehicle. "That bad, huh? Maybe you were right. Maybe I should stay back and review that document you mentioned."

"Oh no, my friend. Get in. If I'm going down, you're going down with me."

Jesse climbed into the seat beside Caleb and reached for the air-conditioning button. The weather had turned extremely hot and humid again over the weekend. Unusual for late December, but weather patterns had changed so much in the last couple of decades it was hard to determine what really was unusual anymore.

Jesse swiped at a bead of sweat that had started down the side of his face. *Somehow I doubt Caleb's cure will work.* However intimidating this Scorcher might be, no one, not even her, would be able to drive thoughts of Meryn O'Reilly from his head.

———•———

Jesse studied the squat, industrial-looking building as they crossed the parking lot. Graffiti covered the grey-brick walls, partially obscured by waist-high weeds.

Caleb stopped with his hand on the knob of the steel door at the back entrance to the warehouse. He tapped Jesse's arm lightly with his fist. "Let me do the talking."

"She's all yours."

Caleb pulled open the door.

A long hallway stretched before them, dimly lit with pot lights set into the drop ceiling every few feet. The two men walked down the hall, footsteps muted on the cement floor. A clammy chill swirled around Jesse's feet and seeped into his body.

He shuddered. If he were a movie director looking for a place to shoot a horror movie where two unsuspecting guys walked into an elaborate trap and were never heard from again, he'd be jumping up and down right now.

It wasn't the building itself, exactly, but the *feel* of the place. Like something alive crept around in the shadows between the lights.

He looked down, half expecting to see a snake slithering across his boots. "What is this place?"

"Just some abandoned warehouse, I think." Caleb sounded as spooked as Jesse was. "It was her idea to meet here."

"Well, it's creepy. I can practically hear hissing in the shadows."

Caleb looked back over his shoulder. His face held a grey pallor.

Was that the result of the lighting in the hallway, or something less ... quantitative?

"I know what you mean. There's definitely something strange in the air here."

"Maybe we could suggest a different meeting spot next time."

"If there is a next time."

Jesse threw him a quizzical look.

Caleb grimaced. "I mean, if we think she's going to work out as an informant, not if we live to tell about this." He stopped in front of an unmarked door, knocked twice, paused, then knocked twice more before turning the knob and pushing open the door.

Jesse strode into the room behind him and blinked. The sudden brightness, after the dull light in the hallway, nearly blinded him. Fluorescent bulbs lined the ceiling, reflecting off the whitewashed walls and white, tiled floor. In spite of that, the darkness he'd felt walking toward the room didn't diminish, but only seemed to intensify when he closed the door.

Scorcher leaned against a heavy oak table, the only piece of furniture in the room. She wore a short, pink dress that showed off a curvaceous figure and long, tanned legs to full advantage.

Jesse lifted his gaze.

Blonde, shimmering curls tumbled almost to her waist.

He had to admit that she had been well named. She was quite possibly the most attractive woman he had ever seen. His eyes met her ice-cold blue ones.

Her full red lips turned up slightly. "Well, well, it's my lucky day. The only thing hotter than one good-looking man with a gun is two good-looking men with guns. Good afternoon, gentlemen."

Beside him, Caleb crossed his arms over his chest.

Jesse tried not to let the fact that her gaze was roaming up and down the length of him—like she was assessing him before he went on the auction block—bother him, at least not to the point where she could sense his discomfort. Unfortunately, he seriously doubted that those eyes, that finally came up to settle on his face, missed much.

Caleb cleared his throat. "Let's get down to business, shall we? Do you have anything for us?"

"My, my. So impatient. I always like to get to know the people I'm dealing with a little before I go to bed with them. Figuratively speaking, of course."

Caleb blew out his breath. "Major Donevan." He jerked his head toward Jesse. "Captain Christensen. Now could we—?"

She pushed herself away from the table and walked toward them, carefully placing one silver-stilettoed foot ahead of the other.

Jesse's throat went so dry, memories of doing manoeuvres in the Rigestan Desert in southwestern Afghanistan flooded through him. He'd never wished he was back there again until this moment.

Scorcher held a hand out toward Caleb. "Annaliese Pettersson."

Caleb hesitated before he took it. "You should use your code name."

"Why? I don't have anything to hide." She turned to Jesse and held out her hand again. "Captain."

Jesse shook her hand briefly.

When he tried to release it, she tightened her grip and held it for a few seconds longer before she let him go.

A faint, exotic scent drifted on the air around her, and Jesse's head began to spin.

"See? Isn't that better? Now we're friends. You men, always wanting to dive right into business. You miss out on all the fun that way." She walked back to the table, every movement languid and clearly calculated to have the greatest effect.

Jesse looked over at Caleb and mouthed the word *wow*.

Caleb managed a strained grin as he crossed his arms over his chest again.

Scorcher picked up a piece of paper. "I'm just starting to build up a network here, so I don't have a lot yet. I do have this list of all the Christians"—she wrinkled her nose slightly as she said the word, like it gave off a bad odour—"I've been able to discover so far who still have Bibles in their possession." She held out the paper.

Neither he nor Caleb moved.

She waved it in the air. "Come on, gentlemen. When Bill 1071 passes, making anyone disobeying the order to give up their Bibles at risk of being charged with a hate crime, this list will be gold. Arrests like these will get Headquarters' attention pretty fast. Who wants it?"

Caleb nudged him with his elbow.

Jesse repressed a sigh and stepped forward. When he grasped the paper, she didn't let go until he met her eyes again.

The ice in their blue depths had melted slightly and the look she gave him now was mocking. "That wasn't so hard, was it?"

Jesse didn't answer, just took the sheet and moved back to his place.

She twisted to reach for another piece of paper behind her. "This one is a list of all the people I recommend keeping an eye on—the ones whose actions come across as suspicious, or who I believe are the most likely to break the law or cause trouble for you. I have three names so far."

Caleb nodded at the paper. "And they are?"

"James Fromme, an outspoken Christian businessman with a lot of powerful connections. He has been making some noise about standing up to the soldiers and demanding they stop harassing Christians and stripping them of their rights and possessions. A lot of people are listening to him, so I would keep pretty close tabs on him if I were you." Her voice had grown low and husky and incredibly mesmerizing.

Jesse actually felt his eyes begin to glaze over, as though he were staring at a swinging object in the hand of a hypnotist. He blinked rapidly.

A slow smile crossed her face. Obviously she was aware of the spell she was casting. "The second person, Taylor Rockwell, owns a printing press. Always a danger in the hands of propagandists. I haven't seen anything he has printed that would be considered subversive or hatred-inciting yet, but I'm sure it's just a matter of time."

"And the final one?" Caleb tapped his fingers on his arm.

"Meryn O'Reilly. She owns a bookstore downtown. Another one with connections in the publishing industry you should be keeping under constant surveillance."

Jesse worked to keep his features even, but he couldn't stop his jaw from tightening.

Scorcher scrutinized him. "Is it the listing of names in general, or that last one in particular that you object to, Captain?"

"It's the listing of names of people who have yet to do anything wrong that I object to, Scorcher. It doesn't seem like you have very much to give us at this point. Why don't you contact us when you do?"

"Ah, a challenge. I like that. And I accept, Captain. I will find something concrete on this Ms. O'Reilly you seem so interested in and personally bring her to you as a gift. Her head on a platter, if you will."

Jesse gritted his teeth. "John the Baptist was an innocent victim in that story, sacrificed on the altar of human greed and lust and political power."

"There's no such thing as an innocent victim, Captain. We're all guilty of something, even the saintly Meryn O'Reilly."

"Why do you have such a problem with her?"

Scorcher shrugged delicate shoulders. "She's nothing to me. It's her *kind* that I have a problem with."

"And what kind is that?" Beside him, Caleb shifted, but Jesse ignored the warning and kept his focus on the woman in front of him.

"Do-gooders. Holier-than-thou types that pretend to be so virtuous, while in reality, they are as devious and evil as the rest of us. More so, maybe, since they hide it under that lily-white veneer. The maddening thing is the way everyone falls for that innocent, eyelash-batting act." Her eyes zeroed in on his, as if she could see right into his head and read his thoughts. "You know all about that, don't you, Captain? You've clearly bought into the whole angelic thing she's got going on. Which puts you on very shaky ground. Don't you agree, Major?"

Caleb strode forward and snatched the paper from her hand. "Thank you for your assistance. It is much appreciated. We'll wait to hear from you when you have something new to give us." He spun on his heel and headed for the door.

Jesse started to follow, but Scorcher's heels clicked across the floor behind him.

She stopped him with a hand on his elbow.

He glanced down at the long, slender fingers wrapped around his arm and reluctantly looked up to meet her gaze.

"You did hire me to produce those names, Captain. I'm only doing my job."

"I didn't hire you. The Canadian Army did."

"Still, I apologize if I have somehow offended you. That was not my intention."

"And what was your intention?"

"Simply to provide a service to the dedicated men and women who so selflessly defend and protect this country. Give me a chance, and I'll show you I am capable of offering exceptional service in more ways that you can imagine."

Jesse pulled his arm from her grasp and stepped away from her. "Just make sure you are doing the work you were hired to do and not using government money to pursue some kind of personal vendetta."

Her lips curved upward again. "The wonderful thing about my job, Captain, is that I can do both at the same time."

Behind him, Caleb cleared his throat again.

Jesse bit back a scathing reply and spun around. Neither of the men spoke until they reached the end of the long hallway and Caleb opened the door to the parking lot. The air had grown thicker and hotter while they'd been in with Scorcher, and it slapped Jesse in the face when he stepped outside. He slumped back against the warm brick of the building and exhaled a curse word.

"You can say that again."

Jesse repeated the word.

Caleb smiled grimly.

"What just happened in there?"

"If I had to sum it up in a sentence, I'd say that Scorcher took the first round."

"I've never seen anything like that in my life."

"Any*one* like that, you mean." Caleb shook his arms, as though trying to slough off anything that might have attached itself to him in the warehouse. "Was it just me or did it feel like there were more than three of us in that room?"

The same clammy chill Jesse had felt in the hallway brushed over his skin again. "It wasn't just you."

"She had your number pretty good by the time we escaped her clutches." He punched Jesse lightly in the shoulder. "Good job letting me do all the talking, by the way."

He cringed. "I should have. Now I've managed to put Meryn in even greater danger."

"What's done is done. If Meryn doesn't do anything illegal, even the relentless Scorcher won't be able to touch her."

"Should we warn her?"

"Go and see her, you mean?"

"I'm the one who put her in this position. I should at least let her know she's being watched."

"You realize that goes against every possible rule and guideline ever conceived of by the army. And that's a lot of rules and guidelines, my friend."

"Yes, I know."

Caleb shook his head. "It didn't work, did it?"

"What?"

"My cure for the pining. You want to see Meryn more than ever, don't you?"

"Yes, for some odd reason."

"Same reason I'd give anything to see Natalie at the moment—to remind myself that there are still good, decent women in the world."

"You could be right."

"Could be?"

Jesse started toward their vehicle. "You're right, okay? Happy?"

"You know I am. Nothing makes me happier than hearing you say those words."

"So we can go see her?"

Caleb pulled the jeep keys from the pocket of his camouflage pants. "You know, I miss the days when you'd come whining to Rory and me about the rough time some girl at school had given you, and all we had to do to cheer you up was take you out for ice cream."

Jesse let out a short laugh. "Somehow I don't think a banana split will cut it after what we just went through."

"I guess not." Caleb rested his arms on top of the vehicle and looked at Jesse for a few seconds before pointing a finger in his direction. "Okay, fine. But I'm coming in with you, and we're keeping the meeting off the record but completely professional. Under no circumstances will you mention that we are using an informant. Only that she is being watched, understood?"

"Understood." Jesse slid into the passenger seat and buckled his seat belt before shooting his friend a sideways glance. "And then you're taking me for ice cream."

Chapter Thirteen

Meryn sat on the stool behind the counter in her store, both elbows propped on the cool surface as she chewed on her thumbnail. She still had connections to the Christian book and Bible supplier she'd always ordered from. Was it possible that she could order more, or would they have been shut down already? They didn't have a physical store, but they sold their supplies online, so maybe the army hadn't gotten to them yet.

But what about Captain Christensen?

Meryn batted a hand in front of her face, trying to dismiss the thought that had crashed into her mind.

It didn't work.

An image of his green eyes pleading with her to stay out of trouble shimmered in front of her.

She dropped her face into her hands. This was exactly why she had wanted to avoid contact with him, with any of the soldiers, as much as possible. She didn't want to care what they thought about her or anything else. Somehow, though, against her will, a desire not to disappoint the captain had grown inside her. If she was being honest, she'd have to admit that desire, along with the fear of what could happen to her if she broke one of the new laws, was what paralyzed her now.

Meryn lifted her head. *I have to do this. I have to try.* She was one of the few people in the city with the connections to place the order for more Bibles. If she could get some, she could slip them to the new Christians or the people who came to church looking for more information on what Christians believed. Some of those people had never cracked open a Bible in their lives and had no idea of the powerful truths contained within its covers. She had to do this.

Holding the i-com tightly, Meryn spoke the number of her supplier into the hand-held unit and rested her head on one palm as she listened to the ringing. She'd have to be careful what she said. Public outcry in the thirties against government spying had resulted in the passing of a strict privacy bill. The Canadian government claimed that, since then, they no longer listened in on the i-com conversations of ordinary citizens, but everyone knew better. It was common knowledge that the use of certain words would alert the authorities and draw an investigation. Meryn would have to work hard to avoid raising any red flags.

"Hello?"

Meryn lifted her head quickly. She recognized the voice, but the old greeting with the name of the business was gone. Not a good sign. "Lynne? It's Meryn."

"Meryn, hi there, darlin'. How are things going up there?"

The knot in Meryn's stomach loosened slightly.

"Oh, you know. Same as everywhere, I guess. We're learning to live with the new normal. How are things with you?"

"Yes, us too. Everything's different, of course, but we're adapting. So what can I do for you today?"

There wasn't anyone in the store and she'd already locked the door and turned the sign to *Closed*. Still, Meryn lowered her voice. "I'm calling to see if you have any ... rare books available for purchase."

There was a pause at the other end of the line.

Meryn straightened the stapler and the loose change cup beside the till, heart racing. Lynne, who had been her main book supplier for years and who didn't deal in rare books, should understand what she meant without further explanation. She picked up a pencil and gripped it tightly.

When Lynne spoke again her voice was much more businesslike. "We do have a small selection, yes. But they are so much in demand that we are only shipping them to clients who truly understand their value and are willing to pay the high cost of acquiring them."

"I do." Meryn doodled on the top page of a notepad. "And I am. I have customers willing to pay whatever it takes, as well, so I would be grateful for any you could send me."

Another long pause.

Meryn pressed her eyes shut. She tried to pray, but wasn't sure whether to ask that Lynne would agree to send her the Bibles, or that she wouldn't and Meryn could rest easy, knowing she had done everything she could to try and get them.

"All right."

Meryn's eyes flew open.

"I'll put an assortment of books together for you and ship them out right away."

Meryn let out her breath in a rush. "Thank you."

"You're welcome. And Meryn?"

"Yes?"

"Be careful." The line went dead.

Meryn powered off her i-com and set the device down on the counter with unsteady hands.

It was done.

———•———

Jesse leaned forward to look up at the sky through the front windshield. "It's starting to look a little ominous out there."

"I heard we were supposed to get some kind of storm tonight. Not surprising, since it's been so hot and humid. Check out the satellite map, will you?" Caleb's gaze flicked to the rearview mirror.

Jesse pulled out his i-com and requested the site address. He scanned the screen. "There's a tornado watch out for this area. The worst of it is supposed to hit in an hour or two."

"I think we should probably forget about stopping by Meryn's."

"We're almost to her place. Okay if we drop in quickly? We can warn her about the storm and make sure she's prepared for it before we leave."

Caleb didn't answer.

Jesse held his breath, waiting for the verdict.

Caleb put on the blinker as they neared Meryn's road.

Jesse exhaled.

"Not long, all right? We should get back to base as soon as possible." Caleb shot a glance at the mirror again.

Jesse's eyes narrowed. "What are you doing?"

"Checking to make sure we don't have a tail."

"A tail? Who ...?" His eyes widened. "You think Scorcher would have us followed?"

"I wouldn't put it past her."

Jesse peered out the back window. "You're right. That does seem like something she would do. And having someone follow us to Meryn's house would not be good."

"That's a bit of an understatement. If we're caught there, a tornado will be the least of our worries."

Jesse scanned the road behind them, but no headlights penetrated the gathering gloom. When he was satisfied they were safe, he turned back around in his seat. They pulled up the driveway to Meryn's house. Her car wasn't there and a stab of disappointment shot through him.

Caleb looked over at him. "Doesn't look like she's home. I'm not sure we should wait."

"Can we give her five minutes?"

"No more."

After four and a half minutes, Caleb reached for the power button to start the jeep.

Headlights flashed across the yard, and Jesse twisted in his seat.

Meryn's white Ford pulled in behind them. She parked and shut the headlights off but didn't get out of the car.

She probably didn't know it was them and would be apprehensive about what more soldiers were doing at her home. He pulled off his camouflage jacket and beret and tossed them onto the back seat before getting out of the jeep.

After a few seconds, Meryn's door opened and she climbed out of the car, holding a bag of groceries.

Jesse walked toward her, his lungs working to draw in air. It almost scared him, how happy he was to see her.

The wind whipped her long hair around her face, and she tucked it behind one ear as she tilted back her head to look up at the darkening sky. Something he couldn't quite define flashed across her face before she turned to him. "Captain."

"Hi, Meryn. Caleb and I were wondering if we could come in and talk to you for a minute."

The same look that had crossed her face when she looked at the sky flitted across it again.

Jesse clutched the top of her car door. *Is that fear? What is she afraid of? The weather? Me?* Had their relationship regressed that far since the last time he'd seen her?

"I guess so."

It wasn't the enthusiastic response he would have liked, but it was better than a refusal. He followed her as she made her way up the grey stone walkway to her house. A hot wind swirled around them, stripping the last of the rust-coloured leaves from the maple tree in the yard.

Meryn climbed the stairs to the porch, and he and Caleb went into the kitchen after her.

She set her groceries on the counter and waved her hand toward the table. "Do you want to sit down?"

"Sure." Jesse pulled out a side chair, while Caleb sat down at one end of the table.

"Would you like a drink? Tea, maybe, or something cold?"

"No, thanks. We can't stay long. There's a bad storm coming, and Caleb wants to get back to the base as soon as possible."

Meryn glanced out the window before crossing the room to take the chair at the other end of the table. She folded her hands on the plastic, flowered tablecloth, tightly enough that her knuckles gleamed white. "Is there something I can help you with?"

"Actually, we're hoping we can help you."

"Oh?"

Jesse looked over at Caleb. He'd already messed up badly once today by opening his mouth, and he didn't trust himself not to do it again.

Caleb straightened in his chair. "It's come to our attention that you are being watched."

She blinked rapidly. "Watched?"

"Yes. The army obtained a report that suggested you, among others, have the potential to carry out what have recently been ruled illegal activities."

Her head jerked. "Potential? Based on what?"

"Your contacts in the publishing industry."

"Ah. And who, may I ask, supplied the army with this report?"

Neither of them answered.

Meryn swung her gaze toward Jesse. "Can I ask who this informant is so I know who's spying on me?"

He wiped his palms on his khaki pants, suddenly sorry they had come. He should have known she would figure out what they were saying, even when they were using army lingo. "That's classified."

Meryn let out a short laugh. "Of course it is. So what am I supposed to do with that information?"

Jesse shifted in his chair. "We're hoping you'll be careful, make sure you aren't doing anything that could be considered even remotely subversive. If you are, there's an extremely high chance we will find out about it and be forced to arrest you."

"Is that all?"

"I guess so. We just wanted you to know."

Meryn studied him for a moment without speaking, then she leaned back in her chair. "I'm sorry. I know you didn't have to tell me that. In fact, I'm pretty sure you weren't supposed to." She rubbed her fingers across her forehead. "I really do appreciate you coming all the way out here to warn me. And I will be careful, I promise."

The tension leached from Jesse's neck muscles. "Good. By the way, this storm tonight could get pretty bad. Do you have emergency supplies?"

"I have water and a flashlight and candles in the basement." Her voice was strained and wildness filled her eyes.

Why had his words sparked such fear?

Caleb got up from the table. "We should head back, Jess."

Meryn stood and braced herself with a hand on the back of a chair. "Thank you for coming, Major. I know this visit is well beyond the call of duty. I honestly do appreciate it." She stuck out her hand.

Caleb took it and held it. "You're welcome, Ms. O'Reilly. We really would hate to see anything happen to you."

She mustered a smile that did nothing to alleviate the fear in her eyes. "It's Meryn, please."

He released her hand. "All right then, Meryn. Keep an eye on that storm tonight, okay?"

"I will." When they headed for the door, she walked to the window and gripped the windowsill as she stared up at the sky.

Jesse stepped out onto the porch behind Caleb and pulled the door shut.

Caleb halted at the top of the steps. "Let me guess. You're not coming with me."

"She seems pretty freaked out by this storm. I hate to leave her like that. Do you need me back at the base?"

"I guess not. I can come back and get you first thing in the morning." He shook his finger at Jesse. "But no monkey business, do you hear?"

"Of course not."

Caleb glanced at the sky.

An eerie, yellow glow had fallen over the yard, and the wind had died down. An unnatural silence hung in the thick air.

A shiver moved up and down Jesse's spine. This storm was going to be a bad one.

"I better go. Call if you need me."

"Thanks, Cale. Be careful, okay?"

"You too. And I'm not just talking about the weather."

Jesse gave him a wry grin. "I know."

Caleb bounded across the yard through the rain that had started to pound down and hauled himself into the jeep.

There goes my safety net. Might not be the smartest thing I've ever done. Jesse drew in a deep breath before pushing open the door behind him and going back into the kitchen.

Meryn stood at the window, arms crossed over her abdomen as she gazed up at the sky.

A cold chill passed through him at the look on her face. Something more than fear had settled there now.

She didn't give any indication that she had heard him come back inside.

Jesse walked over to her and laid a hand tentatively on her arm. "Meryn?"

She jumped and tore her gaze from the window to look at him. "You're still here?"

"Yes. I didn't want to leave you. You seemed a little ... concerned about the storm."

Meryn drew in a deep, shuddering breath. "You didn't need to stay. I'll be okay. I ... have a thing about tornadoes. I have since I was a kid." She looked back outside.

The yellowish sky now held tinges of green. "Why don't we go down to the basement? We'll be safe down there. Have you had dinner?"

"No, but I don't feel like eating."

"You might in a bit. We should take something down with us." Jesse walked over to the bag of groceries and pulled it toward him. "Anything in here you'd like?"

"There's some crackers and cheese. Bring them down if you want." Her head jerked up, like the manners she'd been raised with had suddenly clicked in, despite her angst.

He might have smiled if he wasn't so worried about her.

"Have you eaten? Do you want dinner?"

He grabbed the bag in one hand and, with the other, captured her fingers in his. "This will be fine. Let's go. You'll feel better once we're in the basement."

Thunder rumbled in the distance and her hand tightened around his.

Jesse led her down the steps and across a recreation room to an over-stuffed, chocolate-brown couch facing a black, potbellied wood stove. Thick, beige carpeting cushioned their footsteps. Armchairs bookended the couch. A dart board hung on one wall, and a pool table stood at the far end of the room, the balls racked and ready for someone to come and play.

Not a bad place to seek shelter. I could live down here for quite a while.

One small window was set in the wall on the other side of the pool table, between floor-to-ceiling shelves loaded, not surprisingly, with books.

Meryn dropped his hand, sank down on the couch, and pulled both knees up to her chest.

Jesse set the bag of groceries on the coffee table. "Do you have any duct tape?"

She pointed to a doorway off the main room. "There's a work bench in there. I think there's a roll of tape hanging on the wall above it. What do you need it for?"

"I'm going to tape up the window. I figure we've dealt with enough flying glass in the past couple of weeks to do us for a while."

She rested her chin on her arms. "More than enough."

Jesse went to the work room. He couldn't find a light switch, so he felt around in the darkness until he bumped the chain hanging from the ceiling and pulled on it.

A single bulb lit the room. The tape was where she had said it would be. Along with a myriad of other tools.

Jesse studied the wall, lips pursed.

As capable as she appeared to be at many things, Meryn didn't strike him as the handyman type. And it didn't sound like her parents or brothers had ever lived in the area. *So whose tools are these?*

Another rumble of thunder, closer this time, brought him back to the task at hand. After grabbing the roll, he walked back into the main room.

Meryn didn't move, but her gaze tracked him as he crossed the room.

He yanked off a strip of tape, ripped it with his teeth, and stuck it across the window on the diagonal. He tore off another strip and completed the X, then returned the tape to the work bench, pulled the chain to turn off the light, and went back out to her. "Did you say you had water bottles down here?"

She inclined her head toward a small kitchen area in the corner. "In the cupboard."

Jesse went over and opened the cupboard doors. Two cases of water sat on a shelf. He grabbed four of the bottles and set them on the counter. Searching through the drawer below, he found a flashlight, a couple of candles, and a lighter. He carried everything back to the coffee table.

Jesse sat down on the couch and snagged one of the bottles. He twisted off the cap and downed half the water. He hadn't eaten or drunk anything since well before the meeting with Scorcher. He grimaced at the thought and set the bottle down on the table.

"What is it?"

Jesse leaned back against the arm of the couch, facing her. "Nothing. Just a rough day at work."

"Why? What happened?"

"Caleb and I had a meeting this afternoon that didn't go well."

"Do you want to talk about it?"

"I'd rather forget about it, actually."

"That bad?"

He offered her a tight grin. "Worse."

A clap of thunder, close enough to rattle the window.

The colour drained from Meryn's face as she pulled her knees tighter to her chest.

"Meryn."

She didn't respond. Perspiration beaded on her forehead. She almost looked like she was going into shock.

Alarm rose in him. He reached over and took her chin in his hand, forcing her to look at him.

Her eyes were wide, pupils dilated.

"Meryn. Can you hear me?"

Her head dipped almost imperceptibly.

"Stay with me, all right?" He dropped his hand when she took a quivering breath.

"I'm okay."

"You don't look okay. What is it?"

Her eyelids dropped closed.

Would she tell him? He'd been working hard to gain her trust, but he was still a soldier. The fact that he wore a uniform at the moment had to be driving that point home. He wouldn't blame her if—

She opened her eyes. "I grew up on a farm. We had an old chicken coop in the backyard, about a hundred yards from the house, where my mom kept a bunch of chickens for eggs." She glanced over at him, a tiny spark of humour in her eyes. "Do you really want to hear this?"

"Yeah, I really do. Tell me."

Meryn rested her head against the back of the couch. "One day, when I was six, my sister told me we were supposed to go collect the eggs for Mom. I was nervous, because I'd heard thunder off in the distance, and we were supposed to go in the house when we heard that. I didn't want to get in trouble for not getting the eggs though, so I went with her. She held the chicken coop door open for me, but as soon as I went in, she slammed the door shut and locked it. I was always a little afraid of the chickens, and now I was terrified. It was dark inside, starting to storm, and I couldn't get out of the coop. I banged on that door and screamed and hollered as loud as I could, but no one came." Her voice shook.

Jesse reached for one of her hands and held it between both of his, chest aching for that terrified little girl.

She didn't seem to notice his touch. The faraway look in her eyes showed she'd gone back to that day in her mind and was reliving the horror.

He wanted to tell her it was okay, that she didn't need to finish.

Before he could, she started talking again, the words coming out in a rush, like she'd kept them locked deep inside herself for a long time. "The thunder was so loud by then that the walls of the coop were shaking. Through a tiny window near the roof I could see lightning flashing almost continuously, and the small patch of sky that was visible had turned black. The chickens went crazy. They were beating their wings and pecking at me. I could hear my mom and dad yelling for me, but the wind was howling so loudly that they couldn't hear me when I yelled back."

Meryn's eyes were glazed, unfocused, and Jesse's stomach clenched.

Another sharp crack of thunder split the night, and everything went dark.

Meryn inhaled sharply.

He grabbed for the lighter and lit both candles. When the warm glow filled the room, he took her hand between his again and rubbed it gently. "How did you get out?"

She rolled her head on the back of the couch until she was looking at him. "My brothers figured out what my sister had done and came running out to the coop. By the time they got the doors open, I was huddled in the corner, bleeding all over from the chickens' beaks and claws, and I had gone completely into myself. They said later that I was right there in front of them but it was like I wasn't there at all."

"You were in shock."

"I guess so. I came around when Shane picked me up and carried me out of the coop and the rain hit me, all sharp and icy, like bits of broken glass. The only other thing I remember about that run from the chicken coop to the house in the middle of the storm are the colours. Everything was yellow and green: the sky, the house, Shane's face, everything. Exactly like it is tonight ..." Her voice broke and she pulled her hand from his, trembling from head to foot.

Jesse slid over until he was nearly touching her, then pulled the knitted blanket from the back of the couch and draped it over her shoulders.

Another loud crack rattled the house, and she jumped.

"Come here." Jesse wrapped his arms around her and pulled her to his chest. "It's okay, Meryn. You're safe. There's not a chicken in the place, I promise. And this time you're not alone." He stroked her hair and murmured to her until the trembling gradually stopped and she relaxed in his arms. He held her as the storm whipped around the old farmhouse, tightening his grip whenever the thunder roared or the wind howled loudly enough for them to hear it down in the basement.

Meryn pressed her face to his grey T-shirt, but her breathing had deepened from the short, frantic gasps she'd been taking earlier. When the thunder and wind finally stopped rattling the window and the green and yellow hues had given way to the calm dark of night on the other side of the glass, he held her for a while longer, then looked down at her and realized she had fallen asleep. An overwhelming tenderness welled up inside him.

Jesse shifted slightly to get more comfortable. He kept his arms around her and left the candles burning in case she woke in the night with the memory of a long-ago storm fresh in her mind.

CHAPTER FOURTEEN

S unlight streaming around the silver X on the small basement window woke Jesse the next morning. He blinked, trying to get his bearings. Meryn was gone. He rested his elbows on his knees and scrubbed his face with both hands, fingers rasping over the stubble on his chin. Then he rose with a groan.

He slipped into the washroom at the bottom of the stairs and smiled at the toothbrush, still in its package, lying on the counter alongside a tube of toothpaste. He brushed his teeth, splashed water on his face, and ran his fingers through his hair before starting up the stairs. Halfway up, the i-com on his belt buzzed, and he stopped and pulled it out of the holder.

Caleb. *No deaths but a big mess. Need your help. Pick you up in half an hour. Everything ... okay there?*

Jesse reached for the audio input button, then shot a glance up the stairs. He propped a shoulder against the wall and typed. *House—and my virtue—still intact. See you in 30.*

He stuck the device back in the holder and climbed the rest of the stairs to the kitchen.

Meryn leaned back against the counter beside the fridge, a glass of orange juice in her hand. Her hair fell around her shoulders, and she'd changed into jeans and a blue, long-sleeved shirt that brought out the remarkable colour of her eyes. The sun filtered through the lace curtains, bathing her in a soft light that made her seem almost other-worldly.

Jesse swallowed hard as he crossed the room and stopped a couple of feet in front of her.

A new shyness emanated from her, but she smiled at him. "Good morning."

"Morning."

"I'm sorry, the power's not back on yet or I would have made coffee."

"Orange juice is fine. Caleb's picking me up in half an hour."

Meryn reached into the cupboard behind her for a glass. She handed it to him. "The juice is on the table."

"Thanks." Jesse filled his glass from the jug. "How are you doing today?"

"I went out a few minutes ago to survey the damage."

A bit of a sidestep, but he let it go for the moment. "And?" He took a sip of juice.

"The buildings are all standing, but quite a few shingles blew off the roof of the house and two of the upstairs windows are broken. One tree blew over, one of my favourites down by the pond, and there are branches everywhere, but I guess it could have been worse."

"I'm sorry to hear it, but that wasn't really what I meant when I asked how you were doing."

"I know." Meryn stared down at the glass in her hand, as if gathering her thoughts, before looking up to meet his gaze. "I'm fine, thanks to you. I don't know how to thank you for last night. I'm not sure why I got so worked up. I mean, we have these bad storms all the time now, and while I don't enjoy them, I don't usually lose it completely. I guess that storm was just so much like that one I told you about, I couldn't help going back there in my mind."

"You went through a terrifying experience when you were a kid. If that were me, I don't think I could even eat chicken without remembering what happened."

Humour danced in her eyes. "Believe me, Captain, I eat it as often as I can. Even though I told myself for years that they were only animals, terrified themselves and reacting instinctively, I still get a kind of perverse pleasure out of eating them, like they had me beaten then, but I'm getting the last laugh now."

Jesse chuckled. "Good for you. But, Meryn ..." He sobered as he waited for her to look at him. "You just spent the night in my arms. Don't you think you could call me 'Jesse'?"

Tinges of pink appeared on both her cheeks. "That's not entirely accurate."

He raised both eyebrows. "It isn't?"

"The words might be, but the connotation is a little misleading."

"To whom?" Jesse looked around the room. "We're the only two people here, and we both know what happened. And what didn't."

"I suppose so. But no, I think I'd better stick with Captain."

He frowned. "Why? Do you need to remind yourself who I am?"

"I need to remind myself *what* you are, and what your place in my life is."

"And what would that be?"

"You're the authority here, with a mandate to keep me and the other Christians under control. That doesn't set us up well for any relationship other than an antagonistic one."

"What about loving your enemies? Aren't you supposed to do that?"

A small smile flitted across her lips. "That isn't exactly what that passage means."

Jesse placed his glass down on the counter behind him and moved to stand in front of her.

Her smile disappeared.

"When I came out of that awful meeting yesterday, all I wanted was to see you. And the second I did, I felt better."

A vein throbbed in her forehead. "I'm glad, but ..."

He rested his hands on the counter on either side of her, drawing in the scent of fresh citrus from her lips. "Meryn. I'm going out of my mind. I think about you all the time and wonder how you are and if you're staying out of trouble and when I'm going to be able to see you again."

"Well, you have to stop." Meryn dropped her gaze to the glass in her hand.

"Don't you think I've tried? I know how impossible this is, and I keep telling myself that, but it's not working." He took the glass from her and set it down on the counter, then waited until she looked up at him. "Can you honestly tell me you don't think about me too?"

Her lips quivered, and it took everything in him not to lean in and press his mouth to hers. She drew in a shaky breath. "No, but I have to stop too. We can't do this."

"Why not?"

"Because our lives are too different. We're too far apart in our faith. I can't get involved with someone who isn't a believer. After you kissed me outside the store, I realized I needed to make sure you knew that."

Jesse searched her eyes. "That wasn't all me."

She nodded slightly. "I know. But it still can't happen again. Not just because I can't be with you, but also because you can't be with me. If your superiors found out you were involved with a Christian, you would be considered a traitor."

"I'm not sure I care about that anymore."

"I do. You've been incredibly kind to me, and I don't want to see anything happen to you."

He let out a cold laugh. "That's something, I guess."

"It will have to be everything."

"And what if that's not enough?" He reached up and trailed the back of his fingers along her jaw.

Beneath his hand, a shiver moved through her as she whispered, "Don't. Please."

He moved closer, resting his hand on her cheek and rubbing a strand of her soft hair between his fingers. "Why not, Meryn? Because you don't want me to touch you? Or because you do?"

She didn't answer.

After a few seconds, Jesse exhaled and dropped his hand. "I'm sorry." Her eyes glistened, and he kicked himself for making this even harder for her—for both of them—than it already was. "I'll send some people over to fix your windows and clean up outside."

"No, don't. I have friends who can help me. You'll have enough to do taking care of the damage around town. I'm sure there are a lot of people who are in worse shape than I am."

"But—"

She touched his arm. "I'll be fine, Captain. But thank you ... for everything."

Her fingers were warm on his skin, and his resolve weakened. Their eyes locked. What if he pulled her into his arms and kissed her, really kissed her, until all arguments and protests fled from her mind?

A horn sounded outside, her hand dropped from his arm, and the moment was gone.

A pang of loss shot through him as he glanced out the window. "That's Caleb. I better go." He brushed the hair back from her face. "Take care of yourself, Meryn. You have my number. I still want you to call me if there's anything you need or if you run into any trouble. Okay?"

"Okay."

The door opened behind him, and Jesse dropped his hand quickly and stepped back.

"Meryn?" Kate stood in the doorway, an uncertain look on her face.

Jesse forced a smile. "Hi, Kate. Come on in. I'm leaving."

She came into the room and stopped by the table, her hand on the back of a chair. "Don't go on my account, Captain. I just wanted to check on Meryn and make sure she was all right after last night."

"No, that's my ride you passed on the way in. I'm on cleanup duty today so I need to get going." His feet felt weighted down, leaden. He forced himself to walk away from Meryn, push open the screen door, and step out onto the porch without looking back.

Everything he was feeling must have shown on his face, because Caleb nodded but didn't speak when Jesse climbed into the passenger seat. He rested his head against the window and thought about what had just happened, fists clenching.

Meryn hadn't denied having feelings for him. In fact, she'd admitted she thought about him like he thought about her. Still, her faith—and his lack of it—was a barrier between them, an insurmountable one as far as she was concerned.

He had to let her go. Or at least stay away from her and watch from a distance to make sure she didn't do anything foolish to hand Scorcher ammunition. Not that Meryn would. She'd promised him and Caleb she wouldn't, hadn't she?

Jesse jerked upright.

Caleb's questioning gaze turned on him.

Meryn's words from the night before ran through Jesse's mind. She *hadn't* promised not to do anything foolish, only that she would be careful. And that wasn't the same thing at all.

CHAPTER FIFTEEN

On trembling legs, Meryn made her way over to the table and sank onto a chair.

Kate sat down across from her and folded her hands on the tabletop.

The only sound in the kitchen was the ticking of the clock on the wall above the stove.

Finally, Kate leaned forward. "Could you answer one question for me?"

She had a pretty good idea what it was. "Sure."

"Did the captain get here this morning?"

Meryn met her gaze. "No."

There was silence again for a long moment, until Kate blew out her breath. "Okay, I'm going to need answers to more than just one question."

Meryn managed a shaky laugh. "He and the major stopped by last night to talk to me about something. The storm was starting to get really bad, and he noticed I was a little freaked out."

"Because of the chicken coop?"

Meryn shoved the hair back from her face. "Yes. It felt like I was back in that coop again."

"So he stayed with you?"

"Yes."

"Did it help?"

"Not a whole lot, at first. As the storm got closer, and I could hear the thunder and the wind and see that horrible, green sky out the basement window, I got pretty worked up."

"So what happened?"

"He held me and talked me through it. He was amazing, Kate. Incredibly sweet. I finally calmed down. Too much, actually, because I fell asleep. When I woke up this morning, I was still in his arms, which scared me almost as much as the storm had."

"So what were the two of you talking about when I came in?"

Meryn propped her elbows on the table and dropped her head into her hands. "He told me he's going crazy thinking about me all the time, wondering how I am and when he's going to see me again."

"And did you tell him you've been experiencing the same kind of crazy?"

Meryn's head shot up, but her indignant reply died at the compassionate look on her friend's face. "He did get me to admit that I've been thinking about him too, a little."

"A little. So what does he want?"

"I'm not sure. I told him nothing could happen between us before he had a chance to say."

"Did you tell him why?"

"I told him I couldn't be with a man who didn't share my faith, which is the truth."

"Part of it, at least."

The overhead light flickered and buzzed on.

Both women looked up.

"Wow," Meryn said. "I didn't think the power would be back on for hours."

"That's one good thing about the army being here. Things do run more efficiently." Kate tucked her hair behind her ears. "I'll make coffee."

"As much as I could use a cup, martial law is a pretty high price to pay for it."

"Even so, it looks like they're here to stay, so we'll have to appreciate the small mercies." Kate spooned coffee grounds into the filter and added water before flipping on the switch. "I take it from the way he was looking at you, Captain Christensen wasn't too happy with your answer."

Meryn laughed. "How do you know how he was looking at me? His back was to you."

"I didn't need to see it. I could feel it as soon as I stepped into the room."

Meryn inhaled the smell of brewing coffee. It did nothing to ease the sudden ache in her chest. "It doesn't matter. It's over. I'm sure he'll find another woman soon and forget all about me."

"Sure he will." Kate pulled open the refrigerator door.

Meryn walked over to the cupboard and chose two ceramic mugs. They rattled against each other in her hand, and she set them down on the counter quickly. "Where are Matthew and Gracie?"

Kate grabbed the pot out from under the coffee maker. "They're with Ethan, but he's bringing them over. I called him when I pulled into the driveway and saw all the damage. He's rounding up a few guys to come over and help with the cleanup."

"That's great, thanks. Is your place okay?"

"Yes, a few branches down in the backyard, that's all."

"Were the kids scared?" Meryn sat back down at the table.

"Not really. We all camped out in the basement, so they thought it was an adventure. We prayed a lot, and when it got really bad they ran to Ethan. He snuggled down on the couch with them, and they were fine." Her eyes gleamed. "There's something about having the strong arms of a man around you that calms all fears, isn't there?"

Meryn wrinkled her nose at her friend. "I would have been perfectly fine if he hadn't shown up."

"Of course."

"And I'm sure the praying helped the kids as much or more than Ethan did."

"That's true. Still ..."

Meryn got up and carried her coffee over to the window. She stared out the glass at the devastation the storm had left in its wake. "What a mess."

"Love always is."

Meryn spun around, sloshing coffee over the side of the mug and onto her fingers. "I was *talking* about the yard." She set the mug down and stomped over to the sink, grabbed a cloth, and wiped off her hand. After dropping the cloth back over the faucet, she faced her friend.

Kate's lips were pressed together tightly, as if she was trying not to laugh.

Meryn glared at her. "Don't you dare." In spite of the warning, her own lips quivered at the ridiculousness of the situation. *I don't know whether to laugh or cry.* "What have I done?"

"It sounds like you haven't done anything yet. Nothing irreparable, at least."

"Maybe not physically, but mentally I'm reeling. He's a good man, Kate. And I didn't want to know that he, or any of them, were good people." Meryn rubbed her temples with the tips of her fingers. "Do you know he actually apologized for taking the Bibles? He said that order didn't sit well with him. What am I supposed to do with that?"

"I don't know, Mer."

Meryn dropped her hands. "I do. Nothing. That's what. I sent him away and he went. One mess dealt with." She took her coffee cup and dumped the contents into the sink. "Now it's time to go deal with the other one. I need to start doing more and thinking less. It's too much thinking that's gotten me into all this trouble."

Kate's mouth quirked again. "It's too much of something, that's for sure. But I'm not convinced it was thinking. Hormones, maybe."

"Okay, forget I said anything." Meryn marched across the room and plucked the broom and dustpan out of the closet. She thrust them at her friend.

Kate took them from her. "Attraction, definitely."

"I'm not doing this with you, Kate." Meryn headed for the stairs. They could start with the rooms where the windows had broken the night before.

"Fate, destiny, crossed stars …"

Meryn whirled around on the stairs. "What are you doing?"

Kate's face was innocent. "What?"

"Fate? Destiny? You don't believe in those things any more than I do."

"No, I don't, but there does seem to be something powerful drawing the two of you together. What would you call it?"

"How about temporary insanity? Which, thankfully, I have now re-covered from. So can we stop talking and get some work done?"

"Whatever you say, crazy lady."

Meryn tromped up the stairs. She would never convince Kate of something that, in her own head—and worse, her heart—she was pretty far from convinced of herself.

CHAPTER SIXTEEN

When Meryn caught sight of the boxes on the ground at the back door, she pressed her knuckles to her lips and peered up and down the alley behind the store.

No one was there, even though someone had pressed the buzzer thirty seconds earlier.

That was just as well. She didn't want to know who had made the delivery, and she didn't want them to see her either.

Meryn bent down and gripped a box. One by one, she lugged all three into the back room, where there were no windows. It was early yet, just after eight, so the front door was locked, with the *Closed* sign hanging against the small rectangle of glass at the top. Still, her hands shook as she grabbed a knife and sliced open the top of the first box.

One by one, she pulled out the books. Seven Bibles were mixed in with an assortment of bestsellers. When she'd finished opening and sorting through all three boxes, twenty Bibles sat on the table in the middle of the room. Meryn retrieved one of the long, blue plastic containers she had picked up at the hardware store and set it on the table. She pried it open and carefully placed eight Bibles inside.

Her heart pounded as she replaced the lid and pressed her palms to its smooth surface. *God, give me courage. Keep me safe. Show me the people you want me to give the Bibles to. And protect them too. Amen.* After filling the other two containers with Bibles, she took the first one and pushed through the doorway into the main part of the store. She'd given this a lot of thought, and a couple of evenings ago—the night after Jesse had stayed with her—she'd sat bolt upright in bed when an idea struck her. She knew exactly where she could hide the Bibles until she was able to smuggle them to people in need of them.

When Meryn had bought the store, one of the things she had loved the most was the old hardwood flooring. She didn't mind the creaking sound as people browsed around the room. In fact, she found it comforting and familiar, probably because she'd grown up in an old farmhouse with hardwood flooring. There was one spot, however, over near the fireplace, where the creaking was particularly loud and would occasionally get on her nerves. One day she had pounded on the spot with the heel of her shoe, hoping to drive the board more securely into place. Instead, the other end of the board had lifted slightly. Meryn had dropped to her knees and pried it up.

Below the wood floor was about a foot of space and then a hard-packed dirt surface. With a shiver, she had lowered the board back down, not wanting to know what kinds of creatures might be scuttling around down there, and then solved the problem by dragging a forest-green armchair near the fireplace and settling it in place over the spot. As the years had passed, she had forgotten about it, but trying to think of a good hiding place for the Bibles had brought the space back to her mind.

She glanced toward the window at the front of the store before walking behind the bookcase that shielded the fireplace area from the view of anyone passing by on the street. When she reached the spot, she set down the container and went back for the other two. As soon as all three were piled up in front of the fireplace, she shoved the chair over a few feet and stepped on one end of the board. She grabbed the other end and lifted it as high as she could, then reached for one of the containers, turned it onto its side, and slid it into the hole.

When all three were safely lined up on the dirt floor, she dropped the end of the board, pressed it down hard, then stood and wiped the dust from her knees.

With a grunt, she pulled the chair back over the board and dropped down onto it to catch her breath.

A tapping on the glass of the front door brought her head up sharply. *Who is that?* The army couldn't have seen someone dropping a delivery off at her door and gotten here that fast, could they?

The major *had* told her someone was watching her. Had she been discovered already?

Calm down, Meryn. It's probably a customer. Go answer the door. Her knees weak, she made her way to the front of the store.

Drew's head, light brown hair slightly tousled from the wind, hovered on the other side of the glass. The tight knots in her stomach loosened as she turned the lock on the handle and pulled open the door.

"Drew! What are you doing here?" Nerves sharpened her tone.

"Is this a bad time? I was passing by and thought I'd stop in and say hi."

Meryn pushed her hair back from her face. "Of course not. It's good to see you. Come on in."

Drew stepped inside and closed the door. "What have you been up to this early in the morning?"

"Nothing. Why?" Seriously, she was the most hopeless criminal in the world. Even in the presence of a friend who had no authority over her whatsoever, her voice shook. From the way Drew was staring at her, she figured guilt must be written all over her face too.

He reached out.

She flinched.

Drew pulled back his hand, forehead wrinkling. "I was just going to brush some dirt off your chin."

"I'm sorry." Meryn rubbed at the spot. "I got in a new shipment of books and was going through them. There must have been something on the box."

"Need any help?"

"No, that's okay, thanks. There aren't that many and"— she gestured at his suit and tie—"I wouldn't want you heading off to the bank covered in dust and dirt." How long was he planning to stay? She needed to get to the back and cut down the boxes so she could throw the evidence into the Dumpster in the back alley. But she had been rude enough to Drew the other day at church. "Do you have time for coffee?"

Surprise flashed across his face.

A different kind of guilt flowed through her.

"I wish I did." He tapped his watch. "Gotta keep those banker's hours and get to work by nine." He paused. "I could come back after, though, and take you to dinner."

"Drew, you know I don't date."

He held up a hand. "It's not a date. Just two friends who have a lot of catching up to do, eating at the same table. I'll even let you pay for your own meal."

Captain Christensen's face flashed through Meryn's mind, but she shoved the image away. Maybe it would be a good idea to get out, lighten up a little, and take her mind off ... other things. "You know what? That sounds like fun. Let's do it."

"Great. I'll be back at six."

Drew stepped outside and turned back to face her. He reached out again. "You still have a smudge here." He rubbed her chin gently with his thumb before dropping his hand. "So I'll see you tonight?"

"Sure. See you tonight."

Meryn locked the door behind him and forced herself to walk slowly to the back. If anyone happened to pass by and glance through the big front window, nothing could look out of the ordinary. Within minutes, she had flattened the boxes and carried them to the Dumpster that was already half-filled with cardboard. Should she toss them into one of the containers behind another store farther down the alley, in case there was anything on them that could possibly link them to Lynne's company?

She shook her head. If anyone went looking for them, it would only look more suspicious if she appeared to be trying to hide them.

Meryn tossed the flattened boxes into the Dumpster, then, with a sigh, went back in to open the store and begin a new day.

CHAPTER SEVENTEEN

Jesse tossed another branch onto the growing pile in one of the city parks. Caleb hadn't been exaggerating about the mess around town. Trees were down all over, and although they'd worked non-stop on the cleanup for three days, the sound of chainsaws still filled the air around him. He was almost glad. The soldiers had been going a little stir-crazy lately. Rumours that massive clampdowns were coming abounded as several anti-Christian bills continued to be rammed through various stages in Parliament, but nothing big had happened since the night they'd raided the Christians' homes for Bibles weeks ago. Everyone was getting a little tired of patrolling quiet neighbourhoods and keeping an eye on people who were doing nothing more than going about their business and making the best of the military presence in the town.

The storm was a diversion, at least, and provided them with an opportunity to be active and to present a good face to everyone. A reassurance that, while they were there to keep order and to investigate anyone in this area who might have been involved in the terrorist attacks—a possibility that seemed increasingly unlikely—they were also there to help and to contribute to the well-being and safety of all the citizens.

Unfortunately, even the manual labour wasn't eclipsing thoughts of his conversation with Meryn in her kitchen three days earlier. Jesse slammed a couple of branches onto the pile. Staying with her the night of the storm had been a big mistake. Not that he could have abandoned her, and not that, even knowing how it would turn out, he would have done anything differently. Still ...

He rubbed the back of one of his work gloves across his forehead. His life would be a whole lot easier if he'd never met the woman. And he almost hadn't. Of all the soldiers in the church that day, it was his rotten luck that Caleb had chosen to send him down to the basement. And coming across her on the shoulder of the road like that, way out in the middle of nowhere? What were the chances? If he hadn't, he would likely have never found out she wasn't married, a fact that freed him up to think about her far more than he should. Then randomly picking out her store and searching for a book ...

Jesse yanked both gloves on tighter and reached for another branch. He'd never been able to swallow the idea of a higher power orchestrating the events that went on in his life, but the repeated encounters between Meryn and him were getting harder and harder to dismiss as mere coincidences.

The temperature had dropped considerably from the day of the storm. Still, he'd been driving himself for hours and his shirt was soaked. Anything was better than doing nothing, though. He shifted his hands to get a better grip. The branch he had taken hold of was big enough that he should wait for someone with a chainsaw to come and cut it down into manageable pieces.

Using sheer willpower, he began to drag the branch across the grass. A strong hand clapped him on the shoulder, and he nearly dropped the piece of wood.

Caleb tightened his hold. "Had enough?"

It wasn't really a question. Jesse shook off the hand and finished towing the branch to the pile. "I'm fine. There's still a lot to do." He jerked his head in the direction of the stack of wood. "There are a few more branches to gather up, then I was going to burn them and—"

"Jess."

His shoulders sagged. "I'd rather work, Cale."

"I know. But that's enough for today. The work will still be here tomorrow, and I'd really like for you to be too."

Jesse pulled off his work gloves, conceding defeat. "Fine." He followed Caleb to the jeep and slid into the passenger side.

Neither of them spoke until they were halfway back to the base.

Caleb shot him a sideways glance. "You want to talk about it?"

"No."

"Because, even if you didn't end up in bed—and I'm trusting that, since you insist you didn't, you actually didn't—something obviously happened between you and Meryn."

He sighed. "Why do you always frame these things in the form of a question when you're not really asking?"

"Because it's much more fun for me to let you think, briefly, that you have a say in the matter."

Jesse slumped down in his seat and crossed his arms over his chest. "Always happy to entertain."

"Which leads me to my point. You definitely don't seem happy."

"Believe it or not, I don't live to keep you amused."

"I don't mean that, which I think you know. I mean about whatever happened with the two of you that night."

"Nothing happened."

Caleb pursed his lips.

Jesse rested his head against the back of the seat. "She had a traumatic experience with a tornado as a kid, so she was pretty upset. We went down to the basement and talked until she calmed down and fell asleep." He slapped his gloves together before tossing them onto the front dashboard. "When I woke up the next morning, I found her in the kitchen and I ..."

"You what?"

"I laid my heart on the line, and she told me that nothing could happen between us because we were too far apart in our faith."

"So you had a fight?"

"Not really. There was nothing to fight against. She wasn't angry or anything, but she didn't leave any room for arguments either. We can't be together. That's it."

"Can you live with that?"

"I don't have a choice. She didn't let me believe, even briefly, that I had any say in the matter."

"I'm not sure that's true."

He stared at his friend. "What do you mean?"

"I know she hasn't exactly thrown herself at you, but she also hasn't shut the door firmly in your face. Not until a couple of days ago. I can see how you might have thought the two of you had a chance."

Jesse pulled off his beret and ran a hand over his head. "You can hardly blame her for that. I am pretty much impossible to resist. Poor woman has no doubt been wrestling with herself and her feelings for weeks now, and it's taken her this long to gather the strength she needed to end whatever was starting between us."

Caleb rolled his eyes. "A bit delusional, I see. Well, whatever helps you get through this."

"I *will* get through this. I practically have already. It's time to move on. So let me know what needs to be done around town or on the base, and I'll do it. No more moping around. And speaking of which ..." Jesse shifted in his seat to face Caleb. "I'm sorry about that. I know I haven't been focused for a while. And I haven't been totally there for you. That's over now."

"No need to apologize."

"I'm actually glad Meryn and I had that conversation. It was the kick in the pants I needed to remind me that I am here to do a job, and that has to come first."

"I'm glad to hear it." Caleb reached out and grasped Jesse's arm. "But I am sorry the kick had to be so painful."

"I asked for it." Jesse shook his head. "I knew right from the start that the whole situation was way too complicated. And even if I hadn't realized it, you told me often enough that it should have sunk in. Next time I'll listen to you, I promise."

"Don't make promises you're unlikely to keep, my friend. That's only going to get you into more trouble."

"More trouble than this? Is that possible?"

"Don't underestimate yourself. I have every confidence that you can—and probably will—get into far more trouble than this. Likely sooner than later too."

"With you as my biggest cheerleader, I can't believe I'm not controlling the world yet."

"I don't think anybody's doing that. I just got out of a briefing on the state of international affairs."

"And?"

"Not pretty. Canada's not the only one with a terrorism problem, of course. The board showing current global conflicts was so covered with red pins it looked like the world had been repeatedly stabbed and was bleeding profusely."

"Which, in a manner of speaking, I guess it has been." Jesse slumped against the back of the seat. "Any more on this Bill 1071?"

Caleb's face darkened. "Nothing good. It's stalled at the moment in the final reading stage, which is just as well. Apparently it's extremely controversial and appears to have taken over discussions in Parliament."

"Which part is holding everything up, do you think? The defining of hate crimes or the corresponding punishments?"

"From what I hear, the hate crimes portion has been settled. The government's gotten mired down in the other part of it."

"But you don't know exactly what's gotten everyone so fired up?"

"It's supposed to be a closed debate, but there have been leaks, bits and pieces here and there. Enough to make me extremely nervous."

"Why?" Jesse studied his friend's grave features.

Caleb usually shared everything with him, so his reticence to talk about the already notorious Bill 1071 was raising all kinds of red flags.

Please, no. "They're talking about bringing back capital punishment, aren't they?"

Caleb let out a long breath. "I think that's part of it, yes."

"Part of it? What else could there be?"

Caleb shifted in his seat. "Look, Jess, it's all useless conjecture at this point. Maybe it won't pass or, if it does, it won't be as bad as everyone's speculating it could be. Why don't we wait for official notification instead of wasting our time trying to guess what's going to happen?"

Jesse studied him for another moment, but Caleb didn't look over. Clearly he was shutting down the conversation, something he rarely did when it was just the two of them talking. Jesse stared out the front windshield at the gathering gloom.

The sun sank low in the sky, but the obscuring of the light seemed to have less to do with the turning of the earth and more with what was happening on the face of it.

Jesse struggled to draw in a breath, as though the cloud of dust that had hovered around the obliterated mosques for days after the blasts had rippled out across the country and still hung in the air—now invisible, but just as thick and choking.

He shook his head, trying to throw off the heaviness that had settled in his lungs. "Seems like all of humanity is on a mission to wipe itself out and take the planet with it."

"Seems like it." Caleb twisted the wheel to turn onto the base. "So don't worry about trying to run the whole world; concentrate on controlling your own little corner of it, and I'll be happy."

"Which is, of course, all I care about."

"Naturally." They pulled into the parking lot and wheeled into Caleb's space near the back door. "Hungry?"

"Not particularly."

"Good. That's the perfect way to head into dinner in a military mess hall."

Jesse laughed. What would he do without Caleb? If he didn't have his friendship, Jesse would be completely lost.

CHAPTER EIGHTEEN

Meryn bent over the counter, adding up receipts. Business had been steady all day, with no time to process and shelve the novels Lynne had included in the shipment that morning. Now it was almost time to close, and Drew would be there soon to take her to dinner. She pressed down harder on the paper with her pencil.

She should have called him right after he'd left and cancelled the plans. As much as she liked him, she wasn't comfortable with the shift in his attitude toward her. It hadn't been a good idea at all to agree to spend the evening alone with him. But what excuse could she have given?

She swallowed. Nope, no sore throat. She pressed a hand to her forehead. No fever either. Bells jangled. Too late to get out of their evening now. Meryn closed the book in front of her and looked up.

It wasn't Drew.

A soldier in a khaki camouflage uniform, green beret over hair pulled back in a bun at her neck, stood inside the doorway.

"Lieutenant ... Bronson, isn't it?" Meryn's fingers tightened around her pencil.

"That's right."

Another soldier came into the store behind the lieutenant. He closed the door and the two of them strolled up the aisle, as though they had nothing better to do than browse for hours through her selection of used books.

Whatever they were up to couldn't be good. Cold shivers moved up and down her spine. "Is there something I can help you with?"

"Private Whittaker and I were talking about how we could both use a good book to read, so we thought we'd stop in and take a look around."

Meryn turned her wrist to check her watch. "I was about to close. Was there something in particular you were looking for?"

"Not really. Maybe something new? Have you had any shipments recently?"

Meryn dropped the pencil into the holder by the register. She might be a rookie in the underground game, but she did think it would probably go better for her if she told the truth as often as possible. "Actually, I did get a few new books in today. I haven't had time to process them yet, but you're welcome to take a look if you'd like. I can take you to the back room."

"Great, thanks." The soldiers followed her through the store and past the swinging doors.

Meryn gestured toward the table. "Help yourselves."

She hovered near the doorway, trying to stem the rising panic that was sending her heart rate into overdrive. She hadn't paid a lot of attention to the other books in the boxes. Had she gotten all of the Bibles out? Were there any other titles there that might be considered subversive? And why would the soldiers show up today of all days? Was it a routine follow-up after the warning they had issued the last time they had been in her store? Or had they heard something from their little spy?

Surely if the informant, whoever he was, knew about the delivery, he would have passed on that information earlier in the day. It wouldn't have taken them this long to act on it, would it?

Meryn forced her tense muscles to relax.

After several agonizing minutes, the bells at the front of the store jangled again and Meryn jumped.

The lieutenant looked up from the books. "Go ahead and see who that is if you'd like. I think we're almost done with these."

Should she insist that she either be allowed to stay or that they leave the back room? They had no right to be there, especially alone. She hadn't seen a warrant. There really wasn't a way to argue that with the woman without arousing suspicion, though, so she pushed through the swinging doors back out into the store.

Drew stood at the counter. He smiled at her as she approached. "Ready to go?"

"Actually, there are a couple of soldiers in the back taking a look at some of my books. I need to wait until they finish, and then we can leave."

He frowned. "What are they looking for?"

"Something to read, they said."

"You don't have anything in the store you're not supposed to have, do you?"

"Of course not." Meryn worked to keep her voice light. "They came in here a couple of months ago and took all those away and told me they'd close the store permanently if I tried to replace them."

His frown deepened. "What is our country coming to when—?" His gaze swung to the back of the store.

Meryn turned.

The two soldiers strode down the aisle toward them. When Bronson reached the counter, she set down two books. "I know you said these weren't processed yet, but is it okay for me to buy them?"

"Sure. I'm glad you found what you were looking for." Meryn tipped the books onto their sides so she could read the spines.

Jane Eyre and *Tess of the d'Urbervilles*. More classics.

They must offer some serious literature classes in military school these days. She rang up the purchases.

The soldier tapped her credit card on the machine, then took the bag Meryn handed her. "Thank you. We really appreciate you letting us take a look at the new arrivals. It's always interesting to see stock before it hits the shelf. We may try to come more often on delivery day, so we can be first in line. What days do you normally get shipments?"

They know. The thought pressed against her chest like a hand, and she worked to keep her breathing even. "Actually, that varies. I only order books when my stock gets low, so I don't get regular deliveries. You were fortunate to come just when I happened to get some new ones in. It likely won't happen again for a while."

Bronson gave her a tight smile. "Our lucky day, then. We'll have to keep our eyes open for the next time they bring a delivery to your door."

Meryn refused to look away from the lieutenant's penetrating gaze. "Please do."

Private Whittaker tossed a copy of *Uncle John's Great Big Bathroom*

Reader on the counter.

In spite of her inner turmoil, Meryn suppressed a smile. How differently would the conversation have gone with Captain Christensen in her store the night the window had shattered if his taste in books ran along these same lines?

She rang the soldier's purchase through and waited as he tapped his card. "Here you go." She handed him the book.

He grunted in response as he took it from her.

Not exactly a sparkling conversationalist. It was a little early to make a fair assessment, but Private Whittaker appeared to be much more like she had assumed most of the soldiers would be. If all of them had been, her life would almost certainly not have gotten as messy and confusing as it had over the last few weeks.

When the soldiers had gone out the door and were out of sight, she turned back to Drew.

"They make you uncomfortable, don't they?"

"I don't like them being here in town, that's for sure. I feel like they're watching us all the time, like they're waiting for us to slip up so they can arrest us and charge us with being terrorists."

Drew let out a short laugh. "I doubt you have anything to worry about on that front. Obviously you're not exactly a serious threat to anyone."

Meryn's first instinct was to protest, until she realized how ridiculous that would be. These days, the best thing anyone—even those she considered friends—could believe was that she wasn't a serious threat. Insisting she could be one if she wanted to be was not only a childish urge, but a potentially dangerous one. "I hope so." She grabbed her coat from behind the counter and slung it over her shoulders. "All set."

"Great." Drew pulled the door open and waved a hand in front of him. "After you."

Meryn went outside, unable to stop the rogue thought that flitted through her head. *Are you after me? Because if so, things are going to get really tense between us really fast.*

And more tension in her life was the last thing Meryn needed at the moment.

CHAPTER NINETEEN

D ressed in a black T-shirt and beige camouflage pants, Jesse pulled open the washroom door and went into his quarters, still rubbing his hair with a towel. He finished and draped it around his neck, then blinked at the sight of the man sitting in a chair in front of the fireplace, both legs stretched out in front of him.

"Make yourself at home."

"Thanks." Caleb crossed his arms behind his head. "I already have."

"I see that." Jesse dropped onto the chair across from him. "What's up?"

"With all the hard work we've done this week, I'm thinking we deserve a little better than freeze-dried meat surprise for dinner."

"No argument here. What do you have in mind?"

"I thought we could go into town and find ourselves a real steak."

Jesse tilted his head. "Is this really about having a decent meal for a change, or are you trying to take my mind off other things?"

"Two birds, one stone. You coming?"

"Definitely." Jesse got up and walked back to the washroom. He tossed the towel onto the rack, then followed his friend out of the room.

They crossed the parking lot together.

"I could drive, you know." Jesse waved a hand toward his vehicle.

"Yeah, you could." Caleb opened the driver's side door of his jeep and slid behind the wheel.

Jesse sighed and climbed into the passenger seat. "What's on the agenda for tomorrow?"

"More cleanup, I guess. And my source in Ottawa has hinted that Bill 1071"—Caleb's face screwed up slightly, as if the mention of the dreaded bill left a bitter taste on his tongue—"is almost through the House and could be law in the next few days, so we'll have to prepare for that too."

"How are we supposed to prepare when we don't know what we're dealing with yet?"

"We can't, not in any practical sense. But I meant mentally. We need to brace ourselves for what's coming. I get the sense that taking those Bibles was the tip of the iceberg, and we're about to slide down from that into some pretty frigid waters."

"Very poetic." Apprehension curled itself around Jesse's lungs, choking off his attempt at humour. "Any more details you can share with me?"

"It looks as though you were right about them bringing back capital punishment, at least in a limited way."

"Limited?"

"Yeah, only for those convicted under this bill."

"So Christians, basically."

Another long pause. When Caleb spoke, his voice was strained. "I have a bad feeling that's how it's going to play out, yes."

"Did your guy give you any more clues about the rest of the bill?"

"A few."

Jesse's eyes narrowed at the clipped tone. "Anything you can tell me about?"

"No." Caleb pulled into the parking lot of the local steakhouse.

"No?"

Caleb shoved the jeep into park. "Not tonight. I want us both to enjoy our dinner. If and when this bill passes and we have all the details, it may be a while before we feel like heading out for a night on the town again."

———•———

Meryn scanned her menu. "I didn't realize how hungry I was. Now that I think about it, I guess I didn't stop to have lunch."

"Busy day?"

She really didn't want to talk about her day. Or think about the Bibles hidden beneath the floorboards of her store. While she wasn't sorry for a second that she had done it, the whole idea of breaking the law and placing herself in danger of going to prison—or worse—made her feel sick to her stomach. "It was pretty steady. It still amazes me how people want to buy books again after so many years of reading on electronic devices, but I'm definitely not complaining." She looked at him over the flickering candle in the middle of their table. "How was your day?"

"Same old. Money in, money out. The banking business is similar to the book business, I guess. People have gradually been moving back in the direction of wanting personal interaction with a teller instead of spending half their day on hold waiting for an IT guy to explain to them why the transaction didn't go through, or what they need to do to get rid of the virus that's devouring all their files. Go figure."

"Not all progress is good, is it?"

"Definitely not. Of course, on a personal level, I've found that moving forward is almost always a positive step."

Meryn's eyes connected with his. "Maybe, but it's not always possible to move forward. There are lots of reasons why staying where you are can be the right thing to do."

"Of course. It's just that ..." Drew looked up as the waiter approached their table.

"What can I get you tonight?"

Saved by the server. The conversation had gotten a little more pointed and personal than Meryn liked. It better not be a sign of the way the evening was going to go.

She ordered chicken parmesan and a house salad.

After Drew told the server he'd like the pork tenderloin, he reached for her menu and placed it on top of his, then handed them both to the man, who took them with a nod and headed off to the kitchen.

Meryn drew a line in the condensation on her water glass with the tip of her finger. "So, you mentioned something about us having a lot of catching up to do. What's been going on in your life since we last talked?"

For a few seconds Drew didn't answer, then a small smile crossed his face. "Fine, we'll let that go. For now."

Her finger stilled on the rim of the glass. "I'd appreciate it." *I knew this was a bad idea.*

"Okay, okay." He picked up his spoon and tapped it on the ivory linen napkin. "What have I been up to? Not a whole lot. I work way too many hours. When I'm not in the office, I'm usually out in the shop in my back-yard, still trying to bring my dad's old Chevy back to life."

"That's not the same car I used to come over and watch you working on when we were in university, is it?" She'd almost forgotten those days, how much fun they used to have together.

"Actually, yes." He looked a little sheepish. "I know I'm a fool for wasting so many years of my life on it, but I can't seem to let it go."

"I don't think you're a fool. You're just tenacious. You don't give up easily."

"No, I don't. Not when I really want something. And I really want to get that old car running. It's a matter of principle now. I can't let that thing beat me."

Meryn laughed. "Man versus machine—the age-old struggle."

"As it happens, I have a soft spot for age-old struggles: man versus machine, human versus nature, male versus female. Of course, some of those struggles are more fun to take on than others."

"Not going to let it go, are you?" Meryn shook a finger at him. "I thought we were going out tonight as old friends."

"Actually, I was referring to the struggle of man versus machine, but if that's the direction you want to head, fine with me."

"Drew."

"Okay, sorry. Neutral ground. Let's see … What else have you been up to lately, besides selling books to all the re-enlightened readers out there?"

"Good question. Is there life outside the store? I wonder sometimes. Now that we're housebound after dark, I have been catching up on my own reading in the evenings. I also spend a lot of time with Kate and her family."

"Her kids seem to really adore you."

"I love them too. And being the aunt is perfect. All the fun without any of the real work."

"Somehow I think you could handle the work. You'll be a great moth-er someday, Meryn."

"Maybe, someday. With everything that's happened lately and the way the world seems to be going, it's hard to think that far into the future."

He reached over and covered her hand with his. "You're right. Every day, every moment, is priceless, isn't it? Like you don't want to waste a single one of them."

"That's true. But that means making a mistake can be a costly waste of that priceless time. That's why I'm being very careful not to make a move in the wrong direction these days."

"Is that how you see spending time with me? A move in the wrong direction?"

Her forehead furrowed. "No, I ..."

Electricity tingled up and down her arms.

She frowned.

A movement by the door caught her attention and she glanced over. *No.*

All the warmth drained from her body. She pulled her hand out from under Drew's and dropped it into her lap.

———•———

Jesse felt like a hard fist had driven into his gut. Meryn, beautiful in the candlelight, held hands with the man across from her. It didn't matter that she pulled her hand away as soon as Jesse walked in.

Caleb nudged him. "Do you want to go somewhere else?"

Jesse squared his shoulders. "No, that's crazy. She has every right to be here with whomever she wants. She made it clear the other day that there's nothing between us." He perused the restaurant, taking in the artwork on the walls and the candles and white tulips on every table. Soft music and murmured conversation filled the air. "Besides, this looks like a great place. Let's relax and enjoy ourselves. I'm fine."

"Sure you are." Caleb didn't look convinced, but he followed the hostess when she came to seat them.

Jesse trailed after them. When they passed Meryn's table, he slowed and dipped his head. "Ms. O'Reilly."

"Captain." She didn't meet his eyes.

He forced a smile and kept walking.

Thankfully, the hostess seated them on the other side of the room, where he could barely see Meryn and her date around a large fountain and several potted plants. Jesse opened his menu and tried to concentrate on the words that danced in front of his eyes. He finally gave up and closed it.

Caleb was watching him.

Jesse ignored the questioning look in his eyes. "Which steak do you recommend?"

"Does it matter?"

Jesse dropped the menu onto his plate and almost knocked over his water glass. He steadied it and, grabbing the cloth napkin from his lap, dabbed at the drops that had spilled over the edge. "What do you mean?"

"I mean, are you even going to taste whatever you get, let alone enjoy it?"

Jesse doubted it. "Of course. I'm really looking forward to this."

"Yeah, okay." Caleb glanced at his menu. "I've heard the twelve-ounce New York steak is good here."

"Sounds fine." Jesse tossed the napkin onto the table. "For tomorrow, I'll start back at the park where I was today and get that done. Then I'm free to work wherever you want me."

Caleb studied him before nodding slightly and closing his menu. "That works. I'll get an update from the other areas our guys have been clearing out and assess where the greatest needs are. If those Bill 1071 sentences I mentioned come in, though, I'll need you back at the base."

Jesse nodded as the server approached their table. "I'm at your disposal."

———•———

Meryn worked to compose her features before she looked across the table at Drew.

Confusion flitted through his eyes, but he gave her a tight smile. "I thought the soldiers made you uncomfortable."

The corners of her mouth turned up slightly. "Do I look comfortable?"

"No, actually, but it's a decidedly different kind of uncomfortable than how you looked in the store. You obviously know the captain?"

"Not really. I mean, I've run into him a few times, that's all."

"They must have been fairly intense run-ins. You pulled your hand away from mine pretty quickly when he walked into the room."

Meryn didn't answer.

"I guess your hesitation is not with moving on in general, just moving on with me."

Her head shot up. "Drew, no. I honestly have no intention of moving on with anyone. Which is exactly what I told him the last time I saw him. And I believed you when you said we were going out as friends tonight too, or I wouldn't have agreed to come."

"You're right. I'm sorry. I didn't mean to push you. However, as you have probably noticed, my feelings toward you have been growing over the last few months. We were friends first, though, and I'm grateful for that. If that's all you ever want to be, I'll try to accept it."

"Thank you. I appreciate it. I'm grateful for our friendship too. And I would never want to do anything to put it at risk."

"Sometimes you have to take a risk in order to find true happiness. And that's not pushing, that's letting you know that I'm here. That I care about you, a lot. And if you ever decide you're ready to take another chance, I'd like for you to keep me in mind."

Meryn smiled. "I will. I promise." She grabbed her bag from the back of her chair. "Now, would you excuse me for a moment?"

"Of course."

Meryn wended her way through the tables to the ladies' room, careful not to glance in the direction of the captain's table as she went. In the washroom, she splashed a little cool water on her flushed cheeks, then patted them dry with a paper towel. After tossing the paper into the garbage, she shook her fingers in front of her, trying to burn off some of the excess adrenaline that had been pumping through her body since the captain had walked through the restaurant's door.

When she felt ready to face Drew again, she opened the door and stepped into the hallway.

Captain Christensen came out of the men's room at the same time.

They both stopped and her heart rate skyrocketed again.

The captain cleared his throat. "Look, Meryn, we're obviously destined to keep running into each other. I don't want it to be awkward every time."

"Neither do I."

"Good. Then let's call a truce." He held out his hand. "Friends?"

Meryn hesitated before sliding her hand into his. "Friends." His fingers closed around hers, and she struggled to keep her breathing even as their eyes locked.

He let go of her hand and stepped back. "Your date will be wondering where you are."

"Drew isn't a date. He's an old friend."

"He did seem pretty friendly when we walked in."

Meryn raised her eyebrows.

He held up both hands. "Sorry. As you have pointed out on numerous occasions, it's really not my business who you see or what you do." He dropped his hands. "Were you able to get your place cleaned up after the storm?"

"Yes, thanks. Ethan brought a few guys over, and they had everything under control pretty quickly."

"Good." His eyes searched hers for several more seconds.

Meryn finally looked away. "I should go."

"Me too. Caleb's springing for the steaks, and he won't be happy if my dinner gets cold."

"I'll see you around."

"Apparently."

She almost laughed at that. Like Kate had said, there did seem to be a powerful force drawing them together. But that didn't mean they had to give in to it. Meryn forced herself to walk away, feeling his eyes on her until she turned the corner and went back to the table where Drew was waiting.

CHAPTER TWENTY

Jesse rapped lightly on Caleb's door. As soon as he'd read the message on his i-com, he'd known this was it. Parliament had debated Bill 1071 longer than anticipated, but a week into the new year, they must have finally made a decision. The problem was, now that the moment had arrived, maybe he didn't want to hear the details. In fact, as he made his way down the hall toward Caleb's office, he contemplated the idea of handing in his resignation before Caleb could even share the news with him. There were plenty of professions out there he could take up, lots of jobs he could do that wouldn't involve the trepidation he felt now as he waited for Caleb to summon him inside.

"Come in."

Drawing a deep breath, Jesse went into the office.

Caleb stood behind his desk.

The news had clearly come through, and, from the deep grooves etched across his friend's face, it wasn't good.

Caleb waved him toward one of the leather chairs in front of the desk then came around to sink onto the other one. "It passed."

"I gathered that. Have you read it?"

His friend nodded curtly. "Yes."

"Is it as bad as you thought?"

"No."

Relief poured through him.

"It's worse."

"Worse? What could be worse than capital punishment?"

"Capital punishment ... and corporal punishment."

It took a moment for the words to sink in. When they did, Jesse's eyes widened in horror. "Corporal punishment? As in what, the water hose? Bread and water?"

"No. Flogging."

"Here? In Canada?"

Caleb shrugged. "In Canada is all I have the time and energy to worry about right now, so yes, here."

"For these so-called hate crimes."

"That's right. And they weren't kidding about expanding the definition either. It covers everything from proselytizing to faith-motivated acts of violence."

"And other heinous crimes against humanity, like owning and reading a Bible."

Caleb held up a hand. "Easy. That's pretty close to seditious talk."

"I wouldn't say it to anyone else."

"Make sure you don't."

Jesse shook his head. "How are the courts planning to handle all the cases that will be flooding in now? There's already a backlog of several years clogging up the system."

Caleb's hand closed into a fist on the arm of the leather chair. "That's another thing. People charged under this act won't be going through the courts. The government has handed over the responsibility of trying all those charged under the Terrorism Act to the Canadian Human Rights Commission. They've set up tribunals in every major city to review the cases as they come in. Of course, "human rights" is a major misnomer. In reality, the rights of people suspected of a hate crime will be completely waived. They won't have a lawyer or a chance to represent or speak for themselves. Evidence will be presented and considered, but only rarely will the commission hear from witnesses. All the accused will be able to do is sit and wait for the sentence to come through, which is supposed to happen within a week of their arrest."

"A week?" Jesse choked over the words. "How can they possibly hope to get a fair trial in that amount of time, especially if no one is allowed to advocate for them?"

Caleb met his gaze without speaking.

The heaviness that had settled in Jesse's chest since the first mention of Bill 1071 dropped into his gut like a rock. "They're not worried about fairness, are they? All they care about is showing everyone they're implementing a zero-tolerance policy on terrorism while keeping the prisons and courts from becoming any more bogged down than they already are."

Caleb glanced toward the door and lowered his voice. "That pretty much nails it. Politics and economics. That's what this bill appears to be all about." He straightened. "In any case, when the sentences start to come in, we have to carry them out."

"*We* have to?"

"Who else? The country's under indefinite martial law. The Prime Minister is the technical head of the armed forces. The government's still making the decisions, but it's up to the military to carry out the directives without question. That's the great thing about being a soldier—you rarely have to wrestle with the ethical dilemma side of things. You just do what you're told."

"Funny, I never got that part of it from the ads. Although the having to do 'more before nine a.m. than most people do all day' part is pretty accurate."

"That's true. And maybe this won't be as bad as it seems. The punishments are so harsh, after only a few cases, surely people will get the idea that it's not worth carrying out those kinds of acts and they'll stop. This could all die out and go away within weeks."

Jesse shook his head. *I don't know about that.*

Caleb tapped his arm with his fist. "What? You think I'm wrong?"

"I hope not. But the Christian Bible teaches some crazy things, like how suffering is good because it develops character and perseverance, and that those who experience persecution in the name of Jesus Christ—which is definitely how they will view this bill—will somehow be blessed. They may not be as easily frightened away from doing what they believe God is asking them to do as we might hope."

Caleb's mouth thinned to a straight line. "Well, if they know what's good for them, they will be."

"Their idea of what's good for them might be a little different than ours. Believers can be pretty stubborn when it comes to their faith. At least, my parents were."

"We'll see how stubborn they are when they're feeling the sting of the lash across their backs. From what I hear, one good flogging can beat the defiance out of a person pretty quickly."

Jesse pressed his fingers to his forehead to push back a surging headache. "I can't even believe we're having this conversation. It feels like we've been transported back to the Middle Ages."

"Corporal punishment was carried out in this country a lot more recently than that. All they've really done is reinstate a section of the criminal code that was removed less than a century ago."

"So when does it go into effect?"

Caleb grimaced. "Immediately." He grabbed a pamphlet off the desk. "These were delivered this morning. Instructions on how to carry out the sentences." He slapped the pamphlet down on the arm of Jesse's chair.

Jesse reluctantly picked it up.

Caleb jerked his head toward the pamphlet. "There are rigid guidelines that have to be followed, and I suggest you memorize them now, since we could be dealing with these cases within the week."

Jesse slumped against the back of his chair. "Not wasting any time, are they?"

"Nope. The global pressure on our government to take action against whomever bombed those mosques has been unbelievable. Ever since 2006, when the Toronto 18 group was discovered training here, we knew we were a breeding ground for terrorists. The government doesn't have a choice here; they have to do something drastic. Much as I hate to say it, this might do it."

Caleb could be right. Living for decades with the threat of a terrorist attack looming like a spectre over every form of public transportation, every gathering, every sporting event, tourist attraction, mall, crowded restaurant, hotel, and religious institution had driven the citizens of this country to the brink of madness. The latest, most horrific bombings might have pushed them over the edge.

Jesse gripped both arms of his chair, the pamphlet crumpling in his fingers. "I can't believe this is what the Canadian people had in mind, but maybe they really have had enough this time and are out for blood. Literally." He started to get up.

Caleb's hand clamped over his arm. "There is one more thing."

Jesse sank back down and took a breath, bracing himself.

"It's not only the people carrying out these crimes who will find themselves in trouble with the law. Anyone believed to be helping or supporting them in any way could also face criminal charges. And those of us entrusted with enforcing the law will face even harsher punishments than those charged under it if anyone suspects we're not in full compliance."

"And by 'anyone' you mean Lieutenant Gallagher."

"I mean *anyone*. There are eyes and ears everywhere these days. Never forget that. I know you weren't happy when Meryn told you there couldn't be anything between you, but I hope you can see that was for the best. Being together would have been difficult before, but it will be impossible now. You could end up facing a flogging yourself, or worse, if you're suspected of being in league with any known Christians."

"I get it."

"I hope so." Caleb let him go. "We can handle this, Jess. If we stick together."

He nodded, too drained to muster any other response. The walk back to his quarters gave him time to contemplate his conversation with Caleb, which wasn't a good thing. As Caleb often pointed out to Jesse, it wasn't his job to think. As hard as he usually railed against that, in this case it seemed like sage advice.

If he thought too much about this new bill and the horrific ramifications of it, he might walk to the exit at the end of the corridor and keep right on going.

CHAPTER TWENTY-ONE

A blue-and-red rubber ball bounced along the sidewalk. Meryn grabbed it and tossed it to a little boy.

He smiled and waved at her before heading back to the playground.

Sadness rippled through her as she watched him run, the wind ruffling his dark hair. All the terrible things happening in the world, even here in their own country, might as well have been happening on the moon for all they affected him. Meryn whispered a prayer that he would stay that innocent and carefree as long as possible.

She tore her gaze from the children balancing on teeter-totters or hurtling down yellow, plastic slides, their voices happy and excited as they called to each other, or shrieking with delight when an adult pushed their swing high into the sky.

The exuberant backdrop clashed violently with what she planned to do at the park. Could she even do it? Of course, every time she slipped a Bible to someone, that question crossed her mind. A few days after she'd received her first shipment, an elderly woman had come into the store and asked for a Bible. When Meryn explained that the army had taken them off her shelves and warned her against selling them, tears had filled the older lady's eyes. Meryn had talked to her for several more minutes to make sure the need was genuine, that the woman was aware of the risk, before telling her to come to the back door of the store the following day.

After that, word had slowly spread that Meryn had access to Bibles. Hopefully it had also spread discretely.

A month later she'd had to order more from Lynne.

Finding places to meet with people was tricky, though. The church was too dangerous. Soldiers didn't attend every week anymore, but they did show up in the middle of the service occasionally, standing at the back and watching what was going on or patrolling the parking lot when the parishioners came out.

Parks were the best place, and meeting in the open, during the day, while surrounded by the laughter and excited voices of children, helped to ease the thought of breaking the law and putting herself at risk of being apprehended.

Meryn drew in a deep breath of spring-like air as she ambled down the walkway that wound through the playground. Valentine's Day had come and gone a couple of weeks ago, the warmest one on record, which wasn't surprising. Seemed like every year set a new record as winters became milder and shorter.

Like Christmas, her Valentine's celebrations had been subdued, though for vastly different reasons. She'd thought of the captain several times throughout that day and, while she'd been right to push him away, every thought had been accompanied by a dart of pain shooting through her chest.

But she had more important things to think about these days. The small package, wrapped in brown paper, looked innocent enough as Meryn pulled it from her bag. She sank onto a bench next to a woman who appeared deeply immersed in her book.

As Meryn set the package between them on the bench, however, the woman shifted slightly and leaned in. "Thank you," she whispered.

Meryn kept her eyes trained on two teenagers whipping a Frisbee back and forth in the open, grassy area across from the bench. "You're welcome. Do you have anyone to explain it to you?"

"Yes. I have a friend who's been a Christian for years. She and I plan to meet to study it together."

"Good. Be very careful."

"We will. Bless you."

Meryn rested her hand on the bench.

The woman covered it with hers and squeezed. Then she picked up the package, slid it beneath her book, and dropped both into the bag slung over her shoulder. Without another word or glance at Meryn, she stood and walked away.

Meryn slumped against the back of the bench. She had received the second shipment of twenty Bibles six weeks after the first one. No soldiers had shown up at her store that day, but she wasn't able to breathe freely until she had closed up the shop for the night and gone home, leaving the new set of books safely hidden beneath the green chair in front of the fireplace.

Today she had given away her thirty-eighth Bible. Demand seemed to have slowed down a little now. Meryn was well aware that she couldn't keep receiving shipments and passing out Bibles. Their city was too small. Sooner or later she would slip up, or someone would mention what she was doing to the wrong person, and she would be put in jail.

She had told Lynne that the next shipment—expected any day—would be the last one she would place.

She let go of every Bible with a mixture of joy and pain. But she had been raised in a home that taught from the Word of God daily, and she'd attended church her whole life. Large portions of Scripture were locked into her memory. As difficult as it was to give the Bibles away when she didn't have one of her own, how could she keep them from people who had rarely, if ever, read one before the army came to their town?

Some people had fallen away from the church, unable to withstand the watchful eyes of the soldiers, but many more had come, wondering what this teaching was that was so powerful the full force of the Canadian Army had been sent out to try and counteract it.

Meryn rose and started down the path in the opposite direction the woman had taken moments before. Lost in thought, she didn't see anyone coming toward her until someone lightly brushed her shoulder as she passed by. Meryn turned and watched her.

The woman's raven hair reached nearly to her waist. No one she knew had hair like that, yet the lingering thought that whoever that was seemed somehow familiar stayed with her as she headed for home.

CHAPTER TWENTY-TWO

Jesse's i-com buzzed and he glanced down at the screen.

Scorcher.

Come immediately. Valuable intel.

He grimaced. Valuable intel from that woman could only mean one thing—she'd found something on someone else and wanted the military to bring him in. Of course, that was what they paid her for, and she was incredibly good at what she did. He only wished she didn't derive such sadistic pleasure from it.

Last night, desperate to keep busy so he could stop thinking about everything that was going on, he'd dragged Dettmer and Carson out on manoeuvres. This morning he'd promised to take them out for breakfast, but now, with Scorcher's message, that would have to wait. "Sorry guys, change of plans." Jesse did a three-point turn in the middle of the street and swung the jeep around.

In the past six weeks, more than twenty men had been arrested for hate crimes and brought to the base. Two of them had been acquitted and released. One had been sentenced to death and removed from the base. To Jesse's relief, capital punishment sentences were being carried out in Ottawa, at least initially. Details on the death penalty were hazy, as they hadn't been laid out in the bill. More rumours hinted at the fact that authorities weren't using lethal injection, or even the electric chair, but that's all anyone seemed to know.

Jesse was fine with that. He had enough to absorb at the moment. Eight of the local prisoners had been sentenced to a flogging. He and Gallagher had each carried out four of the sentences.

The first time Jesse had done what he'd had to do before retiring to his quarters, it had taken hours for the shaking to stop, and hours more for the sound of the man's pleading voice to fade from his head. An impotent rage had torn through him as he'd stared, unseeing, out his window. This was definitely not what he had signed up for.

The other three hadn't been any easier. He would never reconcile himself to the idea that the punishments being handed down were just or the best way to handle the current crisis in the country.

Jesse pulled into a parking spot behind the warehouse where he and Caleb had been meeting with Scorcher. This was the first time he'd have to go in and face her alone.

He turned to the two men with him. "I have a meeting here that shouldn't take long. We'll go for breakfast as soon as I'm done." He climbed out of the jeep and slammed the door behind him. How exactly did he end up being at Scorcher's beck and call? *This had better be good.*

He straightened his beret as he strode down the hallway, the same unnatural chill he always experienced in this place rising up from the damp floor and swirling around him like a phantom with cold, bony fingers. Jesse shook off the sensation and rapped on the door at the end of the hallway.

As usual, Scorcher leaned against the table in the middle of the room, this time with one high-heeled leather boot crossed over the other. She wore a shimmering, gold, sleeveless top over tight, black jeans. If possible, she looked even more gorgeous than she had the first time he'd seen her. And, somehow, far more dangerous.

He should have messaged Caleb and waited for him before coming in.

The bright fluorescent lights that usually glared from the ceiling were off today. Only the small light beside the door was on, casting Scorcher half in shadows. "Good morning, Captain. Thank you for coming so quickly. I don't think you will regret it."

"What's this about, Scorcher?" Jesse's voice was sharp.

She smiled. "We've been through this before, Captain. It's Annaliese, please."

From past experience, he knew she'd wait as long as it took to get what she wanted. Jesse really didn't have the time or desire to play games with her today. "Fine. What's this all about, Annaliese?"

"That's better." She reached behind her on the table, not taking her eyes from his. "I have a present for you."

A geyser of heat erupted in his stomach. A present for him? That couldn't possibly be good. He didn't want anything the woman in front of him could look so happy about giving him.

Scorcher pulled a shiny object out from behind her back.

Jesse's heart sank.

A silver platter.

———•———

Meryn finished setting the last of the final shipment of Bibles into the plastic boxes and shoved them into the hole in the floor. After dropping the slat firmly into place, she slid the green chair back over the spot on the floor. Done.

When she came out from behind the shelf that blocked the view of the fireplace, she glanced toward the big front window.

A man in a long, brown coat, a woolen hat pulled down over silver hair, leaned against the brick wall of a store across the street.

Meryn walked slowly toward the front of the store, straightening books on the shelves as she went. When she reached the glass, she looked out again.

The man was peering in her direction, but when their eyes met, he looked quickly away and took a long drag on the cigarette clamped between his fingers.

Meryn walked around the counter on unsteady legs and reached for her i-com. She always felt paranoid the day the Bibles came in, but it was clear that the actions of the man across the street were suspicious. She stood for a moment, clutching the device in her hand.

Who could she call? If she contacted Kate or Ethan or Drew, they would come right away. But if someone had found out about the Bibles and soldiers raided the store ... no one she cared about could be there.

What about Captain Christensen? She started to dictate his number then stopped. If she was being paranoid and the man wasn't really watching the store, she'd have a hard time explaining to the captain why she had dragged him all the way over here and why she would even be worried someone could be spying on her.

Meryn set her i-com down on the counter with trembling fingers. The unit might be capable of storing up to 500 billion gigabytes of information—more than the brain capacity of the entire global population—but there wasn't a single thing on it that could help her now.

She was on her own.

———•———

"What is that?" Jesse crossed his arms over his chest, partly in an attempt to appear completely in control of this situation—although he suspected he wasn't fooling either of them—and partly to push back the surge of nausea at the sight of the object in her hands. He had a pretty good idea what it was and what it meant.

"Meryn O'Reilly's head. Symbolically, of course. We haven't quite degenerated to chopping off heads in this country yet. Of course, the way things are going, I'm sure that's just a matter of time."

"What are you talking about?"

"We have her. As you will recall, I warned you that she could use her contacts in the publishing industry to break the law, and she has. She's been smuggling Bibles. I've been hearing rumours about a number of the books circulating throughout the city for weeks now."

Jesse's throat tightened. "Any number of people could be handing out Bibles. Or even printing them, like the man with the printing press you mentioned at our first meeting."

"I know it's her. I confirmed my suspicions when I personally witnessed her handing off a Bible to a woman in a park a few days ago, the details and photos of which are all in my report. Since then, I have been observing her carefully, and about half an hour ago she received a delivery to her store. I have men watching the front and back entrances, and she has not left the building since bringing the boxes inside, so it's a simple matter of going there, finding the Bibles, and arresting her." She twirled the silver object around in her hands. "Her head. On a platter. As promised." She held the dish out to him. "You're welcome."

Jesse made no move in the direction of her offering.

She waited for a few seconds, then, with a cold laugh, she set the tray down on the table behind her.

Jesse's mind spun. If he could contact Meryn, warn her to get out of the building and disappear before they got there, maybe she—

"Time is of the essence, of course." Scorcher interrupted his frantic thoughts. "You'll want to get there before she hides the Bibles or manages to get them—or herself—out of the building somehow. With that in mind, I asked one of your fellow officers to meet us here so that he could assist you in the arrest."

Rage roared through him like an out-of-control inferno. "May I remind you that *you* work for the military, Ms. Pettersson, not the other way around? You have no business giving orders to any of my people. I will call in whomever I wish to—" The words caught in his throat when Gallagher stepped out of the shadows in the back corner of the room.

"She didn't order me to come, Captain. Merely suggested that you might need some backup on this operation."

His words only threw fuel onto the blazing fire. Jesse clenched his fists. "I could have handled this on my own."

"I'm sure. Still, I've always found that it's good to go into these types of situations with a decisive show of unity and force. It also helps to have a second officer on the scene to ensure that proper procedures are followed. There's nothing more frustrating than a criminal getting off on a technicality, don't you agree?"

"Alleged criminal, Lieutenant. And I believe my record will reflect that I am perfectly capable of following procedures without anyone, particularly a subordinate, watching over my shoulder."

"Think of it as watching your back. We are on the same side, you know."

Jesse drew in a stabilizing lungful of air. This conversation was getting him nowhere. Scorcher's eyes were already on him, gauging and assessing his response to her news. The longer he stood there and argued with the lieutenant, the more suspicious she and Gallagher were likely to get. "We'll need to get a search warrant."

"Already done." Gallagher held up his i-com. It had become ridiculously easy to get a warrant over the last few months. Any suspicion of wrongdoing, however slight, was grounds for permission to make an official search. And warrants didn't need to be delivered in person, just scanned and sent to any hand-held device, which could be done instanta-neously. While Jesse had always admired and appreciated the efficiency of the military, today he wouldn't have minded a little less of it.

"I took the liberty of going ahead and contacting the major, letting him know what's going on and asking him to send the required form." Gallagher dropped the device into his shirt pocket.

So Caleb knew what was happening. That might be for the best. Still, the lieutenant took far too many liberties. That issue would have to be dealt with later.

And it would be.

He spun on his heel. "Let's go, then." So much for warning Meryn. He'd have to hope the intel was wrong, or that no Bibles would be found on the premises. The best situation of all would be for them to not find her *or* the Bibles at the store. Unfortunately, with Scorcher's men in place, that wasn't likely to happen.

Jesse flung open the door of the room and marched down the hall, Gallagher's footsteps echoing on the tiles behind him. For the first time in years, Jesse really wished he were a praying man.

Today there wasn't much he wouldn't give for a little divine assistance.

———•———

Meryn reached below the counter and grabbed her bag. Maybe the man across the street had nothing to do with her, but, if he did, she needed to get out of the store immediately and as far away as possible. If she was wrong, she could return in the next day or two and no harm would be done. But if she was right … With a last glance at the man across the street, Meryn started for the back of the store.

She went through the swinging doors and stopped.

Don't go.

The words, so unmistakable they were almost audible, whispered through her. Meryn braced herself on the table in the back room.

Don't go? Could that be right? Soldiers might already be on their way. If she stayed she would likely be arrested, and rumours were flying about how harsh sentences had become for those charged under the Ter-rorism Act. Even if those rumours were exaggerated, the punishments would still be far worse than the lenient prison sentences the justice system had routinely handed out to criminals when she was growing up. Frankly, she had no desire whatsoever to find out.

She took another step toward the door.

Don't go.

There was no mistaking the message. She was supposed to stay and face the consequences of what she had done.

Meryn squared her shoulders. Whatever happened, she wouldn't have to face those consequences alone. God would give her the strength to endure the trials that lay ahead.

Peace flowed through her and she unlocked the back door before slowly making her way to the front of the store and unlocking that door as well. As calmly as she could, she replaced her bag behind the counter and sat down on the metal stool to wait.

CHAPTER TWENTY-THREE

Meryn pressed a hand to her abdomen as a green jeep roared up to the curb outside her front window.

Captain Christensen, in full camouflage gear, gun holstered at his waist, rounded the front of the vehicle and strode toward the store.

Meryn drew in a quick breath. Would he help her?

Another officer—a lieutenant, judging by the two stars on the shoulder of his uniform—with what looked like a perpetual scowl on his face, jumped out of the vehicle and fell into step behind the captain.

The brief surge of hope dissipated. If the captain had been alone, he might have been able to do something for her, but with another officer as a witness, his hands would be tied.

Meryn pressed her fingers against the counter to keep them from shaking and stood up as the men stormed into the store, the bells jangling loudly.

The captain's jaw was set tightly, and he wouldn't meet her gaze.

She didn't blame him for being furious. This was exactly what he had warned her against doing, the kind of trouble he had begged her, on more than one occasion, to avoid.

"Meryn O'Reilly." Still avoiding her eyes, the captain barked out her name.

"Yes."

"We have orders to search this building for contraband items."

"Do you have a warrant?"

The captain jerked his head toward the other man, who stepped forward and held up his i-com screen.

She didn't bother with all the fine print, but the major's scrawled signature at the bottom of the screen clutched at her chest.

Boots thudded on the wood flooring behind her.

Meryn turned her head to see who was coming.

Two more soldiers, the same privates who had taken the Bible from her home, had come in through the back door. They joined the officers in front of the counter.

Captain Christensen stepped closer. "Did you receive a delivery of books this morning?"

For a few seconds she didn't answer, then she raised her chin. "Yes."

"Were there illegal items among them?"

Meryn hesitated.

The captain slammed both palms down on the counter.

She jumped.

"Ms. O'Reilly. We have an eyewitness prepared to testify that Bibles were delivered to this store approximately forty-five minutes ago. If you show us where they are, things will go much easier for you. If not, we will find them. We will pull every single book from the shelves, tear apart every piece of furniture, and rip up every floorboard until we—"

She flinched.

He searched her face, eyes narrowing. When she didn't speak, he turned to the three men behind him. "Check the entire store for loose floorboards. Tear up any you think might possibly—"

"Wait." Meryn's voice cracked. They knew about the Bibles, and they knew where to start looking. If she didn't show them exactly where they were, it would only be a matter of time before they found the spot under the green chair. In the meantime, half the floor in her store would be ripped to pieces. "I'll show you." She made her way around the counter.

The captain moved back to allow her to pass in front of him.

When she got to the green chair, she reached for it, but the captain stopped her with a hand on the sleeve of her sweater.

He jerked his head at the two privates, who each took an arm of the chair and lifted it back a few feet before setting it down.

The lieutenant stepped forward and stomped each board with the heel of his boot until the loose one lifted. He dropped to his knees and yanked the board up.

Meryn winced as it cracked and broke, and he tossed the large piece to one side.

In seconds, the three boxes had been tugged loose from the space under the floor. The lieutenant pried off the lids, looked up at the captain, and nodded.

Captain Christensen pulled a set of handcuffs from his belt.

Knots twisted in Meryn's stomach until she had to bend forward slightly from the pain.

"Meryn O'Reilly, I am placing you under arrest for the crimes of purchasing, possessing, and distributing illegal materials in contradiction to the Terrorism Act. Do you understand these charges?"

Meryn nodded, throat too tight to speak.

"Hands behind your back."

Her eyes stung, but she blinked back the tears and bent her arms behind her.

Cold steel circled her wrists. The handcuffs locked into place with a loud click.

The captain's fingers slid above the metal, and he squeezed gently. He immediately pulled his hand away and grasped her arm again.

The tender gesture, as small and almost indiscernible as it was, lessened the ache in her stomach and gave Meryn the strength to stand up straight.

"Let's go." Captain Christensen directed her toward the front door. He looked back over his shoulder. "Dettmer, Carson, bring the Bibles." When they reached the door, the captain opened it and then pressed the handle in to lock it. "Pull it shut behind you," he instructed the privates as he led her through the doorway.

Several of her fellow merchants peered out their windows or watched what was going on from the sidewalk in front of their stores.

Heat flooded Meryn's cheeks.

The man in the brown coat and wool hat had disappeared, and bitterness burned like acid in her chest. Who was he? And what was his connection to her?

The captain wrenched open the back door of the jeep. "Get in."

Meryn ducked her head and slid onto the cool, leather seat.

The privates climbed in, one on each side of her, holding the plastic boxes on their laps. The two officers swung into the front seats. As soon as the jeep pulled away from the curb, the lieutenant bent his head.

The captain sent him a sharp glance. "What are you doing?"

"Messaging the major. He said to let him know what was going on."

"I will give the major a full report when we get back to base."

"He asked me to update him as soon as we left the scene."

Captain Christensen's jaw worked.

The privates exchanged a look in front of her. The two officers obviously had a history, a tense one, from the way they were glaring at each other.

The captain's gaze flicked to the rearview mirror before he blew out a breath. "Keep it brief. I'll speak to him when we arrive."

"Yes, sir."

Meryn's eyes narrowed at the sneer in the lieutenant's voice.

Judging by the captain's white-knuckled grip on the steering wheel, he was not impressed either.

They drove in silence for several minutes until they pulled into the old psychiatric hospital the military had claimed for their base. The captain flashed his I.D. to the soldier in the booth at the gate.

Thoughts whirled through Meryn's mind like debris caught up in a tornado. What would happen to her now?

The captain parked the jeep, and all of the men got out of the vehicle.

Meryn struggled to follow them, which wasn't an easy task without the use of her hands.

The captain waited for her by the back door and, when she nearly lost her balance on the loose gravel, grabbed her arm. He didn't let go of her as he walked her toward the nearest building. Once inside, he turned to the officer who had come with him to her store. "Thank you for your assistance, Lieutenant. I can take it from here."

A dark shadow passed over the lieutenant's face, but he started down the hall in front of them without a word. Just before he disappeared around the corner, he pulled his i-com out of his pocket.

As soon as he was out of sight, the tightness in Meryn's chest eased. There was something malignant in the eyes of that man.

The captain tugged on her arm, leading her down another long hallway until they stopped in front of a door. He pressed his thumb to the pad on the wall, and the lock disengaged. The captain shoved open the door before turning to the two privates. "Give me the Bibles, then stay with her in my quarters until I get back."

"Yes, sir," said one of the privates.

They both looked surprised, but neither of them asked any questions. They handed him the plastic boxes, then each grasped one of her arms and guided her into the room.

The door shut behind them, and the lock slid into place with a loud click.

CHAPTER TWENTY-FOUR

Jesse raised his hand to knock on Caleb's door as his i-com buzzed. He looked down at the screen.

Caleb.

My office. Now.

Jesse took a deep breath and tapped lightly on the door before opening it and stepping inside.

Caleb looked up from the unit he held in his hand, then tossed it onto his desk and stood, eyes blazing.

Jesse fought back a rising sense of trepidation.

Caleb came around the desk and stopped in front of him. "I don't think I can possibly convey to you how much I detest hearing what you are up to from Gallagher instead of from you."

"I'm sorry. I was bringing in a prisoner. It didn't seem like the best time to stop and send you a message."

"Speaking of the prisoner, Gallagher was more than happy to let me know you brought her into the building instead of straight to the holding cells. Are you planning to let me in on your plans for her at some point?"

Jesse shifted his weight from one foot to the other. "That's what I was coming here to tell you. She's in my quarters."

"Your *quarters?*"

Jesse had known Caleb wouldn't be wild about the plan devised while driving back to the base, but the barely restrained fury in his tone meant it might be even harder than Jesse'd thought to persuade Caleb to give the experiment a try. "Cale—"

Caleb's chin notched up a fraction.

Jesse came to attention. "Major, I know this arrangement is unconventional, but—"

"Unconventional? I believe the word you are looking for is *ridiculous.*"

"Look, the two jail cells we have here are overflowing. Until they finish building the new ones, there are currently eight prisoners in each one, all of them male. If we send her there, you either have to double that number in one cell to clear the other, which will not go over well, or lock her up in an eight-by-ten room with a bunch of men. Even if the situation remained under control and no one bothered her, she would be unable to sleep or let her guard down for a minute." Jesse lowered his voice. "Then there is the lack of privacy, the toileting situation, the possibility of ... female issues."

Caleb closed his eyes. "All right, enough. I get it. We are not currently equipped to handle female prisoners. But the way things are going, that had better change fast." He opened his eyes and pinned Jesse with a hard look. "Unless, of course, you plan to host all of them as they come along?"

Jesse dropped his gaze.

"I didn't think so. And I have to believe there's a better option than your quarters this time too."

"Why? Meryn is comfortable with me. Maybe if we have the opportunity to talk about what happened, she might open up, give me more details about what went on today. The trail to those Bibles is going to get really cold really fast. She may tell me something, or let something slip, that will help us track them all down."

"Which brings up another matter I'm not sure you are bearing in mind. Her alleged illegal activities are considered hate crimes, meaning that, if convicted, she will be officially considered a terrorist. As such, she does not merit preferential treatment in any way."

"You know as well as I do that her so-called crimes are arbitrary, manufactured, and propaganda-driven." Jesse's voice rose in frustration. "Passing around Bibles isn't exactly a threat to society, and the person who does that shouldn't be treated the same as someone who has blown up a building or released rounds from an automatic weapon into a crowd of innocent people. Have we completely lost perspective in this country?"

Caleb spun around and stalked across the room to slam his window shut. When he came back around the desk, he stopped inches in front of Jesse and lowered his voice, pushing out the words through clenched teeth. "If you don't want to end up in a jail cell too, Captain, you will keep your mouth shut and try to get a little *perspective* yourself. You are not thinking clearly here. Whether or not the new laws are just is not for us to say. The only thing we are required to do is follow them and ensure that everyone under our authority—even those with whom we might happen to have a personal relationship—does the same. If we fail to do so, we are in grave danger of being in breach of those laws ourselves. Do you understand me?"

Jesse's shoulders slumped. "Yes."

"Good." Some of the fire went out of Caleb's eyes. "Listen, I understand that you are concerned about her, and I'm sorry this has happened, I really am. But Meryn knew the law and she willfully broke it. She also knew there would be consequences if she was caught, and now she'll have to face them."

"I know. And whatever the Commission decides to do with her, I will respect their authority. I do plan to send them my report, which will include testimony that she voluntarily showed us where the Bibles were and did not resist arrest. That might help to get her a lighter sentence, at least."

"You do what you have to do, as long as it falls within the guidelines of the law. I will not stand by and watch you throw away everything you have worked so hard for because you are letting your personal feelings interfere with your professional mandate."

"Understood. And in the meantime, until her sentence is handed down, if she stays with me she'll be safe and you won't have to worry about her."

"Are you sure about that?"

"Yes. Like I said, she's made it clear that I'm the last man she would be with voluntarily, and I hope you know me well enough to know I would never pressure her to do anything she didn't want to do. And none of that matters anyway, since this would be a purely professional arrangement, so any kind of personal interaction would be strictly off the table."

"Purely professional."

"Yes."

"What about leaving her locked in there while you bunk down on my couch?"

Jesse frowned. "Wouldn't that look more suspicious? Everyone will definitely know something is going on if I move out of my quarters."

"We could make it known that you moved out because we had no other place to keep a female prisoner."

"News like that will reach Headquarters fast, and I'm sure they won't be impressed when they hear we're housing a terrorist suspect in an officer's quarters. I really think this has to be kept a secret."

Caleb blew out a breath. "What about security?"

"My room has a two-way lock that can only be opened with my thumbprint or with the key card in the safe in my office. I'll make sure the lock is engaged night and day."

"And the windows? Do they still have bars on them?"

He hesitated. "The bedroom does. The washroom doesn't."

"How is that going to work?"

"I'll lock the door at night and when I leave the room. It opens with my thumbprint too, so she won't be able to get in when I'm not there. When I am, I'll put the fear of God into her to leave the door open a crack, so I'll hear her if she tries to escape that way."

Caleb let out a short laugh. "*You'll* put the fear of God in *her*? Good luck with that. I'm substantially more concerned that she will put the fear of God in you."

"That's the last thing you need to worry about. I've heard it all before and haven't fallen for it yet."

Caleb shook his head. "I have no idea how you talk me into these things, but fine. We'll try it." He held up a hand when Jesse started to speak. "Under the following conditions: One, you promise to steer clear of conversations about faith or religion. Two, we establish some kind of patrol in that area. Are there still empty rooms in your hallway?"

Jesse nodded. "A few. There's one across the hall and a couple of doors down."

"Good. We'll set it up like an office, so the soldiers we appoint—and we'll have to choose them carefully—can come and go without arousing suspicion."

"That should work."

"You better hope it does. Three, you give me your word that if you don't feel things are going well, you will come to me and tell me, so we can make alternate arrangements. Four, when her sentence is handed down, you will accept it without hesitation, questions, or dissension of any kind."

"Is that all?"

Caleb glared at him. "I can do this all day. Any other sarcastic comments you'd like to share?"

Jesse dipped his head. "No. Sorry."

Caleb made him wait several seconds. "Five, I reserve the right to terminate this situation at any point if I feel it is becoming detrimental in any way to the prisoner, you, or the company in general. Lastly, but most importantly, no one other than the soldiers we appoint to patrol the hallway hears about this. We'll have to put it out there that she is a high-level political prisoner and has been put in solitary confinement. Anyone wanting to go into that area has to have clearance from me, so that should keep out any unwanted visitors, especially Gallagher. Hopefully he'll believe that story. If he doesn't and he reports us to Headquarters, both our careers will be on the line. At best. Is all of that understood?"

"Understood."

When Caleb relaxed his stance, Jesse followed suit, breathing freely for the first time since stepping into Caleb's office. "Thank you, Cale. You won't regret it."

"I'm already regretting it." His friend shook his head. "I trust you, Jess, with my life. You know that. But I have a bad feeling you're playing with fire here. She may have told you there couldn't be anything between you, but it's clear you still have feelings for this woman—strong feelings. I hope you know what you're doing."

"Me too."

Caleb slung an arm around Jesse's shoulders and walked him to the door. "One thing I can say about you, you never let things get dull for me, do you?"

"It's my life's mission." He reached for the door handle.

Caleb smacked a palm against the door, a smirk on his face. "Female issues?"

Jesse sighed. "You were married. It's a legitimate point."

Caleb's lips twitched. "I suppose it is. Of course, you realize if those ... issues do come up, you're the one who has to deal with them now?"

Jesse winced.

Caleb laughed and moved his hand so Jesse could open the door. As he walked out into the hall, Caleb slapped him on the back. "Good luck, my friend."

Even if his parting words were more mocking than sincere, Jesse was willing to take them.

Because, from everything he knew about Meryn O'Reilly, he had a feeling that he was going to need all the luck he could get.

CHAPTER TWENTY-FIVE

Meryn sat on the black leather chair at the captain's desk, hands still cuffed behind her back.

Dettmer and Carson had settled on the couch in front of the fireplace, but, when the door flew open and the captain marched into the room, they both scrambled to their feet.

Without a glance in her direction, he motioned to the two privates, who walked over to the door. "Thank you, gentlemen. You can go now. I apologize about breakfast. We will do it another time."

"No problem, sir." Dettmer strode out the door, Carson right behind him.

"And, gentlemen ..."

They both turned back to face him.

"This is a highly confidential situation. The major has cleared you both to know what's going on, but no one else is to hear anything about it. If they do, you will face criminal charges for leaking classified information. Is that clear?"

"Yes, sir."

Captain Christensen shut and locked the door behind them before spinning around to face Meryn, anger churning in his eyes.

She tried to swallow, but her throat had gone paper-dry.

"What is it exactly that you don't comprehend about the words 'stay out of trouble'?" He stalked across the room and stopped in front of her.

"I guess it's the part about seeing the opportunity to do the right thing and not doing it."

"So you call flagrantly disregarding the law the right thing? Don't you have some kind of rule about obeying authority or something?"

"Yes, we do. But ultimately we have to obey God rather than man."

"You didn't look surprised when we came into the store today."

She blinked. "What?"

"When the lieutenant and I arrived, you almost looked like you were expecting us."

"I did think there was a possibility you might be coming, yes."

"Why?"

"A few minutes before, shortly after I had hidden the Bibles, I looked out the front window and saw a man in a brown coat leaning against the wall across the street. He seemed to be watching the store, so I knew there was a chance you had found out about the delivery."

"So why would you wait there for us to come and get you? Why didn't you leave?"

"I was told not to."

Deep lines appeared in his forehead. "What are you talking about? Who told you not to?"

Somehow she didn't think the words "the Holy Spirit" would erase the look of confusion from his face. "Is it so hard to believe that I could be willing to accept responsibility for what I had done?"

He didn't answer right away, just pursed his lips as he considered her. "That is a fairly uncommon occurrence, yes."

"Maybe in the circles you travel."

He lifted a hand, face incredulous. "Does insulting me really seem like the best idea at this point?"

"What better time than this? I have very little to lose at the moment."

"You might be surprised at how much you have to lose. Did you not stop to consider, when you were ordering those Bibles, that you could end up here?"

"Actually, no, not here exactly." Meryn glanced around the room. "Aren't you going to take me to a cell?"

"Not yet. The few cells we have are overflowing with male prisoners at the moment, so we don't have a place to hold you. If you can possibly stay in line for five minutes straight, you can remain here for now. But don't make the mistake of thinking you aren't a prisoner. You don't have any more rights or privileges here than you would in a cell. If you forget that, we'll toss you in there with the rest of them, female or not."

She nodded slowly. "All right."

He pulled a set of keys from his pocket. "Stand up and turn around."

Meryn forced herself to her feet and turned her back to him.

He unlocked the cuffs and removed them.

When she turned back around, rubbing the wrists that had gone numb, he was tucking the handcuffs into his belt.

"There will be a soldier patrolling the hallway outside at all times, with orders to shoot your pretty little head off if you so much as crack open the door. Do you understand?"

"Yes." Meryn was relieved to see that the anger had faded slightly from his eyes.

"Is there anything you need?"

She pointed in the direction of the washroom. "May I?"

"Yes. But leave the door open a couple of inches."

Meryn's throat tightened. If he thought for a moment—

"I won't come in. Unless the door closes. If that happens, in ten seconds I'll have it kicked in and then I'll hand you over to the soldier outside the door. He will take you to the prison, where I will no longer have any control whatsoever over what happens to you."

Meryn sighed and went into the washroom. She pushed the door shut as far as she dared, even though the small act of defiance likely wasn't wise under the circumstances.

When she came back out, the captain walked over and pulled the door shut behind her.

The lock engaged with a loud click.

"I have to go out for a while. I'll be back in a few hours." Before she could respond, he crossed the room, pressed his thumb to the pad, yanked the door open, and strode into the hallway, slamming the door shut behind him with enough force to make her jump.

Meryn exhaled loudly and dropped onto the nearest armchair. Of all the possible consequences she'd contemplated before deciding to order those Bibles, ending up in this room was not one of them.

The captain's quarters were sparsely decorated and impeccably neat, not surprisingly. An antique desk sat in one corner, so small that she guessed he must have an office somewhere else. A chocolate-brown leather couch and armchairs were arranged in front of the floor-to-ceiling stone fireplace. The room was considerably nicer than a regular jail cell, of course, although she would be cooped up with an armed man, a trained killer no less, who was so angry with her at the moment he could barely stand to throw a glance in her direction. Not exactly comforting.

Meryn closed her eyes. *Father, give me the strength to face whatever lies ahead. I know you are in control of all things, so you have put me here, in the middle of the enemy camp, for a purpose. Help me to accomplish that purpose, whatever it may be. Amen.* She propped her elbow on the arm of the chair. Resting her chin on her hand, she settled in to wait.

For what, she had no idea.

A soft tapping on the door woke her, and her eyes flew open. Meryn turned her arm to look at her watch. Two thirty. Or maybe, given her new residence, she should say fourteen thirty. She conjured up a grim smile and rose as the door opened. One of the privates who had brought her here stepped into the room, carrying a tray with a sandwich and a bottle of water. The sight of the food made her stomach rumble.

"The captain's been held up." The private sounded apologetic as he dropped a key card back in his pocket and carried the tray over to the table under the window. "He asked me to tell you he'd come by in about an hour."

"Thank you, Private ... Dettmer, is it?"

"That's right." He spun around and headed for the door, pulling it shut behind him.

Nice chatting with you. Meryn sighed. Already the enforced solitude was starting to get to her. She meandered over to the table and sat down on one of the chairs. If she was going to survive this, she would have to make a mental shift. For years she had wanted to go on a spiritual retreat. If she could think of this experience in that light, instead of as a punishing isolation, she might actually be able to draw something valuable from it.

Appetite gone, she picked at the food for a few minutes before leaning back in her chair. Meryn stared at the grey wall in front of her, barely resisting the urge to grab fistfuls of her hair and pull.

She really had to be careful what she wished for.

———•———

The captain had come into the room twice, briefly. At 4 o'clock he'd brought her a pot of tea and some cookies, then he had delivered a tray with chicken, vegetables, and bread for dinner. He was there and gone in less than five minutes both times. When he spoke to her, his words were clipped and to the point.

How could she break through the rage that still radiated from him? She couldn't undo what she had done, and she couldn't bring herself to lie and say she was sorry she had done it.

Meryn paced in front of the fireplace. A long walk outside in the fresh air would be better, but she'd have to settle for getting exercise any way she could. She pressed her hand to her mouth to stifle a yawn. It was almost time for bed. She hoped the captain would be back soon so she could ... Meryn spun around to look at the bed.

There was only one in the room. What exactly were the sleeping arrangements going to be if he was planning to keep her here for a while?

Meryn steadied herself with a hand on the fireplace mantel.

The door handle turned and the captain marched into the room.

She froze.

He hung his jacket and beret on a hook by the door, then crossed over to the washroom door and pressed his thumb to the pad. "Do you want to get ready for bed?"

His words sent a fresh wave of apprehension through her, but she walked past him and into the little room. She didn't have any toiletries or pyjamas, so she splashed water on her face and rinsed out her mouth before coming back out.

"Get some sleep." The captain jerked his head toward the bed before turning on his heel and heading for the couch.

Meryn didn't move.

He sat down on the edge of the couch and unlaced one boot, then raised his head. When their eyes met, his face softened. "No one will bother you tonight, including me. You have my word." He let out a short laugh. "If the word of a *pagan* means anything to you."

"It means a lot to me, Captain. We may not agree where faith is concerned, but I do know that you are a man of integrity." She paused before adding, more softly, "I trust you." She took a step toward the bed, then paused. "I could take the couch. I didn't mean to kick you out of your bed."

"You didn't *kick* me out of my bed." He yanked off one boot and tossed it onto the floor. "I told you that's where you would be sleeping."

Okay. He was in charge. She got that. Meryn stayed where she was until he looked at her again.

"Is there something else?"

She twisted her fingers together tightly. "What's going to happen to me?"

Captain Christensen reached for his other boot. "I don't know, Meryn. Everyone's trying to figure out how these human rights commissioners are going to deal with people charged under the new Terrorism Act. Each case is handled differently, and there is no predicting the sentences that will be handed down. We'll have to wait and see."

"Okay." The softness that had crept into his voice gave her hope that he might be getting over his initial fury. She shot a look at the couch. Maybe a good night's sleep would make everything look better in the morning.

At this point, it certainly couldn't make things worse.

CHAPTER TWENTY-SIX

Meryn tucked the navy sheet under the pillows and pulled the grey duvet up to the headboard. She hadn't needed the army blanket, so she left it folded neatly at the foot of the bed. She looked down at her black dress pants and lavender sweater.

They were a little rumpled.

She smoothed them out as best she could.

The captain wasn't in the room. The washroom was closed, but there was no water running. Likely he had gone out and left the door locked. So how was she supposed to freshen up?

At least she wouldn't have to waste time wondering what to wear.

If she asked for a change of clothes, the captain would likely say that having her personal items brought to her from home fell into the category of rights and privileges she shouldn't expect to receive.

She bent closer to the mirror above his dresser, combing her hair with her fingers.

Two framed photographs, the only personal items on display in the room, caught her eye, and she dropped her hands and looked closer.

The first photograph was of an older couple, Captain Christensen's parents probably, taken in front of an apple tree in full bloom. The man had his arm around the waist of the woman, and, while she looked straight at the camera, his eyes were fastened on her. Meryn's breath caught at the sight of the man's emerald eyes—so like the captain's—glowing with obvious love and affection for the woman at his side.

Smiling, Meryn reached for the other picture.

The major stood between the captain and another man so similar to the captain in looks that the two of them could almost have been twins. His older brother, Rory. The major's arms were slung over the shoulders of his two friends, and all three were laughing. Rory looked strong and full of life.

And that life had been tragically torn away from him. Meryn pressed her fingers to her mouth. Looking at the three of them, the closeness between them so obvious, a glimmer of comprehension of the hole that must have been ripped in both the captain's and the major's lives—and hearts—when Rory had been killed shivered through her.

Meryn lowered her hand to her chest, pressing her palm against the ache carved there. A memory of the grief etched across Captain Christensen's face when he told her about Rory's death flashed through her mind, and the ache deepened.

The door to the room opened.

Meryn set the picture down quickly.

The captain came into the room carrying a tray with fruit, juice, and coffee on it. He set it down on the table by the window and turned to her, something else in his hand. "I thought you might want this."

Meryn looked down at the object he held out. "My purse! How did you get it?" She walked over and took it from him.

"I was thinking about yesterday while I was out for my run this morning, and it occurred to me that we had left the back door of the store open, so I sent Privates Dettmer and Carson over there this morning to lock up. I figured this would be behind the counter and asked them to grab it."

Meryn gripped the bag tightly. Now she had some lip gloss, at least, and her toothbrush, items that had suddenly become pure luxury. "Thank you."

"You're welcome." He strode over to the washroom door, laid his thumb on the pad, and opened the door. "There you go. When you're done we can have breakfast."

She started for the washroom.

He waited for her to pass by, close enough that she could see the muscles that rippled up and down his arms and feel the warmth of his body beneath the navy T-shirt he wore. He had obviously showered after his run, since he now smelled of soap and a faint, citrusy musk.

Meryn swallowed hard and went into the washroom, leaving the door open slightly behind her. When dishes rattled on the tray he had brought in, she freshened up quickly.

By the time she came back out, he had set the table with plates and glasses of orange juice. He pulled one of the chairs away from the table and held it.

Meryn smiled at the chivalrous gesture, set her bag down, and walked to the table.

The captain poured coffee into her mug. He was still keeping his distance, but the hostility appeared to be gone.

Drawing courage from that, Meryn wrapped her hands around her mug. "Captain."

"Yes?" He took a sip from his glass of orange juice.

"I'm sorry."

He leaned back in his chair.

She kept her eyes on the steam rising from the hot coffee. "I'm not sorry for what I did, but I am sorry that you've been dragged into it." Meryn stopped and drew in a deep breath. "I struggled with whether or not to order those Bibles, not because I didn't believe it was the right thing to do, but because I didn't want to disappoint you or let you down after you had been so good to me. I know that's exactly what I've done, so I apologize for that."

For a long moment he didn't answer, then he set down his glass. "Meryn."

She forced herself to look up and meet the eyes that were watching her intently.

"You haven't disappointed me. To be disappointed, you have to expect or hope for something that doesn't end up happening. And frankly, pretty much from the moment I met you, I knew better than to expect you wouldn't do something like this."

She offered him a wry grin.

"I was angry, though, when I came to the store yesterday."

"Yeah, I got that."

He grimaced. "I'm not very good at hiding what I'm feeling. I never have been. It's a failing, I know."

Meryn shook her head. "I don't think that's a failing at all. I think it's a rare and beautiful thing. I wish I had the courage to be that transparent."

"I wish you did too." His smile tempered the words.

A warm fluttering sensation rippled through her stomach.

"But when those feelings are … ill-advised or unwelcome, it can be a detriment, believe me. The point is, I *was* angry when I found out what you had done, not because I felt let down, but because I was worried sick about what you had gotten yourself into and what you would face as a result. And I'm still worried."

"But not angry?"

"Do I look angry?"

"No."

"There you go."

She laughed. "I'm glad to hear it. I didn't mean to make you worry either, but I'll take that over the anger any day."

He grinned and drained the last of his juice before pushing back from the table. "I have to get to work. I'll check back in with you in a couple of hours." He pulled the washroom door shut and locked it, then walked across the room and out into the hallway.

When the lock clicked behind him, she slumped against the back of her chair, feeling as though she had run a marathon. Maybe it had been a mistake for her to apologize to him. His coolness had been a barrier between them. She glanced around the room where she would spend the next few days alone with him and bit her lip.

Leaving that barrier there might have been a really good idea.

———•———

Meryn jolted upright in bed. What had woken her?

A moan came from the couch.

She flung the covers aside and climbed out of bed.

The captain had been in and out of the room every few hours all day. When he had finally come in for the night, around ten, lines of exhaustion had creased his face. He hadn't done much more than pull off his boots before stretching out on the couch and falling asleep.

Meryn had lain in bed for an hour, listening to his deep, even breathing, before finally succumbing to sleep herself.

She caught a glimpse of the face of her watch in the moonlight streaming through the window as she passed by. Three o'clock.

The captain moaned again and turned onto his side.

She hurried over to him. The blanket had fallen to the floor, and Meryn picked it up and spread it back over him.

"Stop!" His arm flailed through the air.

She stepped back quickly.

Distress splashed across his face.

Was it bad to wake someone up during a bad dream? Or was that when they were sleepwalking?

He cried out again and flopped onto his back.

She had to do something. Meryn knelt down by his side. "Captain," she said softly, resting her hand on his upper arm.

He didn't open his eyes, but he didn't lash out either. The horror that had been flashing across his face gradually faded. His arms stopped twitching, and he stilled beneath her hand. After a couple of minutes, his breathing evened out again and his features grew calm.

Meryn took her first full breath since his moans had woken her. His arm was hard under her fingers, even in rest, and she pulled her hand away. Bracing herself on the couch, she started to rise.

Another moan froze her in place. The captain's face twisted again, and she quickly touched her hand to his arm. When the lines on his face smoothed out, her shoulders slumped. She couldn't leave him.

Meryn reached for the cushion on one of the chairs and tossed it on the floor, then lowered herself onto it and leaned against the side of the couch. If his arm thrashed around again, she would be directly in the line of fire, but as long as her hand was touching him, he seemed to be calm.

She sent up a silent prayer that the calm would last, then settled herself more comfortably on the cushion and closed her eyes.

———•———

Jesse opened his eyes and blinked at the sight of Meryn's face, relaxed in sleep. Now *that* was something he could get used to waking up to every morning.

Not very likely, Christensen.

An ache settled in his gut. He glanced down at her hand, resting on his upper arm. Her fingers were warm and he revelled in the feel of her soft skin pressed to his below the sleeve of his T-shirt.

Before he could enjoy the sensation nearly long enough to suit him, she stirred and raised her head. When her eyes met his, she yanked her hand away.

"Not that I'm complaining, but what happened? Did you get lonely in the night?"

Pink tinged her cheeks and she scrambled to her feet. "No, I ..."

"You what?"

"It wasn't me. It was you."

His forehead wrinkled.

"You were moaning and tossing around on the couch, like you were having a terrible dream."

"Ah." Jesse swung his legs over the side of the couch and sat up. He rested his elbows on his knees and drove his fingers through his hair before looking up at her. "Sorry about that. A souvenir from one of my tours. I should have warned you that could happen, but I hadn't had a bad dream in months and didn't really think about it."

"It's okay." She lowered herself onto the armchair behind her.

His gaze dropped to the cushion on the floor. "You must have been uncomfortable. You should have woken me."

"You got agitated whenever I wasn't touching you, so I figured the easiest thing was to stay here and let you sleep."

"What makes you think I was asleep?"

She stared at him.

He laughed. "I'm kidding. While I admit it was a nice thing to wake up to, I wouldn't have tricked you into sleeping on the floor all night just to see your face first thing when I opened my eyes."

"I appreciate that."

He sobered. "Thank you, Meryn. When I've had a nightmare like that in the past, I've always woken up drenched in sweat, my heart pounding so hard the sound of it echoes in my head. Even when I do calm down, the images in my head often take days to fade. The fact that I can't even remember having this one is something of a miracle." He reached over and took her hand in both of his, studying it as his thumbs rubbed circles over the back of it. "There must be some kind of magic in these fingers." He looked up at her, and his breath wedged itself in his throat.

Her eyes were wide and soft, her chest rose and fell rapidly, and her lips were parted slightly. Her gaze locked with his.

Jesse moved closer, desperate to close the space between them, to pull her into his arms and press his mouth to hers.

The loud buzzing of the alarm clock on the table at the end of the couch shattered the moment.

Jesse bit back a curse word as Meryn pulled her hand from his and took a shuddering breath. He slammed a hand down on the top of the clock, shutting off the noise, and pressed his eyes closed as she rose and walked to the bed. Dropping his face into his hands, he dug his fingers into his forehead.

"Could I use the washroom?"

He lifted his head.

Her face was pale, and she clutched her bag to her chest as if she felt the need to protect herself from him.

Of all the things that had happened in the last few minutes, that bothered him the most.

Jesse went over to the washroom and jabbed his thumb at the pad until the lock disengaged. When she approached the doorway, he pressed the palm of his hand to the frame on the far side, preventing her from going in. "Meryn."

She wouldn't look at him. "I can't."

For a few seconds he didn't move, then he dropped his arm, letting her pass.

While she was out of the room, he changed quickly and sat down on the edge of the couch to pull on his boots. Bringing her here had been a terrible mistake. Having her this close, catching glimpses of her vulnerability when she let down her guard, seeing her, listening to her breathe as he lay on the couch in the dark ... all were affecting him far more deeply than he'd thought they would.

As much as he dreaded getting the news that her sentence had come down from the Canadian Human Rights Commission, part of him hoped it would come soon. Something was going to have to give.

She wouldn't be able to keep going on like this for much longer.

And Jesse was absolutely certain that he couldn't.

CHAPTER TWENTY-SEVEN

Meryn paced the captain's quarters from end to end. The room might be bigger than a jail cell, and considerably more comfortable, but the fact was that she was still confined within its four solid walls against her will.

She stopped in front of the large painting that dominated the wall above his bed. It depicted a small ship being tossed about on stormy waters out in the middle of a sea. Behind the boat, rays gleaming from a lighthouse flashed a warning, but the prow of the ship was pointed toward the opposite shore. Far off in the distance, so pale it was barely discernible, a soft light glowed. Home, perhaps. The light calling to the weary sailors, drawing them through the storm to where the ones who loved them waited and prayed for their safe return.

Meryn stepped back, grief flooding her. Who was on their knees tonight, wondering where she was and praying for *her* safe return? Kate, probably. And Ethan. Her parents and brothers would be if they knew what was going on. Did anyone? When the captain got back, she would ask him if she could call someone to let them know she was okay.

She turned away from the picture abruptly and stared out the window at the darkness. The moon was a tiny, yellow sliver in the sky, barely penetrating the thick blackness that seemed to dance against the glass like a living thing, mocking her with its freedom.

Meryn stepped back from the window. The darkness was mocking her? She was already starting to lose her mind, and she'd only been locked in this room for four days. Of course, if she were being honest, what was driving her the craziest might not be the confinement, but something else entirely.

Meryn sank down on the side of the bed. What had happened—or almost happened—the morning before with the captain didn't mean anything, did it? She had helped him and he'd been grateful, that was all. They'd both gotten caught up in the moment again.

The problem was that there had been so many moments between the two of them it was becoming increasingly difficult—ridiculous, even—for her to keep trying to pass them off as something unlikely to occur again.

She got up and walked over to the fireplace. Why wasn't there anything to read in this room? He was a booklover, right? Did he keep his books somewhere else?

Meryn glanced over at the drawers in his desk, then let her gaze travel to his dresser and bedside table. More than likely she would find a book in one of those places if she looked, but even though he had left her here unsupervised, she didn't feel right about invading his privacy like that.

As soon as he got back, she would ask him about it. Even prisoners in a real cell were given books to read, weren't they?

At the sound of the doorknob turning, her head shot up.

Good. Now she could—

Three men burst through the door, black ski masks pulled down over their faces.

Every muscle in her body stiffened rock-hard. Before she could scream or call for help, the first man levelled a pistol at her face.

"If you even think about making a sound, you will be dead before it leaves your throat."

Since she was in the middle of a military base, chances were good that the man in front of her was a trained soldier perfectly capable of carrying out his threat. Her heart hammering in her chest, Meryn backed up slowly until she felt the mantel above the fireplace pressing into her shoulder blades, her eyes not leaving the gun in his hand.

"Here." He tossed a roll of duct tape to one of the other men who had come into the room with him. "Do her mouth and hands."

Meryn looked around wildly. *What can I use for a weapon?*

The other two men reached her. One gripped her elbow and pulled her away from the fireplace, then grabbed her other arm and twisted them both behind her back. The second man shoved his mask high enough up on his face to rip a piece of tape off the roll with his teeth. He slapped it over her mouth.

Meryn struggled, but the man behind her tightened his hold until it felt like the pressure would break her arms. She stopped fighting him and groaned as the other man moved around behind her and wrapped the tape around and around her wrists until they were locked together.

Then the man who'd been holding her arms let go of one and dragged her by the other to the bed and tossed her down on it.

Oh, God, no! Don't let them do this! Meryn dug her heels into the covers, pushing herself away from him, but the man with the tape grasped her ankles and held them while the other guy knelt beside her, pinning her to the bed with a large, latex-encased hand around her throat.

Meryn gasped for air. What was going on? What did they want? And where were the soldiers who were supposed to be patrolling the hallway? *Please, God, bring the captain back. Quickly.*

The man who had come into the room first still hovered near the doorway, an i-com in his hand. "Hurry up. He could come back any time."

Something sharp pricked her skin. A cry of pain rose in Meryn's throat as the man pushed the tip of a knife into the side of her neck.

The sound, muffled by the thick tape over her mouth, only brought a low, rumbling laugh from the man. "We're here to deliver a message to you, gorgeous."

Meryn tried to twist her head, to look away from the hard, cold eyes that peered through the slits in his mask, but his hand, and the sharp blade biting into her flesh above it, held her in place.

"We want to make sure you know that we can get to you anytime we want, no matter where you are. There is no safe place for you, not anywhere."

"Yeah." The man at her feet pressed his fingers deep into her ankles.

Meryn gritted her teeth, refusing to give them the satisfaction of crying out again.

"We know you're the captain's little pet at the moment." His voice was mocking. "But he'll be tired of you soon. And when he tosses you aside, we'll be waiting."

Please, God. Help me. Don't let them …

"All right. Let's go." The man by the door tossed the i-com he'd been holding onto the captain's desk.

The knife slid deeper and warm blood dripped down her neck.

The man wielding the knife lowered his head, breath hot against her cheek. "Maybe next time we won't be in such a hurry." He jerked the blade out and clambered off the bed.

The tape over Meryn's mouth smothered her gasp of pain.

The other man let go of her legs abruptly, and Meryn turned onto her side and dug her elbow into the mattress, scrambling into a sitting position.

"Hurry up!" The man at the door commanded them.

"Don't forget. There's no safe place." The one with the knife spit the words at her as he retreated toward the exit. The three of them disappeared into the hallway, not bothering to pull the door shut behind them. Their footsteps echoed on the tile floor, growing fainter until the hall went silent.

Meryn pushed against the mattress with her heels until her back rested against the headboard of the bed. She pulled her knees to her chest and leaned her head against the board behind her. *Thank you, God. Thank you, God.*

The pounding in her chest gradually diminished. The tape still covered her mouth, but Meryn sucked in as much air as she could through her nose. *Did that really happen?* Her eyes darted toward the open door. They could come back any time, and there would be nothing she could do to stop them from doing whatever they wanted to her. She closed her eyes and dropped her forehead onto her knees.

The men were right. There was no safe place.

CHAPTER TWENTY-EIGHT

The door to his office flew open and Jesse looked up. "Cale? What is it? What's wrong?"

"What do you mean, what's wrong? You messaged me that there was some sort of emergency."

Jesse glanced down at his belt.

The holder was empty.

"I didn't message you. I must have left my i-com at the gym this afternoon. Why would someone—?" He whipped his head toward a shelf of books, behind which he kept the key card to his room in a small safe in the wall.

A few of the books had been shoved aside and the safe door was hanging slightly open.

Meryn. He shoved back his chair. "Weren't you supposed to be patrolling down the hall from my quarters?" He strode across the room.

Caleb followed him into the hallway. "I was. I just left for ten minutes to grab a coffee."

Jesse shook his head. Ten minutes. Nothing too terrible could happen in ten minutes. Could it? The long jog from one end of the building to the other felt like miles. *Who would do this, and why?* If something had happened to her ...

He broke into a sprint as his quarters came into view.

The door wasn't closed.

His stomach clenched.

Someone had been there.

When he burst into the room, Caleb on his heels, Meryn looked up. Heat surged through Jesse's chest. She was on the bed. Her hands were tied behind her back and her mouth was covered with duct tape, but the blue eyes that met his were surprisingly calm. He tugged his knife out of his pocket and flipped it open. Pressing one knee into the mattress, he worked the blade through the tape around her wrists. When her arms were free, he went for the duct tape over her mouth.

She waved him off and pulled it from her face with one swift movement. "Ouch." Tossing the tape onto the floor, she covered her mouth with her hand.

Jesse cupped her shoulders. "Are you okay?"

"I'm fine."

"Did he ...?" He couldn't finish the thought.

"No." She dropped her hand from her mouth, wrapping both arms around her knees and pulling them to her chest. "And there were three of them."

Caleb spoke up from the doorway, voice tight with anger. "What did they look like?"

"I don't know. They wore ski masks."

He swore softly. "Did they say anything?"

She looked back at Jesse. "They said they wanted to make sure I knew they could get to me anytime they wanted, that there was no safe place." Her voice shook slightly.

Rage tore through him. If he found out who had done this to her, he was going to rip them apart piece by piece. "Just like on the brick."

"Yes. And they said ..." Her gaze flicked to Caleb and back to him.

Jesse looked over at his friend.

Caleb cleared his throat. "I'll go talk to the patrols, see if they saw anyone."

"Thanks, Cale."

One hand on the door frame, he turned back to Meryn. "I don't suppose it would help to dust for fingerprints?"

"No, they all wore gloves."

Jesse angled his head toward the hall. "Surveillance cameras?"

Caleb shook his head. "They're being installed next week." He pushed away from the door frame. "If I find out anything, I'll come back and talk to you; otherwise I'll be in the office down the hall for the rest of the night."

Jesse waited until the door clicked shut before turning back to Meryn. His hands slid from her shoulders to her arms, and he rubbed them gently, wishing he could do more to comfort her. "You're shaking. Are you scared or mad?"

She managed a weak grin. "Do I have to choose?"

"No, actually. You have every right to be both." He hesitated. "What else did they say?"

"That they knew I was your ... little pet, but that you would soon be tired of me, and when you tossed me aside they would be there, waiting."

Jesse gritted his teeth. "Anything else?"

"No."

A flash of red on her neck caught his eye. He lifted her chin with one hand, prickles of ice tingling across his skin. "They had a knife?"

"Yes."

He forced himself to speak softly, to not let the helpless fury roaring through him come out in his voice. "Hold on." Jesse got up and went into the washroom, wrenched open a drawer, and snagged some disinfecting ointment and a box of Band-Aids. He set them down beside the sink and pressed both palms against the cool countertop, inhaling deeply to push back the anger.

She's okay. This time.

But somehow, in spite of their attempts to keep it secret, someone had found out Meryn was being held in his quarters. He didn't even want to think about what the ramifications of that would be. And they'd somehow hacked into his i-com to retrieve the combination to his safe. Who knew what other information they'd been able to acquire or what damage they could do with it?

Shaking his head, Jesse picked up the first-aid supplies and went back to the bed.

Meryn gathered her hair in one hand and pulled it out of his way.

He cleaned the small cut and covered it with a Band-Aid. On impulse, he leaned in and pressed his lips to it. "All better."

Meryn blinked, then offered him a tentative smile. "Yes, I think I am."

He studied her face, wanting to believe that was true. "Can I run you a bath?"

Her smile wasn't tentative this time but reached deep into her eyes. "A bath would be great."

"And a glass of wine?"

"That would be even better."

"Bath and wine. Coming up." He started for the washroom.

She grabbed his hand. "Jesse."

He turned back to her, unable, for a second, to retrieve a breath. The sound of his name on her lips for the first time was the most precious gift he had ever been given. "Yes?"

"Thank you."

Not trusting himself to speak again, he squeezed her hand before letting go and heading into the washroom to run the water. While the tub was filling, he walked back to his small fridge and took out a bottle of wine and poured her a glass. He'd wait to pour his own until she had left the room. The last thing she needed was to mistake his actions for some kind of seduction.

Meryn came toward him.

His heart pounded as she crossed the room, dark hair shimmering. He held out the glass.

"Thank you."

"You're welcome." His eyes were drawn to the slender fingers curled around the stem and he looked away quickly. "Here." He opened the top drawer of his dresser and rummaged through it before pulling out a royal-blue T-shirt and plaid flannel pyjama bottoms. "These are clean, if you want to put them on when you're done. You'll sleep better if you're more comfortable."

She reached for them and tucked them under her arm. "Thanks."

"Your bath should be ready. I'm sorry I don't have any bubbles or anything."

"Or candles? What happened to always being prepared?"

"Um, I believe that's the Boy Scouts. Not the army."

"Sorry." She looked anything but.

How could she have that mischievous glint in her eyes after everything she had been through that evening?

"I'm assuming you used to be a Boy Scout."

Jesse grinned. "Actually, I was. For years."

"I knew it. That explains a lot." Her mouth turned up in an impish smile. "I guess I'm glad you're not prepared for entertaining women in your quarters."

His grin faded. The truth was he *had* entertained women in his quarters before. Not since he had come here, but in the past, occasionally.

After a few seconds, understanding dawned in her eyes and her smile faded too. She waved a hand in the direction of the washroom, like she was trying to wave away the sudden awkwardness between them. "I'm off. I won't be long."

"Take all the time you need."

She disappeared into the other room, leaving the door open slightly.

He shook his head. How, even now, could she display such trust in him, or any man? He squared his shoulders. Maybe it was time for him to do a little trusting himself. He walked to the door and pulled it shut, barely restraining the urge to stand there and bang his head against it.

With a deep sigh, he turned back and poured himself a glass of wine before dropping onto a chair in front of the fire. Somehow it had never occurred to him, until that moment, that when he did meet the woman he wanted to spend the rest of his life with he would bitterly regret every other encounter he'd ever had.

Jesse set down his glass of wine so hard some of the scarlet liquid splashed onto the end table. Where had that come from? He wanted to spend the rest of his life with her? The question Caleb had asked him the night the brick came through the store window, about whether or not Meryn was "the one" for him, bounced around in his head. *I guess that's my answer.* He picked up the glass and downed half the wine.

What did she mean she was glad he didn't entertain other women? Would she care if he did? For the first time, he didn't immediately move to extinguish the tiny flicker of hope that ignited deep inside of him. It wouldn't be easy, of course, but maybe ...

He focused on the glowing embers for what felt like hours, letting the warmth of the flames and the wine seep slowly through him, thawing the ice that had formed in his gut when he'd seen drops of blood sliding down her neck.

He gripped the leather armrest. That wouldn't happen again. From now on ...

He slumped against the back of the chair. He couldn't keep Meryn here in his room forever. He should never have brought her here at all.

He thumped his fist down on the armrest. If he had done things by the book and let her go to jail, none of this would have happened.

Except maybe it would have. She would have still been vulnerable there, and he would have had even less control over what happened to her.

The best thing would have been if she had never ordered those Bibles in the first place.

Or if the army hadn't been called in to take control of this area.

Or some radical zealot group hadn't decided to bomb all those mosques.

Jesse set down his glass again and scrubbed his face with both hands. What had happened had happened, and none of them could do anything to change the past. Not the events that occurred in the world around them, washing over their lives in devastating waves, or the small wounds they inflicted on each other daily with their weak and selfish actions, their repeated failures. Those last ones were more painful than catastrophes on a global scale, because of their personal nature.

The future loomed ahead as a big, black hole, and he felt even more helpless and out of control than before as he stared into its abyss. He groaned.

"Jesse?"

His head shot up.

Meryn stood in front of him, head tilted to one side as she looked at him. "Are you okay?"

She swam in his T-shirt and pyjama bottoms. She looked so adorable his first instinct was to laugh. His second was to stand up, pull her to him, and kiss her the way he'd wanted to since the day he'd first laid eyes on her. The way he almost had the morning after he'd woken up with her hand on his arm.

He stayed where he was. "I was thinking about everything that's happened since that day I saw you in the church and how out of control it all feels."

Her smile was gentle. "Nothing is out of control, Jesse. It's just not in *our* control. Personally, I've always been happy that responsibility doesn't rest on my shoulders."

"So where is God in all of this?" Jesse waved a hand toward the window.

"He's here. He's always been here."

"Then why is he letting this happen?"

"Jesse." She walked over to the couch and sat down in front of him, waiting until he met her gaze before continuing. "God isn't *letting* this happen. God is *making* this happen."

"Why?" Agony and confusion came out in his voice.

Compassion flitted across her face. "To show himself to us. To call people—and nations—that have turned their backs on him to return to him." She pointed at the painting above his bed. "It's like that picture. I know it feels like we're being beaten and tossed around by the overpowering wind and waves right now. But if we keep our eyes on that distant light—the promise that we are not alone and that, whatever happens, the one who created the wind and the waves *will* bring us home to that safe harbour—then the storm has no real power over us."

"So God bombed the mosques and killed all those people?"

"No. Don't get me wrong, there is a prince of darkness, who has been given temporary power over the world and who is wreaking all the havoc and destruction that he can. But God is sovereign over that too and can use even what is intended for evil to work for good."

"But you're one of his followers. Why would he make you go through all this?"

"This is the way he planned it, long before I was born, before even the creation of the world. He decided that I would be here, in this time, in this place, for a purpose. All of this—you, me, everything that's happening out there—is unfolding exactly according to plan. And I know it's crazy and scary, but it's also incredibly exciting. This is God pulling out all the stops. Time is running out, and he will no longer be ignored. Every single person on the face of the planet will have to decide whether to accept his son, Jesus Christ, now, before it's too late, or reject him and be lost forever."

It was all too much for him to comprehend. Jesse got up. "Are you hungry?"

She shook her head. "No, only tired."

"Come on, then." He reached for her hand, led her to the bed, and held up the sheet and dark-grey duvet. After she lay down and curled up on her side, he pulled them up to her chin.

She rested her head on one arm and looked up at him with a smile. "It's been a long time since anyone has tucked me into bed."

Jesse crouched down beside her and brushed a strand of hair back from her face. "I'm sorry, Meryn."

"It wasn't your fault."

"You're in my custody. It shouldn't have happened. And I promise you it won't again. You're safe now."

Meryn smiled, but there was a sadness in it, and in her silence, that tore at his heart. They both knew he couldn't really make that promise to her. "You know what bothers me the most?"

"What?"

"When things started going crazy, it occurred to me that something like this could happen. And I've been trying to prepare myself for it. I even thought I *was* prepared, but tonight I realized—"

"You can't prepare for something like this."

"Right. Although ..."

"What?"

"Somehow you've made it okay." She reached out and brushed her fingers through his hair. "For a killing machine, you're kind of a softie, you know that?"

"Don't let it get out." Jesse caught her hand and pressed a kiss to her palm. "Can you sleep?"

"I think so."

When he let go of her hand, she slid it under the covers.

Her eyelids looked heavy. Maybe she could find rest, in spite of everything.

"Sleep. I'll be here if you need me." He stood up and let his fingers linger on her head until her eyes closed. Then he made his way back to the chair by the fire.

Rest would not come to him so easily.

He stared out the window, at the thick blackness pressing against the glass. Chaos and confusion and pain and fear swirled not just outside that window, but even inside the room with them now. He glanced over at Meryn, lying still beneath the covers, and protectiveness rose up in him. For the first time since he was a kid, he found himself hoping there actually was a God and that he *was* in control of everything that was going on. It sure would be nice to be able to believe that somebody was.

Jesse's head jerked. *What are you doing?*

This was exactly why Caleb had warned him against having anything to do with Meryn O'Reilly. If Jesse had listened to his friend for a change, he wouldn't be sitting here now, entertaining traitorous thoughts that could cost him not only his job, but his life.

No, he couldn't give up everything. He wouldn't. Not to believe in a God who had never shown an ounce of interest in him.

Not even for her.

Chapter Twenty-Nine

Meryn opened her eyes when a sliver of sunlight shafted between the curtains and fell across the bed late the next morning. Her hand went to her neck. When her fingers brushed over the bandage, memories came flooding back. She pushed aside the twinges of fear and helplessness that resurfaced and smiled. Last night had been terrible, but God had protected her during the attack. And afterward, Jesse's kindness had been like a healing balm to her body and spirit.

Slowly, she lifted her head, not wanting to disturb him if he had been able to get some sleep. She frowned.

He still sat in the brown leather chair he'd gone to after putting her to bed the night before, his fingers clutching the empty wineglass that rested on the arm. His face was turned toward the fireplace, so she couldn't tell if he was awake or not, but even if he wasn't, his sleep couldn't have been terribly restful in that position.

Lifting the covers, she clambered out of bed, then almost laughed at the way Jesse's pyjama bottoms hung several inches below her feet. She took a moment to roll them up before standing and padding toward the washroom.

When she had drawn almost even to him, he turned his head.

His drawn face and bloodshot eyes sent a pang through her. "Did you sleep at all?"

"I don't think so."

"Give me a minute, okay?"

"Do I have a choice?"

She wrapped her arms around her waist. "What does that mean?"

"Nothing. Forget it."

"Jesse."

His head snapped up. "Maybe we should go back to Captain, at least try to pretend that you're still a prisoner here."

Meryn examined his face. What had changed in the night?

He looked away and wouldn't meet her eyes.

Fine. She went into the washroom and started to push the door shut, then stopped and left it open a crack. Probably best to go forward as if last night hadn't happened at all, since that's what he seemed intent on doing. She shoved her hair behind her ears with both hands. Actually, that might be for the best.

She had been far too open with him the evening before, too vulnerable. Leading him on like that, making him believe they could possibly have a future together, was cruel and wrong. She'd known it, even as he kissed her neck and pressed her hand to his mouth, but somehow she hadn't been able to pull away. If she was being honest—and she might as well be with herself, since she wasn't with him—she wanted to feel his lips against her skin as badly as he wanted to kiss her. She wanted the two of them to be together.

The problem was, they couldn't be.

She'd been able to fool herself, and him, for a while, but clearly Jesse had come to the same conclusion sometime in the early morning hours.

And he was right.

Meryn brushed her teeth and washed quickly, then changed out of his pyjamas and left them folded in a neat pile on the laundry hamper before pulling on her own clothes.

She straightened her shoulders, praying for calm and strength, and stepped back into the room.

He didn't appear to have moved while she'd been gone, but now he stood up, locked the washroom door, and turned toward the doorway to the hall. "I'll get us some coffee, and I need to grab some papers and my laptop so I can work in here today. Will you be okay for a few minutes?"

"I'm sure I'll survive. I don't really need you to babysit me."

He glanced back at her sharply.

She pressed her knuckles to her lips. Mouthing off was not going to help the situation.

198

He looked as if he was going to reply, but then he spun around and headed out the door, closing it harder than necessary behind him.

Meryn sank onto the edge of the bed and didn't move until the door handle turned. Then she jumped to her feet and pressed back against the wall.

Jesse came into the room, a leather bag hanging on one shoulder and a tray in his hand. He shoved the door closed and strode over to the small table by the window, walking past her as if she wasn't even there, every muscle in his back tight. He set the tray on the table, grabbed a Styrofoam cup of coffee and a muffin, then walked over to his desk in the corner and pulled his laptop out of the bag without a glance in her direction.

Meryn sighed. It was going to be a very long day. She crossed the room, tossed some grapes and a banana on a paper plate, and picked up the other cup of coffee. She took her breakfast over to the chair by the now cold fireplace and sat down.

Jesse was only a few feet from her, in plain view, yet he was as far away as home, which she suddenly missed desperately. *What is Kate doing today? And Gracie?* The thought of the little girl's arms tight around her neck brought a lump to her throat. She set the cup down on the table beside the chair. "Does Kate know I'm here?"

Jesse glanced over at her. "I doubt it. It's not our policy to send out updates on our prisoners to their friends."

His abruptness stung more than the tip of the knife had. "She must be worried sick."

This time he didn't look up. "She likely is. Maybe next time you'll think about that before you break the law."

Heat surged through Meryn. "An unjust law deserves to be broken."

His face darkened. "Say something stupid like that again and there won't be anything I can do to help you."

"Help me? How exactly are you doing that? Seems like all we've been doing here the last few days is delaying the inevitable."

He slammed a fist down on his desk.

She jumped.

"Maybe you're right. If you're so eager to feel the lash across your back, why don't we go and get it over with?"

Coldness crept through her extremities, and she crossed both arms over her abdomen to push back a sudden, stabbing pain. "What are you talking about?"

Jesse shoved his chair back from the desk and jumped to his feet. "Have you even read Bill 1071?"

She shook her head. "No. I've heard rumours, but only things I couldn't believe were true."

"Well, believe it. For starters, the bill added a whole new section to the Terrorism Act called Hate Crimes. Largely based on its stance on homosexuality, the teachings of your Bible fall into this category. They haven't had the nerve to come right out and say it, but for all intents and purposes, Christianity has now been outlawed. Which means that you can be arrested and punished for pretty much anything you do that is affiliated with Jesus Christ. You might want to disassociate yourself from that name as much as possible."

"Jess—" She stopped herself. "Captain. I *carry* his name. How am I supposed to disassociate myself from it?"

He raked his fingers through his hair. "I don't know. But I would advise you to try and find a way."

"I can't. And you might as well know now that no true believer will. We don't answer to the ones that can hurt our bodies, or even kill us, but have no power to control what happens to us after death. We only answer to the one who does."

"Well, good. As long as you're not worried about those types of things, you won't mind hearing the rest of it. The bill goes on to outline prescribed punishments for those crimes it defines as acts of hate."

"Which are?"

"Flogging and death. Those are the options now."

For a moment she couldn't speak for the horror that threatened to close her throat. When she did, her voice came out barely above a whisper. "What is this, the fifteenth century? How can they justify that?"

"Economics." His laugh was cold. "They can justify anything if they can show that it will save the country money. And those consequences are a pretty strong deterrent to anyone considering breaking the law too." He swept an arm around the room. "What did you think we were waiting for here? Your case is before the Canadian Human Rights Commission now, and I'm expecting word that your sentence has been handed down any day. So, no, I haven't been sitting around here doing nothing but delaying the inevitable. I sent in my report outlining the fact that you willingly turned over the Bibles, didn't resist arrest, and have otherwise maintained a clean record with the law."

She swallowed hard.

"I've also been trying to figure out how to best deal with a sentence that is overly harsh, if that's what comes down. The CHRC won't hesitate to make an example of you, especially since we haven't been able to track down any of the Bibles you gave out." His mouth clamped shut as if he hadn't meant to give her that information.

"Don't I get to testify on my own behalf?"

"No. That's not how it works anymore, not since that bill passed. If your alleged crimes fall under the Terrorism Act, your rights are basically waived. All you can do is sit and wait to hear what they have decided to do with you."

"So you have been helping me."

He shrugged. "I don't know if anything I've done has made a difference, but I had to try."

"I'm sorry." Her voice broke. "I didn't know."

Jesse gazed at her, his face softening slightly. Then his features settled back into granite. "Now you do. And as sentences for those charged under this act come down within a week of arrest, we are dangerously close to running out of time to try and convince them to show you leniency. If you could not talk for a little while, so I can get some work done, maybe we'll be able to find a solution to this situation before it's too late."

"I won't bother you if—"

Jesse held up a hand. "You're not in a position to make any demands."

"I know. I was going to ask if you had a book I could read."

He blew out an exasperated breath and went to the little table beside his bed. After pulling open the drawer, he drew out a leather book.

Meryn pressed a trembling finger to her lips. Was that ...?

He carried it over to her and held it out.

Her heart sank. It was a beautifully bound copy of *Moby Dick*. "I thought—"

"I know what you thought," he said curtly. "And I know what you want. But you'll have to make do with this for today. And if you know what's good for you, you'll put that other book out of your mind forever."

The tears that had hovered just below the surface all morning sprang into her eyes. "I can't."

When she didn't reach for the book, Jesse tossed it onto the small table beside her chair. "Don't do that, Meryn."

The sharp words felt like a slap across her face. She stood up, tired of him towering over her. "Don't do what?"

"Try to manipulate me. It won't work."

Shock streaked through her, dragging anger after it like the tail of a comet. She swiped away a tear that had started down her cheek and pulled herself up to her full height. "Manipulate you?" She ground the words out through clenched teeth. "That is *not* what I am doing."

"I think it is." Jesse took a step closer to her. "I think it's what you've been doing since the moment I brought you here, maybe from the moment I first saw you in the church."

Too furious to speak, Meryn just stared at him until he started to turn away. The movement shook her out of her silence and she grabbed his elbow, turning him back to face her. "What, exactly, have I manipulated you into doing?" she asked, voice shaking. "Sticking a gun in my face? Arresting me? Keeping me captive here?" She let go of him and held up both hands in a gesture of surrender. "You're right. This has all been an elaborate scheme to force you to strip me of my rights, my life, and my freedom. You got me. You've just been a poor, innocent victim here, while I've been playing you like a chess piece."

"Stop it." He seized her by the arms and shook her. "Just stop it, Meryn. That's not what I meant. I meant that you've been playing with my heart, making me fall in love with you so you'd have an officer in your pocket to do your bidding. And to protect you when you decided the law didn't apply to you like it does everyone else, or to smile and pat you on the head when you made comments that bordered on sedition."

"What are you talking about? I never asked you to do any of that."

She planted her palms against his chest, struggling to free herself. His heart pounded beneath her hands. "Let go of me!"

His grip on her arms tightened. "I can't even fathom letting you go to jail or face the sentence you deserve like every other criminal I bring in, that's how twisted around and backward you've got me. I'm risking everything I've worked for my entire life by having you here. By not being man enough to do my job." His breath came in short gasps. "And if that isn't bad enough, you've got me thinking about your God, about whether or not he actually could be real and as powerful as you claim. And why he'd have any interest whatsoever in a nobody like me. Talk about risking everything." He let go of her abruptly.

She stumbled back a step, balanced herself with a hand on the back of the chair, and stared at him, trying to work her way through the murky waters he'd created by stirring up all the mud he possibly could. The heat in her chest subsided. "That's what this is all about, isn't it?"

"What?"

"You're starting to believe the truth you've been sent here to try and stamp out. This isn't about you and me at all. This is about you and God."

He clasped his hands behind his head and gaped at her. When he dropped his arms and spoke, his voice was more weary than angry. "We're not discussing this anymore. I've said everything I'm going to say, which is a lot more than I should have." He wheeled around and headed back to his desk. "Now I have work to do."

Trembling violently, Meryn sat back down on the chair, thoughts spinning wildly. Reeling from everything Jesse had said to her, she tried to pray for him, and for herself, that they would find the strength to somehow work their way through all of this.

In the end, the only words she could drag up from her hurting soul were *help him, help him.*

Maybe that was enough. She rested her head back against the chair. The anger drained away and her thoughts gradually cleared as peace worked its way through her.

A loud thud shattered her reprieve and brought her head up sharply. Jesse had removed the running shoes he'd been wearing, dropped his boots in front of the couch, and sat down. "I'm going out. I need some air." His voice was still hard and cold.

What could she say that wouldn't set him off again? She nodded.

He picked up one boot and pulled it over his grey, woollen work sock.

Restless, Meryn stood and walked around the room, stopping in front of several framed certificates hanging on the wall above his desk. "What does the *E* stand for?"

"What *E*?"

"In your name. *E*. Jesse Christensen."

He bent down to tie up his boot. "Eli. And no."

She tilted her head. "No?"

"Not like the priest. In fact, it's short for Elijah, but I'm no prophet either. That's why I started going by my middle name when I went into the army." He finished tying the laces on his second boot with a hard pull and stood.

"You realize that Jesse was also—"

"Yes, I know. I figured it was the least of the three"— he shot her a quick look—"options. At least he was a lot lower profile than his son."

"That's true." She almost smiled. "But you kept your last name."

"Of course. That's my father's name. I wouldn't dishonour him by changing ..." His jaw tightened. "It's not the same thing."

"Isn't it?"

He reached for his belt and slung it around his waist.

Meryn pursed her lips. "You know your Bible."

He snorted. "I ought to. I was weaned on it."

"And yet you've rejected it. Why?"

"The usual reason, I guess. The hate-mongering."

She let out a humourless laugh.

Jesse looked up from buckling his belt. "What?"

"That's the media talking. You strike me as a man intelligent enough to form his own opinions, not just blindly follow what he hears on the news. Or has your military training driven that out of you?"

"Watch yourself, Meryn."

The step he took toward her trapped the air in her lungs.

"I can think for myself."

She prayed for the right words. "Good. Then there's hope for you yet."

His fists clenched.

When he took another step toward her, she forced herself not to move back.

"I'm not the one without hope in this situation."

"Are you sure about that, Captain? Are you absolutely sure which of us is the prisoner here and which of us is free?"

"That's it." Jesse stalked toward her.

Meryn's mouth went dry and she shot a glance toward the door as she backed away from him. Should she run? She took another step back and bumped against the cold wall.

There was nowhere to run to.

Instinctively, she raised her arms in front of her as he approached.

Jesse grabbed both her wrists and pinned them to the wall on either side of her head. "You need to stop talking."

Meryn summoned up every ounce of her rapidly waning courage and lifted her chin to meet his flashing eyes. "You're right about one thing."

"I said stop talking, Meryn. Now." His fingers tightened around her wrists.

She willed herself not to look away. "You *have* rejected the truth for the usual reason. But the usual reason isn't hate-mongering. It's fear."

Jesse let go of her left wrist and yanked his pistol from its holster. Before she could move or scream, he pressed it to her temple. "I swear, if you say one more word, I will put both of us out of our misery." The weapon trembled against her skin.

She couldn't draw in a breath. Had he cocked the weapon? Did he have to with that kind of gun? Was it even loaded?

His eyes, inches from hers, were glassy and unfocused.

Don't flinch. Don't say a word.

He was probably close enough to losing it completely to carry out his threat given the slightest provocation.

Neither of them moved for several seconds.

Then he dropped her wrist, pulled back the gun, and jammed it into his belt. Without a glance in her direction, he turned and stormed out of the room.

CHAPTER THIRTY

Meryn staggered over to the bed. She crawled onto the mattress and collapsed against the headboard. After pulling her knees to her chest, she rocked back and forth, playing over everything that had happened again and again in her mind, trying to make sense of it. Shadows lengthened across the room as she waited and prayed.

The door opened hard enough to bang against the wall behind it.

Jesse hadn't calmed down any.

Meryn shivered, as though an icy wind had blown into the room with him.

He slammed the door and crossed the room toward her. His clothes were rumpled and his eyes wild, a soldier clearly at war with himself.

Her shoulders relaxed. She wasn't the one he was fighting so hard against.

Jesse paced back and forth at the end of the bed before stopping and clutching the top of the footboard. "I will not be bewitched by you!"

Meryn shook her head. "I don't have either the power or the desire to bewitch you."

"Then what are you doing to me?"

"*I'm* not doing anything to you."

He shoved himself away from the bed. "Then I won't be bewitched by your God."

"He's not bewitching you either."

"Then what is he doing?"

"He's pursuing you."

"Why?" His voice was anguished.

Her heart went out to him. It wasn't easy, the choice he was being forced to make. Rejecting the God he'd convinced himself didn't exist was no longer the default position he could take. The other option, though, of submitting his life and will to that God would require turning his back on everything he had worked so hard to achieve.

Both choices came with a high cost, and only Jesse could decide which one he was willing to pay.

"The same reason he's doing all of this. Because he loves you, and he wants you for himself."

Jesse came around the side of the bed and dropped to his knees, burying his face in his hands. "I don't want him to love me."

Meryn didn't answer.

He raised his head and looked at her, his face lined and weary. "This will cost me everything."

"Yes."

His eyelids dropped shut. "Can I fight him?"

"What do you think you've been doing your whole life? The question is, do you really want to keep fighting?"

For a few seconds he didn't answer, and the battle that raged inside him played out across his face. Then a look of peace settled over him.

He had made his choice.

"No." He opened his eyes and met her gaze. The confusion and weariness were gone, replaced by a soft light. Jesse got up and sat down on the edge of the bed. He reached for her arm, pulled it to him, and gently massaged the wrist he'd gripped hard enough earlier to leave red marks.

Warmth flooded through her, dispelling the chill that had tormented her throughout that whole, long, terrible day.

He finished with one arm and reached for the other one.

Her heart rate accelerated as he worked, his fingers as gentle around her wrists now as they had been unyielding before. Meryn swallowed hard at the feel of his warm hands on her arms, the touch that sent electricity tingling across her skin.

Finally his hands stilled and he looked up at her. "Meryn, I'm so sorry. I don't even know how to begin to ask you to forgive me."

She drew in a shaky breath. "I understand. It's a terrible thing to wrestle with Almighty God."

"Yes, it is. And surprisingly exhilarating to give up the fight. Which you won't hear a soldier say very often." Lines of exhaustion were etched across his face. "Still, I said some terrible things to you. Things that weren't true. I know you haven't been manipulating me. Other than ordering the Bibles, you haven't chosen any of this. You're right. It's your life that has been invaded, your rights that have been violated without anyone asking for your input or approval. And grabbing you, and pulling a gun on you ..." He cringed. "After last night, especially, you must have been terrified."

"A little scared, maybe. Mostly because I had no idea what you were going to do."

"I don't blame you. *I* was scared of me. I had no idea what I was going to do either. I've never felt like that before, like I was going to explode or ... well, I didn't really know what. That's why I had to leave."

"Where did you go?"

"The shooting range. Usually a great place to release pent-up tension. But today, not so much." He offered her a sheepish grin. "I took out every bad guy—and a few of the good ones—put three or four straw dummies out of commission permanently, and ended up feeling even more wound up than when I'd started. God wasn't going to let me off the hook that easily, I guess." He took a deep breath. "You were right about that, too. It *was* fear that was keeping me from admitting how much I needed God. Fear of everything I would have to do without. But now that I understand how much I have received, everything I have to give up seems a pretty paltry sacrifice, like ashes in my hands."

Meryn nodded. "I know that feeling."

Jesse squeezed her arm before letting her go. "I'm sorry it took me so long to figure it out. Here." He stood up and walked over to the washroom. Pushing open the door, he left it and returned to sit on the edge of the bed. "Tomorrow I'll go see Kate and tell her what's going on."

"Thank you."

"Everything is different now. We have to try and figure out what to do."

"We will. Tomorrow. Right now you need rest."

He contemplated her with tired eyes, then smiled weakly and started to get up.

Meryn touched his arm. "Stay here. You need a good sleep. I'll take the couch tonight." She moved over to the other side of the bed, so he could lie down.

Jesse paused before he bent, untied his boots, and tugged them off. With a groan, he stretched out on top of the duvet, his eyes closing immediately.

Meryn slid to the edge of the bed.

Jesse reached out and covered her hand with his. "Don't go. I'll sleep on top of the blankets. Not that I have the energy to try anything." He opened one eye and looked at her. "Unless you put my pyjamas on again. Then I just might rally."

Heat flooded her face. "Jesse."

"I'm kidding. Sort of. I'll be good, I promise. But I need to be close to you tonight, Meryn. I need to know that you're right here with me. Please."

He sounded so sleepy, as if he could barely get the words out.

She squeezed his hand. "I'll be right back, okay?" Meryn went into the washroom and got ready for bed. When she came out, she crossed the room, plucked the woolen army blanket from the foot of the bed, and spread it over him.

"It's been a long time since anyone has tucked me into bed," he murmured.

Meryn smiled and walked around to the other side. She crawled under the sheet and duvet and rested her head on one bent arm. She watched Jesse for a while, mesmerized by the rise and fall of the blanket over his chest, and the way the lines on his face smoothed out as he finally began to relax. More than anything, she wanted to reach out, stroke his hair or the side of his face, comfort him in some small way, but she forced herself to keep her arm at her side.

He lay so still, as if asleep, but suddenly he reached out and grabbed her hand again. Eyes closed, he said, "Don't kid yourself, lady. You have me completely and utterly bewitched, and have since the first time I laid eyes on you."

Meryn clasped the grey duvet tightly. Was he awake, or talking in his sleep? Either way, he was dragging them back into dangerous territory.

When he didn't let go of her hand, she gave in with a sigh. For tonight, she wouldn't worry about what the future held. She'd just be close to him—like he'd asked and like she wanted anyway—watching him sleep and feeling his strong fingers holding hers.

She contemplated what had happened between her and Jesse that day, every word they had said to each other. He was right. Everything was different now.

He was a believer. What that would mean for him? For them?

Her eyes widened. There was one thing that Jesse had said to her that he hadn't apologized for or retracted, something that had almost gotten lost in the midst of the heated words flying back and forth between them. He had said he was in love with her.

CHAPTER THIRTY-ONE

Jesse woke at dawn and slipped out from under the blanket to shower. When he came back, he sat down on the edge of the bed. Meryn's hair spread across the pillow, and one hand was curled up with the backs of her fingers resting against her slightly flushed cheek. He wanted to touch her so badly he had to clutch the arms of the chair so he wouldn't.

The last few days had changed everything for him. He'd made a radical turnabout in his faith and life path, but he'd also lost the heart he'd only had a tenuous hold on since the day he'd first seen Meryn. And he'd told her as much yesterday. Of course, his timing hadn't been perfect, given that he'd grabbed her and was shouting in her face at the time.

Little wonder she hadn't responded to his revelation in any way.

Had she even heard him? It was possible the words hadn't penetrated her hurt and confusion. It might be better if they hadn't. Even if what he had said was true, he probably shouldn't have said it. Not yet.

Meryn stirred, then stretched and slowly opened her eyes. A startled look crossed her face before she smiled. "Good morning."

"Morning."

"What time is it?"

Jesse glanced down at his watch. "Eight thirty."

"You should have woken me."

"Not a chance. I was having way too much fun watching you sleep."

The flush on her cheeks deepened as she propped herself up on one elbow. "Was I snoring?"

He laughed. "No, sadly. You were just being beautiful."

Her answering laugh was light and sweet. "If that's the sort of thing you say to all your prisoners, you're going to have a huge crime problem before you know it."

"I think the streets are safe for a while. There's only one prisoner I'd say that to. Mostly because the rest of them are big, sweaty guys that have been sharing a cell with other big, sweaty guys for days, and beautiful is not the word I would use to describe any of them at the moment."

"I thought they were moving people through the system a lot faster now."

"So far that's only for prisoners convicted under Bill 1071, but I wouldn't be surprised if it gets extended to all convicts before long. Although the sentences are pretty brutal—or because they're so brutal, I guess—they are remarkably effective at emptying the prisons. The economic impact of that will be too appealing to ignore."

She frowned.

"Meryn, I want you to know that what happened to me yesterday … that was real."

Small lines appeared across her forehead. "I do know that."

"Good. Because I'm aware that our difference in beliefs has been a barrier between us, I didn't want you to think I was pretending something had happened, or that I was something I wasn't."

A shadow crossed her face. "Jesse, there's something I need to tell you. I—"

The i-com on his belt buzzed, cutting off whatever she was about to say.

Jesse pulled it out of the holder. "It's Caleb." He scanned the screen quickly, then looked up and met her eyes.

"What is it?"

"Your sentence has come in. He wants me to come to his office right away. I'm sorry."

"Go. It's okay."

"What were you saying?"

Meryn waved a hand through the air. "Later. It's not important now. Go talk to the major, find out my fate." She attempted a smile that didn't make it anywhere near her eyes.

A warning niggled in his gut. If they didn't finish this conversation now, they never would. It was cruel to make her wait to find out what she might be facing, though. He stood up. "All right. I'll go. We'll finish this conversation later, I promise."

"Is it okay if I take a shower while you're gone?"

He hesitated. He'd promised Caleb to lock the washroom door when he left the room, so … Jesse nearly laughed. He'd broken so many promises to his friend the last few days, what was one more? At this point, he'd almost be glad if she did crawl out the window and escape. "Sure."

"Thank you."

The slight quiver in her voice ripped through his chest, and he couldn't help himself. Bending down, he cupped her face in his hands and pressed his lips to her forehead. Her skin was warm and soft under his fingers, and he had to force himself to pull back. "It'll be okay, Meryn. Whatever happens, we'll face it together."

The shadow flickered across her features again. Was it because of the verdict she was about to be given, or did it have something to do with them?

His i-com buzzed again and he let her go. "I'll be back as soon as I can."

———•———

Striding down the hall toward Caleb's office, Jesse pressed a hand to his stomach, trying to quell the apprehension churning there. *Please, God, don't let them come down on her too hard.* His head shot up. He hadn't prayed since he was a little kid, but the words had come as naturally as if he'd done it yesterday. He reached the office and knocked.

"Come in."

Caleb's voice was grim, and Jesse's apprehension level ratcheted up. Drawing in a steadying breath, he turned the knob and opened the door.

"Sit." Caleb waved a hand toward the chair in front of him before sitting down behind his desk.

Jesse swallowed. Caleb almost always came around his desk to talk to him, even if he was keeping the meeting formal. The fact that he felt the need to put a buffer between them was not a good sign. Jesse sat down on the leather chair.

"I know you're anxious to hear this, so I won't keep you in suspense."

Caleb picked up a piece of paper off his desk. "The CHRC has sentenced Meryn to fifteen lashes."

Jesse shut his eyes for a few seconds, then opened them and dug his fingers into the leather armrests, bracing himself for the rest. "When?"

"Tomorrow, eleven hundred hours. And the following stipulations are included in the directive. There are to be three officers and one female medic present. The prisoner is allowed up to four friends or family members in the waiting room to take her home afterward. A government official will be present to ensure the punishment is adequately carried out. If the officer assigned to carry out the sentence fails to do so to the government official's satisfaction, another officer will be assigned the role, and the sentence will be carried out again, from the beginning, at eleven hundred hours the following day."

Bile rose in Jesse's throat and he swallowed it back down. "Who has to do it?"

"The commanding officer is supposed to supervise, as you know, so that leaves you and Gallagher. I'll let you decide who it's going to be."

"Some choice." Jesse considered his options for two seconds before he grimaced. "I can't let Gallagher do it. He'd enjoy it too much."

"That's what I thought you'd say." Caleb gave Jesse a moment. "You have your orders, Captain. Do I need to remind you that you promised to accept her sentence without hesitation or dissension?"

His shoulders slumped. "No."

"Good." Caleb's face softened. "I'll be there."

"I know. I appreciate it."

"There's one more thing. It is possible for the sentence to be reduced."

"How?"

Caleb eyed the sheet in his hand. "You will give the prisoner the opportunity to cooperate with us. Five lashes will be deducted from the sentence if she reveals the name of her supplier, and an additional five if she gives us the names of at least ten people who received the Bibles."

Jesse sagged against the back of the chair. "She'll never give us that information." And as much as he'd give anything for Meryn's sentence to be reduced, he wasn't sure he wanted her to.

The price the Christians she named would have to pay would be too high.

Unable to sit any longer, he crossed the room to the window. Caleb's office had a view of the rolling practice fields, and Jesse studied the soldiers doing push-ups, cleaning their weapons, performing yard work ... all the ordinary, mundane activities he'd done himself a thousand times.

Suddenly the world on the other side of the glass seemed as far removed from him as his childhood home. Another place where he had once belonged but which he no long fit into and to which he could never return.

With a heavy sigh, Caleb walked over and nudged Jesse's shoulder. "It could have been worse, Jess."

He nodded.

"Last week a woman in Vancouver was sentenced to thirty lashes, and another one in Montreal, to death. With the courts still figuring out this new law and the best ways to implement and apply it, anything could have happened."

Jesse faced him. "I know, but if you'd had to do this to Natalie, how would you have felt?"

Caleb studied him. "About as sick and helpless as you look, I guess." He pressed his palm against the wall beside the window, as though he needed the support. "I've assigned soldiers to carry out *special training* at the back of the building, outside your windows, from now until tomorrow morning. No one needs to know why they're there. Of course, with someone breaking into your quarters, that may be a moot point. In any case, it is standard procedure to tighten up security after a sentence comes down."

Jesse stared at him.

Caleb dropped his gaze. "Look, Jess. It's not that I don't trust you. But if you feel for this woman anything close to what I felt for Natalie—and I'm starting to see that you do—I know that there are very few lengths you wouldn't go to in order to protect her. I get that, believe me, but my main concerns are protecting the law and protecting you. Even if that means protecting you from yourself."

Jesse exhaled loudly. "Maybe you're right, Cale, I—"

Caleb held up a hand. "Don't tell me if you would have considered letting her go. If I know that, I have to report it." He ran a hand over his face. "Standard procedure or not, this was my idea, and the extra security presence comes on my orders. To be honest, taking that step had far less to do with protecting the law than with making sure you didn't have to make one more difficult decision this week."

"What does that mean?"

Caleb stepped closer and lowered his voice. "It means that I've been watching you since the day you met Meryn O'Reilly, and more than ever since you took her into your custody. I saw you yesterday morning when you came into the mess hall, looking like a man who'd been up all night fighting with his demons. Or maybe with something at the other end of the spectrum?"

Jesse met his gaze.

Caleb pursed his lips and nodded. "Later in the day reports started coming in about you ripping through the shooting range, which, by the way, Hamilton is not happy about, since he spent the last few weeks setting it up. Took you all of an hour to tear it apart, apparently."

"Sorry about that. I'll help him fix it."

"Yes, you will. But the point is, as soon as you walked into my office today, I could see something in your eyes that wasn't there yesterday. Something that I don't think I've ever seen there, in fact. You were done fighting and you'd lost, or won, depending on how you look at it."

The two men gazed at each other, able, as always, to say more without words than with them.

Caleb reached out and grasped his shoulder. "It's a tough road you've chosen, Jess. But I guess you don't need me to tell you that."

"No, I don't. But I'm happy to talk to you about it anytime."

"I want to hear about it, actually. But not now. Let's get through the next couple of days, okay? After Meryn's ..." He stopped and drew in a deep breath. "After Meryn goes home tomorrow, we'll talk more."

"Thanks, Cale."

"For what?"

"For not saying 'I told you so.'"

"Much as I would have enjoyed that, I couldn't. Not this time."

"Why not?"

"Because that's what you say to someone who realizes he made a mistake not listening and wishes he had done things differently. And something tells me, however rough it gets for you and Meryn in the next day or two, you don't regret defying me in this for a single minute."

"You're right, I don't. Not in this."

Caleb squeezed Jesse's shoulder before dropping his hand. "I guess you and I have been through worse things together."

"I guess. But at the moment it doesn't feel like it."

"Go tell her what's going on. I'm sure she's wondering."

Jesse turned and made his way across the room.

"Jess?"

With his hand on the doorknob, he turned back to Caleb.

"You know where I am if you need me."

"I always do."

"What, know where I am or need me?"

"I'd tell you, but I don't believe your ego needs the boost at the moment."

"That's all I wanted to hear."

Jesse shook his head as he pulled open the door. What would he do without Caleb and his never-ending ability to lighten his mood, even if only slightly? The walk back to his quarters seemed to take forever, but that suited him fine. When he broke the news to Meryn, the shadow crossing her face that morning would morph into something a lot worse.

Or maybe it wouldn't. She had shown remarkable strength under fire so far. What was about to come was her biggest test yet, though. The next twenty-four hours would either break her or prove the power she drew on was not coming from within her but from a much greater source.

And the same was true for him.

Chapter Thirty-Two

Jesse shut the door to his quarters quietly behind him. The room was empty. Had Meryn run? The thought that he might never see her again shot through him with the sharp, tearing pain of an arrow penetrating flesh.

Then the washroom door opened and she came out, her hair gleaming damp and hanging around her shoulders. "How did it go?"

Jesse gestured toward the chairs in front of the fireplace. "Why don't we sit down?" When she had settled onto one of the chairs, he took the other one and turned to face her. "The Commission has sentenced you to fifteen lashes."

The colour drained from her face, but otherwise she didn't react.

"It could have been worse. They've been routinely handing out harsher sentences, even to women, under Bill 1071, but I know that's a small consolation."

"When?"

"Tomorrow. Eleven in the morning."

Meryn stood and walked over to the window.

Jesse stayed where he was, giving her time to process what he'd told her.

When she turned to him, her face was anguished and she had both arms wrapped around herself tightly. "Are you going to tell me who did this?"

"Who did what?"

"Who turned me in? Who was this eyewitness you mentioned, who was so eager to testify against me? Your informant? What did I ever do to him that he would want me to suffer like this?"

He got up and walked over to stand in front of her. "The informant is a she, actually."

"A woman? Who?"

"I'm not supposed to—"

"Jesse, please. I need to know."

He sighed. "All right." Right or wrong, he guessed she did have a right to know. "Her name is Annaliese Pettersson. Technically one of our assets, but—"

Meryn looked the way she had the night of the tornado.

What had he said? When she swayed on her feet, he grasped both of her arms. "Do you need to sit down?"

She didn't answer.

Jesse let go of her arms and reached for her hands. They were ice cold. "What is it? Do you know her?"

She seemed to be trying to draw in one unsteady breath after the other. She trembled, and he was about to insist they go and sit down when she looked up at him. "Yes, I know her. She's my sister."

Jesse's eyes widened. "Your sister?" For a moment he could only stare at her, his mouth slightly open, as he tried to grasp what she was saying. Now that he thought about it, there was a resemblance, yet Meryn was so dark and Annaliese so fair, and their personalities were so completely opposite. He never would have connected the two of them. He dropped one of her hands and tugged her by the other one toward the fireplace. "I need to sit, whether or not you do." He sank onto the couch and pulled her down beside him.

For a long moment, the faint ticking of the clock on the mantel was the only sound in the room.

Jesse shook his head. "Annaliese is your sister. I can't believe it. Of course, traumatizing you by locking you in a chicken coop does sound exactly like something Scorcher would do." His fingers tightened around Meryn's as anger swept through him.

"Scorcher?"

"Her code name." He shook his head. "I'm sorry, Meryn. I had no idea she would come after you for personal reasons, or I would have warned you about her a long time ago."

"It's not your fault. I always knew she hated me, but I didn't know until this minute how much." Her voice shook.

He let go of her hand and pulled her to him.

She laid her head on his chest.

He held her for several minutes, until she sat up, pushing the damp hair away from her face.

Her laugh came out more like a sob as she swiped at his white T-shirt. "I'm sorry. You're all wet."

He caught her hand. "It doesn't matter. Tell me about Annaliese. What happened between the two of you? Or would you rather not talk about it?"

"No, it's okay." She shifted on the couch until her head rested against the back of it. "My mother is a beautiful, godly woman, but she didn't become a believer until she was in her twenties. Before that, she was a little wild. During her second year of college, she became involved with a Swedish exchange student, Emil Pettersson. Around Christmastime, she found out she was pregnant. The day she told Emil, he packed his bags and went home, and she never heard from him again.

"She had Annaliese a few months later and raised her on her own for a year. Then she met my father. He is one of those larger-than-life characters, a booming Irishman with hair as black as coal and the tendency to storm in and command everyone's attention like a steam engine roaring through the room."

Ah. That explained Meryn's dark, Irish looks. And Annaliese's fairness.

"He tried so hard with Annaliese. My parents decided to let her choose whether or not she wanted my father to adopt her, so when she was old enough, he offered. He loved her and would have made her his own daughter if she'd been willing, but she wasn't. Somehow she'd built her birth father up in her mind until he was the king of Sweden. She expected him to show up at the door any day and sweep her off to her rightful place as royal princess and heir to the throne. As my brothers came along, and then me a few years later, she treated us like the subjects she felt she deserved."

Fascinating. Meryn wove her way in and out of her memories as if they were geographical locations she could actually go to and visit. Jesse tightened his grip on her fingers.

"She hated me the most, maybe because my father hadn't left me like hers had, or because my brothers always stood up for me against her. She felt like she didn't belong in our family, that it had all been a terrible mistake only her father could rectify, and that he would, as soon as he came for her. Which of course he never did, so she only grew more and more angry and bitter over the years." Her eyes widened. "That must have been her, in the park that day."

"Yes. She told me she was there. Did you see her?"

"Not her face. But someone brushed by me right after I gave a Bible to a woman. There was something familiar about her, but her hair was jet black, so I didn't recognize her." She let out a cold laugh. "She was always doing that when we were kids, dressing up, pretending to be someone else. Who she is was never good enough for her."

"I don't blame her. She's a total psycho." His face warmed. Probably should have kept that thought to himself. "Sorry."

"It's okay. I don't think she's crazy, though, just extremely ambitious. Unfortunately, she has never seemed to care who she crawls over on her way to the top."

Was that sadness in Meryn's voice? Surely, after everything her sister had done to her, she couldn't feel anything but contempt for her. Could she?

Meryn drew in a quivering breath. "She made all our lives miserable. Then one day she packed her bags and disappeared. It broke my mother's heart, but it was a relief to the rest of us. Life at home became a lot more peaceful after that. I didn't see her again until I moved here. She's shown up in town a few times. Every once in a while, she'll do something to try to get to me, like spreading a rumour about me or something. Mostly it's been fairly harmless harassment. Until now."

"Yeah, she's definitely moved past harmless."

Meryn offered him a mirthless smile. "She's gorgeous, isn't she?"

His military training had given Jesse a highly developed radar—and healthy respect—for minefields, and he approached this one with extreme caution. "I wouldn't know." He lifted one shoulder. "I'm strictly a brunette man myself."

Amusement danced across her face. "Good answer." She tapped his arm with her knuckles. "But you don't have to pretend you didn't notice. It's not a matter of opinion, she's just beautiful. When I was little, I thought she was like a doll, with her big blue eyes and long blonde curls." She pulled her hand from his and twined her fingers together in her lap, staring down at them. "I always wanted to play with those curls. I'd try to touch them all the time, but she would push me away. The day she slapped me across the face I learned to admire her from a distance."

The acid that always flowed through him at the mention of Scorcher's name burned in his gut now. "I think you can safely drop the admiration part, but keeping your distance from her still seems like an excellent idea."

Meryn wrapped her arms around her knees. "Jesse, tell me everything you can about tomorrow, please. I want to be prepared."

He exhaled. "Caleb and I will be there, as well as Lieutenant Gallagher. There will also be a medical officer, a female. And there will be a government agent present. Since all of this is so new, the agent is there to watch that the sentence is carried out legally and ... adequately."

"Who will do it?"

His throat tightened and he couldn't answer.

She must have read it in his face, because she laid a hand on his arm. "That's good. I'm glad it will be you."

"I'm glad you're glad. Personally, I can't feel anything but sick about this whole thing."

She squeezed his arm.

He shook his head. How amazing that she was the one trying to comfort him under these circumstances.

"Have you had to do this before?"

"A few times. All men, and no one I really knew, so it was completely different, but I still detested every second of it."

"Is there anything else I should know?"

"You can have up to four friends or family members waiting in a room down the hall for you. Think about who you want, and I'll contact them for you."

"I'd like Kate and Ethan to come if they can." Her head jerked up. "I can go home with them afterward, right?"

"Yes. It will all be over. Provided you stay out of trouble, of course."

Meryn smiled wanly.

He didn't return it. "Seriously, Meryn. They'll be watching you closer than ever now. You cannot break the law again, or the consequences will be far more serious next time."

Her smile disappeared. "Will they shut the store down permanently?"

"I'm not sure. Caleb hasn't said anything about that, but I'll find out."

Meryn rubbed her temples with the tips of her fingers. "I don't know who else to suggest. Could you ask Kate if she can think of anyone?"

"Sure."

She regarded him in silence, her face serious.

"What is it?"

"Will I see you again, after tomorrow?"

His chest clenched. "I'll leave the army. After what happened yesterday, I really can't stay here. I'll find another job in the area, and we can see each other whenever we want."

"You can't, Jesse."

"Why not?"

"Think about what you could do if you stayed in the army, if no one knew you were a Christian. If things get worse, you could really help us. We'll need someone in power, someone with the ability to get things we might not be able to get much longer, or to help make things easier for people who get arrested. Someone who still has some influence over the way things are run in this town."

He drummed his fingers on the leather armrest of the couch. "But we wouldn't be able to see each other. Not very often, and not without being extremely careful."

"No. Which might be for the best." She rose and walked back to the fireplace.

Jesse went to her. After grasping her by the shoulders, he turned her to face him. "For the best? How can you say that? After everything that has happened between us, can you still tell me you don't want us to be together as much as I do?"

She wouldn't meet his gaze.

He let go of her with one hand and slid his fingers under her chin, forcing her to look at him. "Meryn?" He couldn't keep the pain he was feeling from his voice.

A sharp knock on the door shattered the moment.

He searched her face, desperately looking for an answer. Then he turned and walked to the door.

Caleb stood in the hallway, a tray in one hand and a package in the other.

"Cale." Jesse ran his fingers through his hair. "Come in." He stepped back so his friend could enter the room.

"I didn't see you in the dining hall, so I brought breakfast for the two of you."

"Thanks." Jesse closed the door as Caleb crossed the room to his desk and set down the tray, then tossed the package onto the chair.

Caleb turned to Meryn. "Are you okay?"

Her lips quivered as she attempted a smile. "I'm fine."

"I'm sorry about all of this, Meryn."

"It's not your fault, Major. I knew what I was doing."

"I don't just mean about that."

Her eyes glistened but she met his gaze steadily. "Oh. Then thank you."

His gaze shifted to Jesse. "I brought you the shirt. For tomorrow."

The burning in his gut intensified. "Thanks."

"Is there anything else you need? Either of you?"

"Meryn was wondering about the store. Do you know if they are going to let her keep it open?"

"I haven't heard yet. I'll let you know as soon as I do."

"Thank you, Major," Meryn said. "I appreciate it. And there's nothing else I need."

"Okay, then. I'll come by around ten forty-five in the morning."

Jesse walked him to the door and out into the hallway. "Do you have anything you want me to do today?"

"No, things are pretty quiet. I'll message you if something comes up. Otherwise, take the day off. You're due one, and I'm sure you'd rather be here than anywhere else."

Jesse's smile was strained. "Yeah. I do need to go see Meryn's friends and let them know what's going on and that she wants them to be there tomorrow, but I'll be here if you need me." He held out his hand and Caleb grasped it.

"We'll get through this, Jess. Together." Caleb squeezed his hand, then headed down the hallway.

Caleb was right. If Jesse did decide to stay in the army or Meryn wouldn't agree to see him again, then today was all they had.

So there was nowhere else in the world he could be but here with her.

CHAPTER THIRTY-THREE

J esse forced a smile as he waited for the door to open.

"Captain?" A look of surprise flashed across Kate's face, but she stepped back. "Come in."

"Thanks, Kate." Jesse followed her down the hallway and into the small kitchen of her home.

"Do you want to sit down?"

"Sure, thanks." Jesse pulled a chair out from the table. "I've come to let you know what's going on with Meryn. And I apologize, because I should have contacted you days ago. It's been a ... crazy week."

Kate shoved her short red hair behind one ear, her mouth pinched with anxiety as she settled onto the chair across from him. "I've been so worried. Drew ... some people who work in the neighbourhood around her store told us she had been arrested. I've tried calling the base a dozen times, but no one would let me talk to you or tell me anything about what was going on. I even went there once, but they wouldn't let me onto the property. Is it true? Was she arrested? And is she okay?"

Was Meryn okay? He had no idea how to answer that. "Meryn was arrested last Monday morning. Someone who witnessed her passing out Bibles, then watched her bookstore while a shipment came in with more Bibles in it, turned her in."

Kate sucked in her breath. "She was arrested for smuggling Bibles? That can't be right. She never said anything to me about that. Could she have been set up?"

He shook his head. "It's true, Kate. When we went to the store and confronted her, she showed us where she had hidden them beneath the floorboards. We figure she received at least a couple of other shipments and probably managed to hand out thirty or forty copies before she was caught."

The colour drained from Kate's face. "I can't believe it."

The kitchen door flew open. "Kate?"

They both turned toward the doorway.

A tall man with sandy-brown hair and a face etched with concern stalked into the room. "Is everything all right?"

Jesse stood up. He'd intentionally dressed in jeans and a long-sleeved T-shirt, but he didn't have any vehicle other than the jeep to drive, so he couldn't hide the fact that he was with the army.

The man stopped and eyed him with clear distrust.

Jesse didn't hold that against him. In his place, Jesse wouldn't trust himself either, not for a second.

"We're fine." Kate's voice shook slightly.

The man's eyes narrowed.

"Come and join us. Captain, this is my husband, Ethan Williams. Ethan, this is Captain Christensen. He's the soldier I told you about, the one who let us go from the church that day."

The muscles across the man's broad shoulders relaxed. "Oh. Then I guess I owe you a debt of gratitude, Captain." He held out his hand.

Jesse met him halfway across the room and grasped it. "It's Jesse, please. And you don't owe me a thing. If anything, I owe you an apology for everything that has gone on the last few months."

The eyes that met his softened. "Jesse." He shook Jesse's hand firmly, then let him go and waved toward the chair Jesse had vacated. "Please, sit." Ethan walked over and sat down beside his wife. "What is it?"

"It's Meryn. She's been charged with smuggling Bibles."

Ethan stared at Kate. "What? Did you know about that?"

"Of course not. I would have told you. But I can't believe it."

Her husband gave her a grim smile. "Actually, knowing Meryn, I have no trouble believing it." His smile faded as he turned to Jesse. "What's going to happen to her?"

"Are you familiar with Bill 1071?"

A dark look passed over Ethan's face. "I know it's the revised Terrorism and Hate Crimes Act and that anyone charged under it is likely to face corporal punishment."

Kate's eyebrows drew together. "Corporal punishment? Meaning what?"

Ethan took one of her hands in his, his eyes not leaving hers. "Flogging, even death."

She blinked, as if she was processing that information, then turned to Jesse, her voice calm. "Are you saying Meryn could be given the death penalty?"

"No, but ..."

"What?"

"The Canadian Human Rights Commission has convicted her and sentenced her to fifteen lashes."

Kate propped her elbows on the table. After dropping her head onto her hands, she pressed her fingers into her temples. "You have got to be kidding me."

"Trust me, I wish I were."

"I can't believe this is happening. Not here. And not in this century. What is going on in this country? Has everyone gone crazy?"

"I know it seems like that, but according to Meryn, this isn't collective national or global insanity. This is God, pulling out all the stops, trying to get everyone's attention. And I believe she's right."

Kate raised her head. "You do?"

"Yes."

"I guess some good has come out of all of this, then."

Ethan slid his arm around Kate's shoulders and looked at Jesse. "When is this supposed to happen?"

"Tomorrow morning, eleven o'clock. She is allowed up to four friends and family members in the waiting room, and she has requested that the two of you be there. She can go home with you afterward."

Kate nodded. "She'll want to go to her place, so maybe Ethan and I can take the kids to the farm and stay with her for a few days, until we know she's okay." She looked over at her husband.

"Sure. The kids love it there."

Jesse clasped his hands on the table. "That would be good. Thanks, Kate."

"You're welcome." She tilted her head, studying Jesse. "You really care about her, don't you?"

He dropped his gaze to the tabletop. "Yes, I do. I wanted to leave the army so we could be together, but Meryn convinced me I can do more good if I stay where I am." He shifted in his seat. "She said to ask you if there's anyone else you think should be there."

Kate looked at Ethan. "What about Rick?"

"Yeah, it would be a good idea to have her doctor there if he can make it. He's older, though, and might not be able to help us much if she needs support." He tapped his fingers on the table. "We could ask Drew."

Kate shot a glance at Jesse. "I don't know if that's the best idea."

"It's okay, Kate. I know he cares about her and that the two of them are friends. If he can help her in any way, then he should be there."

"Okay. I'll call them both and make the arrangements." When Kate met his gaze again, her hazel eyes had gone hard. "Who turned her in?"

Revealing an informant's name broke every code of confidentiality he could think of, but he couldn't bring himself to care one bit about Scorcher's right to privacy and anonymity. Besides, if she hated Meryn enough to betray her, Scorcher likely wouldn't have any qualms about going after her sister's friends. It would be a good idea for them to be prepared. "Annaliese Pettersson."

Shock and disgust registered on both Kate and Ethan's faces.

"I take it you know who that is."

"Meryn's sister." Ethan smacked his hand on the table. "She's been out to get her for years. It's hard to believe a person could be capable of stooping that low, but if anyone is, it's Annaliese."

"Yeah, she's something, all right. I shouldn't have revealed her name. Don't pass it on. But I wanted you to know, so you could be extra vigilant. I don't think she would hesitate to go after anyone Meryn cares about."

"You're right." Ethan pointed a finger in his direction. "Which means you should be careful of her too. If Annaliese were to find out you were involved with Meryn, she'd use that information against you in a heartbeat."

"I'm hoping to have as little to do with that woman as possible from now on. After what she did to Meryn, I'm not sure I could be alone with her without tearing her head off."

Ethan grinned. "That's a show I'd love a front row seat for."

Jesse returned the grin before pushing back his chair. "I better get back. Meryn's waiting to hear that everything's set for tomorrow."

Kate stood and held out her hand. "Thank you for coming, Jesse. What's happening is horrible, but I feel better knowing what's going on and that Meryn isn't going through any of this alone."

He squeezed her hand before letting her go. "And I feel better knowing you'll be taking care of her." He reached into the back pocket of his jeans and pulled out a business card. "Here's the direct line to my i-com. Don't hesitate to use it if there's anything you need, okay?"

Kate took it from him and set it on the table.

Jesse nodded at her husband. "Good to meet you, Ethan. I hope we'll have a chance to talk again soon."

"Me too." Ethan followed him back down the hallway to the door. "Give Meryn our love, and tell her we're praying for her, okay?"

"I will."

What was it about Ethan Williams that seemed so familiar? Jesse studied Ethan's face for a moment before it hit him. Something in his eyes reminded Jesse of Rory. And of their father.

Jesse stepped outside. Did he have the same look in his eyes now too? He really did hope to talk to Ethan again soon. It would be dangerous, of course, to see either of them after tomorrow.

But nothing about his new life would be easy or safe from now on.

CHAPTER THIRTY-FOUR

It was late in the day when Jesse arrived back at the base. Keenly aware that night was approaching and his time with Meryn was drawing to a close, Jesse sent up a quick prayer for calm and strength as he shut the door to his quarters.

Meryn sat on the couch, holding his leather-bound copy of *Moby Dick*.

Jesse walked over and dropped down beside her.

Weariness lined her face, but she managed a smile. "Hey."

"Hey yourself. How's the book?"

She looked down at the novel in her hand and wrinkled her nose. "I can't seem to get past the first few paragraphs. Not Mr. Melville's fault. I can't focus long enough to get into the story." Meryn closed the book and set it on the arm of the couch. "Too bad. I've always wanted to read it, and I don't usually have this much free time."

"It's a good one."

"So I've heard. I don't have to consume a novel to experience the depths of darkness the human soul can sink into though. Seems I don't have to look any further than my own family to find it these days."

The sheen in her eyes made his gut ache. Yeah, he'd gladly rip Scorcher's head off. Maybe put *it* on a silver platter. The thought made him smile. He squeezed Meryn's arm.

She lifted her chin. The sadness dissipated as if she'd simply made the choice to banish it.

If only he could do the same.

She touched the back of his hand but pulled her fingers away quickly. "Did you talk to Kate?"

"Yes, and Ethan. He seems great. I'd like to get to know him better."

Her eyes lit. "He *is* great. You'd really like him." She pressed her hands together on top of her bent knee and rested her chin on them. "Will they be there tomorrow?"

"Of course. And Kate is going to ask Rick to come. And Drew."

She blinked. "Okay. I guess it would be good to have him there as well."

Which him? Jesse mentally slapped himself. What was he? Back in seventh grade? Maybe he could pass a note to Ethan, asking him to ask Kate to ask Meryn if she liked Jesse or the cute boy who sat in front of her in math class better. He rubbed the side of his hand across his forehead. When he looked up, Meryn was watching him, the corners of her mouth twitching.

"I meant Rick. I'm glad he'll be there, in case I need him."

He could have kissed her for knowing how much the clarification would mean to him. It cost him, but he forced himself to respond. "It's good that Drew will be there too. The more friends you have around you when you go home, the better."

"That's true. You can't have too many *friends* around when you're going through a crisis."

"Especially when the people who love you the most can't be there for you."

Her eyes widened.

He waited a heartbeat before saying, "You know, like your parents and your brothers."

"Ah." A pink flush crossed her cheeks. "Yes, my family."

Jesse couldn't resist. "Who did you think I was talking about?"

The flush deepened, but her blue eyes gleamed when they met his. "That *is* who I thought you were talking about, of course. Why? Who else could it have been?"

She'd turned the tables on him nicely.

"Well played, lady."

Meryn laughed—under the circumstances, a pretty remarkable thing.

Jesse reached for her hand. She didn't resist when he intertwined his fingers with hers. "Speaking of your family, do you want me to call any of them? Let them know what's going on?"

"I think it would be better to wait. I'll call them in a couple of days, when it's all over. Otherwise they'll be worried tomorrow, and there won't be anything they can do when they're so far away." Sadness flickered across her face. "Although, I have to admit, there isn't much I wouldn't give to see my brothers at the moment." She gently pulled her fingers from his. "Thank you for offering to call them. That was sweet."

His hand felt suddenly cold and empty, like this room would after she had gone. Especially if she left without offering him any hope that they would see each other again after she returned home.

Meryn pointed to the washroom. "I'm going to get ready for bed, okay?"

Jesse forced a smile. "Sure." When the door clicked shut behind her, he blew out a deep breath.

That was it, then. She was closing the door, literally and figuratively, on him. On them.

Jesse crossed the room and looked out over the courtyard, dark now except for the soft glow haloed around the lampposts that lined the walkway from the building to the practice fields.

Well, he'd given it his best shot. He couldn't push her any further or harder than he had.

Pain shot through his chest. As much sense as that line of reasoning made, somewhere along the way his heart had clearly untethered itself from his brain, because the thought of all that time and space apart from Meryn didn't feel like a good thing at all.

CHAPTER THIRTY-FIVE

Meryn changed into the royal-blue T-shirt and flannel pyjama bottoms and paced in front of the washroom counter. She had to answer the question he'd asked her earlier, about whether she could tell him she didn't want them to be together as much as he did. She detested game-playing, and leaving Jesse hanging with no idea where he stood with her was the worst—and cruellest—type of game. Something had been happening inside her since the day he had stormed into her life ... a destabilizing of the walls she'd built around her heart to try and keep everyone out.

There had once been good reasons for making that attempt, but suddenly, as Kate had pointed out months ago, those reasons were starting to seem like nothing more than excuses. Tonight, when he'd taken her hand and she had studied their entwined fingers, struck by how perfectly they fit together, she could almost feel the breach, the crumbling into dust of those walls. Instead of the expected terror, a deep, consuming joy filled the void.

Not that she had intended for any of this to happen. She hadn't asked Jesse to fall in love with her; she hadn't even wanted him to. And she certainly hadn't meant to develop feelings for him that were so strong she couldn't fight against them. The problem was, now that she had those feelings, she had absolutely no idea what to do about them.

Stop lying to yourself, Meryn. She stopped pacing and turned to stare at her reflection in the mirror. She *had* been lying to herself. She knew exactly what she had to do. What she wanted to do.

Meryn opened the door and stepped out into the main room.

Jesse stood in front of the window, both arms folded over his chest as he gazed out the glass.

Heart pounding, she walked over to stand behind him. This was what she would remember after she had gone home. This was how she would picture him, standing strong and silent. She would miss him so much. Her courage began to wane and she spoke up quickly before it could slip away entirely. "Before the major came to the door, you asked me if I could still tell you I didn't want us to be together as much as you do."

He didn't turn around. "Yes, I did."

"I'm ready to answer that now."

He took a deep breath, as if he was trying to fortify himself for what she was about to say. "Okay."

"The answer is … no." Pushing away every thought, every obstacle, every hesitation that had held her back from the moment they had first met, Meryn reached out and rested her hands on his hips, letting the warmth of him seep into her cold fingers. "I can't tell you that I don't want us to be together as much as you do. Because that would be a lie."

A shudder moved through him, but he didn't speak.

Meryn rested her forehead against the back of his long-sleeved, grey T-shirt. "That was my attempt at transparency."

He covered both her hands with his and let out a choked laugh. "It was a pretty good one." Jesse pulled her fingers to his mouth and kissed them, then wrapped her arms around his waist and held them there.

Meryn drew in the scents of soap and citrus before lifting her head. "I have no idea what that is going to look like for us, but—"

"We'll figure it out. I promise." Jesse turned to face her. "I just need-ed to hear that answer to my question." He cupped her shoulders. "We could run away. Caleb would cover for us. We'd have hours, maybe even enough time to cross the border, before anyone knew we had left. We could find someplace safe and start a new life together."

Briefly, Meryn allowed herself to think that such a thing could be possible.

His green eyes darkened. "Let me guess, we've been told *not* to go, haven't we?"

She offered him a sad smile. "Yes."

"You know what? I think I'm actually beginning to get that. I'm not quite sure whether that thought encourages or terrifies me."

Meryn sobered. "We have work to do here. And besides, there is no safe place, remember?"

His hands moved up and down her bare arms before he slid them to her neck, both thumbs rubbing softly over her collarbone. "Nice pyjamas."

"Thanks. They're my new favourites." Warmth rushed through her. The look in his eyes weakened her resolve as quickly as it weakened her knees. "We can't." Her voice was hoarse and she cleared her throat.

His thumbs stilled. "I know."

"It's not that I don't want to." She clutched the hem of the T-shirt to keep from reaching out for him. "In fact, I'm a little terrified by how much I want to, how easy it would be. But it would be wrong and ... complicated."

"Well"—Jesse stepped back—"we wouldn't want this situation to get complicated, would we?"

Meryn forced a grin.

"Okay then." He took her hand and led her across the room. "It won't be easy, but how about I attempt to drive those wanton thoughts from your head with a story?" He let go of her hand and dropped down on one end of the couch, grabbing his pillow and settling it on his lap.

"A story?"

"Yes." Jesse smiled at her. "I'm a closet storyteller, didn't I mention that? Do you want to hear it?"

"I'd love to."

"First things first. You know how you said there is no safe place anymore?"

She nodded.

"That isn't entirely true. There is one." Jesse patted the pillow. "For tonight, there is one safe place."

Meryn blinked back tears as she sat down in front of him and rested back against his chest.

Jesse wrapped his arms around her. He held her and began to speak, his breath warm on the top of her head. "It's not so much a story maybe, as a picture. Close your eyes."

Her eyes shut as she relaxed back into his embrace.

"Are they closed?"

"Yes."

"Okay, imagine this scene. An old man and woman are sitting together on a couch much like this one. Only they aren't in cramped military quarters, they're in their own home. There's a floor-to-ceiling stone fireplace with a blazing fire that crackles and sends sparks shooting upward every few minutes, and there's no other light, only the soft glow of the flames flickering off the log walls. The ceiling is exposed beams, and the house is small and cozy, the type of rustic house the woman always wanted to have, growing up."

Meryn drew in a quick breath and twisted her head to look up at him. "How did you—?"

"Shh." Jesse tapped her on the nose. "Close your eyes. No interrupting the storyteller."

She turned and settled back against his chest, heart pounding. How was it possible that he could know her so well after such a short time? It was as if he could read her thoughts and feelings, that he could see down deep inside of her where she kept all her hopes and dreams for the future. A future she had believed she would never have.

"The man has his arms around the woman, and she is resting against him. The warmth of the fire is lulling them both to sleep, which isn't hard. Their three dark-haired, blue-eyed grandchildren have just left after spending the day with them, and the couple are exhausted."

In spite of the emotions roiling through her, Meryn laughed.

"But not so exhausted that he isn't willing to scoop her up, carry her into the bedroom, and prove to her that, in spite of his white hair, he still has the constitution of a forty-year-old."

She slapped his knee. "Behave. You're supposed to be getting those thoughts *out* of my head, not putting them in."

"Can't blame a guy for trying." He tightened his hold. "All right then, they stay where they are. Gradually, the woman stills in his arms, and he knows she has fallen asleep. And the man looks around the room, at the dog stretched out on a rug in front of the fireplace, the light flickering off the logs of the cozy home, and the pictures of their children and grandchildren that cover the walls. Then he looks down at his wife, the woman he loved before he even met her, before he knew her name, and his heart is full. Because he knows that, whatever might happen in the future, for this moment in time he is holding everything he has ever wanted in his arms, and he is content."

A tear slid down her cheek, and Meryn pressed the side of her face against his soft, cotton shirt.

Jesse touched his lips to the top of her head, then shifted slightly against the arm of the couch, settling in.

His heart beat against her cheek, the strong, steady rhythm of it soothing her. She let the strength of the arms that held her flow through her. Breathing a prayer for both of them, that they would have the courage they needed to face whatever the light of day would bring, she drifted off to sleep.

CHAPTER THIRTY-SIX

Meryn lay unmoving for a long time before even contemplating getting up from the couch. Sunlight streamed through the window, bathing Jesse's quarters in a golden light.

The window was cracked open, and cool, spring air filled the room. Birds chirped loudly in the trees along the walkway.

She blinked several times. The bright, cheerful sounds clashed with the sense of foreboding that hung in the room like a heavy cloud overshadowing the beauty of the morning.

Her gaze flitted around the room.

These four grey walls imprisoned her, held her against her will. Still, even within their confines, last night she had found the strength to break away from the shackles that had held her captive, figuratively speaking, for so long. She would soon be handcuffed and taken where she did not want to go to face a punishment she had no desire to endure, but that memory sent a glorious feeling of freedom soaring through her. Her fear and trepidation dissipated in the warm sunlight.

Lying there against Jesse's chest, she took several minutes to summon the energy to move. When she did stir, his arms tightened around her, and she settled back against him with a small smile.

Finally he kissed the top of her head and let her go.

Meryn sat up and faced him. "Did you sleep?"

"Surprisingly, yes. You?"

"I did, actually, really well. Which I hadn't been expecting."

"Good." His gaze probed hers. "How are you feeling about today?"

"That's a loaded question. I may need to have coffee before I answer it."

A slow smile crossed his face. "We can do that. I'll go get us some breakfast."

"Okay. I'm going to take a shower while you're gone." She started to get up, then stopped and turned back to him. "This morning when, you know …"

He nodded.

"Do I have to take off … I mean, will I be …?" She couldn't bring herself to say the word.

"Naked? Oh no, that wouldn't be *civilized*." Jesse got up off the couch and walked over to the chair in front of his desk. He picked up the package the major had left there the day before and pulled something out of the white paper wrapping. "This may all be very barbaric, but it's civilized barbarism." Shaking out the folded cloth, he held up a pale-blue shirt with ties at the back.

Like a hospital gown, only shorter.

"I should have shown you this before. You wear this into the room and then, just before the sentence is carried out, the three outer ties are undone and retied at the front so the shirt is held open. The elastic on the sides, and the inner ties at your neck and waist, hold the cloth in place, so nothing but your back is exposed."

Meryn rubbed her damp palms on the flannel pyjama bottoms. "What is it like?"

"What?"

"The lash, or whip, or whatever it is."

Jesse draped the shirt over the back of the chair before lowering himself onto the couch beside her. "They're using the old cat-o'-nine-tails. It's made up of nine cords of rope, designed to inflict pain with minimal permanent damage to the skin. And it isn't really lashed across the back, it's flicked. It's done with a wrist action, kind of like fly-fishing."

Meryn pressed her fingers against her forehead. "I still can't believe they're doing this in Canada."

"It's not new. This type of punishment was in the criminal code of this country until the early 1970s. They put back in the section that had been taken out then, with no changes to any of the subsections except for one."

"Which is?"

"Subsection number six used to read that it was prohibited for women to be whipped. Now, thanks to the equal rights movement, I guess, that prohibition has been removed."

Meryn smiled weakly. "Not exactly what Susan B. Anthony had in mind, I'm sure."

"Probably not." He hesitated. "There's something else."

"What?"

"I'm supposed to tell you that you can have your sentence reduced."

"How?"

"If you give us the name of your supplier, they'll take off five lashes, and another five if you tell us who you gave the Bibles to."

"I can't."

"I figured you'd say that. But you might change your mind."

"Can I?"

"Yes. I'll ask you after every five strokes. If you can't take the pain and decide to talk, no one would blame you."

"Except maybe the people whose names I give up." Meryn drew in a deep breath. "No, I have to go through with this."

"You won't be alone."

"I know."

He reached out and brushed back a strand of hair from her face. "Anything else you want to know?"

"I don't think so. I don't really want to think about it anymore until I have to."

"Fair enough. Go have your shower, then we'll eat breakfast."

She went to get ready.

If such a thing were actually possible.

———•———

When she came out of the washroom, Jesse had set the table in front of the window for them. Meryn looked at her watch. Almost ten. The major would be coming by for them in less than an hour. She banished the thought. This would be their last meal together in this room, and she didn't want to waste precious time worrying about what would come after.

Jesse held out a chair for her.

She sat down. The eggs and bacon might have been appealing under other circumstances, but today the smell turned her stomach.

Jesse's hands covered both of hers. "Can I pray for us?"

Only a couple of days ago, she never would have thought she'd hear the man across from her say those words. She nodded.

For a few seconds after he had bowed his head, she watched him, heart overflowing with something even stronger than the joy that had flooded through her the night before. Something she still couldn't name but that she could no longer deny. Then she bowed her head and let the words wash over her.

"And, God, you know this is a hard day for us. I pray for Meryn. Give her the strength and the courage to endure what lies ahead. Help me to do what I have to do. God, you've brought us together, and we're more grateful for that than we can say. At least I am." He squeezed her hands. "We're not sure what is going to happen after today, but you know, and we trust you to guide us and show us the way we are supposed to take. Amen."

It was by far the most beautiful and powerful prayer she'd ever heard. She blinked back tears as she raised her head. "Thank you."

He let her go and reached for her plate. After setting it off to one side, he lifted up a smaller plate and held it toward her. "Toast?"

"Thanks. That's all I can handle today."

"I get it." He sipped his coffee and leaned back in his chair. "That felt good."

"What?"

"Praying. I've been doing a lot of it the last couple of days, but I haven't prayed out loud in years."

"It felt good for me too, listening to you."

The same look she'd seen in his eyes that night the brick came through her store window—the one that was either remorse or regret—darkened them again.

"What is it?"

He set down his mug. "I was thinking about how happy my parents would have been to hear me praying. It hurt them a lot that I didn't believe. I wish they could know, somehow, that I've finally come to realize that everything they taught me was true."

Meryn rested a hand on his arm. "Jesse. The Bible says that the angels in heaven rejoice over one lost person who is found. Don't you think someone, maybe even Jesus himself, would have told your parents who the party was for? I'm pretty sure they would have been invited to be there to rejoice along with everyone else."

"I never thought of that." Light flowed back into his eyes. "That means Rory would have been there too."

Her eyes widened. "Rory?"

"Yeah. He was a believer. He talked to Caleb and me about it all the time, but we were both too pigheaded to listen."

Meryn grasped his arm. "That's so great. You're going to have quite the family reunion someday."

"Yeah, I guess we will." He lifted her hand to his mouth and kissed the back of it. "Not too soon, though, I hope. I suddenly find myself with a lot more to live for than I've ever had before." He pushed his own plate away. "It's not a good idea for me to come by your place anymore. We need to think of somewhere we can meet."

She tapped her fingers on the table. "There's an abandoned property about a kilometre down the road from my house, with an old cabin set back in the woods. I've never seen anyone around there, so it should be a safe place for us to go. Have you noticed a big house with beige siding on my road, on the way to town? The barns on the property have green roofs."

"I know the one."

"It's the property just past that as you're heading toward my place, same side of the road. There's an old gate and a lane beyond it. It's overgrown, but you should still be able to drive down it."

"I'll find it." He blew out a long breath. "If I'm going to try and convince everyone I'm still a loyal soldier in the Canadian Army, I won't be able to go there very often, but I'll message you whenever I think I can get away."

"Don't take any chances." Her next words clung to her throat, but she forced them out. "You have the opportunity to really do some good, to help a lot of people. Don't risk that so we can see each other."

"There isn't much I wouldn't risk to see you, but you're right. This thing is bigger than either of us, and we're going to have to try not to be selfish. It won't be easy."

"No, it won't."

Jesse held her gaze for a moment before glancing down at his watch. When he looked up at her again, pain was etched across his face. "Caleb will be here in a few minutes."

Reluctantly, Meryn set down her mug and stood up. "I'll go get changed." She rummaged through her purse for a hair elastic, then zipped the bag shut and took the blue shirt Jesse held out for her. She went into the washroom and changed quickly, pulled her hair up in a loose knot, and came back out.

"Here." He reached for the clothes she clutched in her hand and lifted the white cloth bag he was holding. "I'll put these in here with your purse and give them to Kate for you." He added her lavender sweater to the cloth bag and set it down by the door.

She pointed to her back. "I couldn't reach the middle ties. Would you ...?"

"Sure."

She turned around.

Instead of tying the middle strings, though, he tugged on the top ones, and slowly spread the shirt open as far as the tightly elasticized sides would allow.

Meryn struggled to breathe.

He ran his hands gently over her bare back. After a moment, he leaned in and whispered, "I'd a thousand times rather it be me."

"I know." Her voice broke.

Jesse tied the strings and pressed his lips to the curve of her neck.

Meryn turned to face him.

He wrapped his arms around her and pulled her close.

She rested her head on his chest, then looked up and met his gaze. "I'll be thinking about that old man and woman in front of the fireplace."

His eyes were sad but he smiled.

Ah. That was why he had told her that story. It was a kindness, his gift to her, the only way that he could help her get through what lay ahead. She rested a hand on his cheek, hoping he could read in her eyes how grateful she was, feel it in her touch.

A knock sounded on the door.

Her stomach clenched.

Neither of them moved until he touched his forehead to hers. "If I kiss you, I won't be able to do this."

Meryn stepped back, head high. "I'm ready."

CHAPTER THIRTY-SEVEN

Meryn faced the door as the major came into the room.

"All set?" His blue eyes, filled with compassion, settled on her face.

Meryn nodded and took a step forward.

He pulled a set of handcuffs from his belt. "I'm sorry, Meryn, but it's regulation."

"It's okay." She held her hands out in front of her.

He snapped the metal around her wrists and raised his gaze over her shoulder.

The empathy in the look he gave Jesse draped over her too, a temporary shelter from the pain.

The major nodded toward the door. "Let's go."

Meryn walked into the hall and stopped, a cold shiver spreading across her skin.

Lieutenant Gallagher, the one who had come to her store with Jesse the day she was arrested, stood outside the door. His dark, hooded eyes raked over her, like clammy fingers groping her body.

She suppressed a shudder and looked back as Jesse came out of the room, holding the white cloth bag in one hand.

He took in the two of them, and a shadow passed over his face. He grasped her elbow, turned her away from the lieutenant, and started down the hall. The major fell into step on the other side of her.

She couldn't see the look Jesse gave his subordinate over his shoulder, but the temperature in the hallway dropped.

After several turns through the maze-like building, they stopped outside a room with big double doors. The major pressed his thumb to the pad on the wall and opened one of the doors, holding it for the rest of them as they passed through into a large room.

Meryn's breaths came in shallow spurts.

It was the most sterile room she had ever seen. Fluorescent light gleamed off bare, white walls. No paintings or certificates broke up the endless starkness, and nothing absorbed the sound of their echoing footsteps.

A short man with a shaved head and pale, blue eyes, business-like in a navy suit and red tie, waited for them in the room. A woman with the high cheekbones and long, glistening black hair—pulled back in a sleek ponytail—of a native Canadian stood just behind him. She wore a camouflage jacket and pants, and a stethoscope hung around her neck. Both of them regarded her with solemn faces.

A large, metal pole in the middle of the room extended from the floor almost up to the low-hanging ceiling. A crossbeam, both ends angled slightly forward, extended out from either side of the pole, about five feet off the ground. Another crossbeam was bolted into the pole a couple of inches from the floor.

Meryn's heart hammered in her chest.

The man in the suit stepped forward and glanced at the i-com in his hand. "Meryn O'Reilly?"

She nodded.

He looked down again. "You have been convicted of purchasing illegal hate literature for the purposes of distribution and sentenced to fifteen lashes. Do you understand this?"

Meryn nodded again.

"Have you been informed of the fact that this sentence can be reduced if you cooperate with the Canadian government by revealing the name of your supplier or those of the people to whom you distributed these illegal materials?"

"Yes." The word came out in a raspy whisper, and she cleared her throat.

"Do you wish to supply us with that information now?"

She met his gaze. "No."

"You will be given two more opportunities to cooperate as the sentence is carried out. Should you refuse to comply, the full fifteen lashes will be given." He stepped back and motioned to the medical officer.

The woman stepped forward. "I'm going to check your blood pressure and heart rate to ensure it is safe to carry out the sentence." She wrapped a blood pressure cuff around Meryn's arm. When the woman finished, she nodded, and the government agent inclined his head toward the officers.

The ties came loose at the back of her shirt, and heat flared in her cheeks.

Jesse moved around to the front of her and began retying the strings.

She lifted her cuffed hands out of his way. The cool air in the room brushed across her back, and she shivered.

He met her eyes briefly, then focused on his task. When he had finished, he took her elbow again.

The major reached for her cuffs and unlocked them, then tucked them back into his belt as he moved out of the way.

The lieutenant grabbed her other arm, and he and Jesse led her toward the pole.

They stopped in front of it, and Jesse squeezed her elbow before letting go of her. "Place your wrists on the pads of the crossbars."

She hadn't realized she was shaking until she set her hands where he had told her to, one on each side of the main beam, so that her arms were stretched out to the sides and forward, following the slight angle of the beams.

The lieutenant closed the top metal piece of the ring attached to the pad around her left wrist and locked it into place.

Jesse snapped the other metal ring around her right wrist.

"Step forward."

Meryn moved closer to the bottom crossbeam.

Both men crouched down and locked the metal rings around her ankles.

She closed her eyes. *Father, give me strength.*

From behind her came the rustling of plastic, the unwrapping of the cat-o'-nine-tails Jesse had told her about.

"Are we ready?" The voice of the man with the i-com, the government agent, boomed through the room.

Was she expected to respond?

Jesse answered the man with a terse "yes" before she could.

"Then let's begin."

Meryn focused on the image of the elderly couple Jesse had described to her, trying to prepare herself.

A whooshing sound broke the silence in the room. White-hot, prickling pain exploded across her upper back. A cry of shock rose in her throat, but she pressed her lips together tightly as the second stroke landed on her skin.

Three more strokes came in rapid succession, as if Jesse was trying to get it over with as quickly as possible. The lashes coming so close together made it difficult to draw in a breath between the flashes of searing pain.

When he stopped, she gulped for air and blinked, lightheaded.

Jesse stepped in front of the metal pole. "Do you have anything you want to tell us?" His face was impassive, almost cold, but pain roiled deep in his green eyes.

"No."

He dipped his chin curtly and disappeared behind her.

She squeezed her eyes shut, knowing now what was coming and that there was no way to prepare for it. Her heart pounded so loudly it almost blocked out the sound of the whip whistling through the air again. Meryn bit her lip until the metallic taste of blood coated her tongue.

Paul. Silas. Jesus. Those greater than she had endured the same punishment and more.

Seven strokes. Eight.

Each of those men had done so much for the kingdom. She didn't even deserve to be listed among them.

Nine.

What have I done? So little. But that could change.

Would change.

The tenth stroke sent waves of shock shooting through her. Her entire body shook. If her arms hadn't been securely attached to the bar, her legs would not have held her up.

How does anyone endure thirty lashes or more?

Jesse came into sight again. "You have the right to request medical assistance if you need it. Do you want to see a medic?"

The whip in his hand, the cords speckled with fresh blood, hypnotized her. She shook her head slightly, the instrument of her torture blurring as a fog drifted in front of her eyes.

"Is there anything you wish to say?"

A single word from her and this would all be over. Jesse was right. No one would blame her. *God, help me.* She blinked away the dizziness. "No."

He blew out a rush of air as he turned away, as if he'd been holding his breath while waiting for her response.

Meryn's fists clenched when the tips of the cords slashed against already broken and tender skin. Warm blood trickled down her back, and she couldn't hold back a groan of pain as the next stroke sent tongues of flame licking across her flesh. *God, give me strength. Help me get through this.*

The trembling in her legs stilled. A warmth like the rays of sun that had flooded Jesse's room that morning spread through her. Overwhelming peace deadened the pain of the lash as it flicked over her skin again.

She blinked, in wonder this time, at the deep breath she was able to draw in spite of the fourteenth stroke that sent needle pricks of fire skittering across her shoulders.

The whip whistled through the air one last time, the cord tips sparking over her lower back, but all Meryn felt was an overwhelming gratitude welling inside her.

It was done, and she had endured. Not on her own strength, which had failed, but on the power that had come to her when she had called out for it.

Meryn rested her forehead on the cool metal pole in front of her as Jesse and Lieutenant Gallagher freed first her ankles and then her wrists. When the manacles fell away, she turned to face Jesse.

The officer who had checked her vitals stood behind him.

"Do you wish to receive medical attention here at the clinic on the base?"

The only thing she wanted at the moment was to go home. "No."

The government agent standing off to the side held out his i-com and a stylus.

Jesse took them from him. "You need to sign this waiver stating that you were offered medical treatment and refused it." He handed her the stylus and held the screen in front of her.

Her hand was steady as she signed her name.

Jesse returned the unit to the agent and reached for the strings of her shirt.

She waited as he moved around behind her and pulled the cloth loosely over her throbbing back.

The agent stepped in front of her. "Meryn O'Reilly, you have received your sentence in full and are now released from custody."

"Thank you."

Surprise flashed through his eyes as he stepped back.

Jesse took her by the arm. "This way." He directed her through the double doors and into the hallway.

Footsteps echoed on the tile floor behind them as the other officers filed out of the room.

They walked past two doors before Jesse stopped, rapped lightly on a third one, and pushed it open.

"Meryn." Kate's eyes filled with tears as she crossed the room toward her. "Are you okay?"

"I will be, once I'm home."

Kate looked at Jesse. "Can we leave?"

"Yes. She's free to go."

Ethan held out a jacket.

Kate took it from him and draped it gently over Meryn's shoulders.

"Thanks, Kate."

Jesse held the white cloth bag out to Kate. "Her personal effects."

Kate took the bag, and her eyes held Jesse's for a few seconds before he stepped back.

Rick shuffled up behind Kate, his lined face soft with compassion. "I'll come back to your house with you, Meryn, and make sure you're all right."

"Okay, thanks, Rick." Meryn offered him a small smile that faded as Drew approached, his eyes hard. "Drew. Thank you for coming."

"Of course." The words were addressed to her, but his gaze, filled with hostility, was directed over her shoulder at Jesse.

He must have caught the look, but when he spoke, Jesse's tone didn't reflect any animosity. "I'll help you find your way out."

Drew moved closer to Meryn. "I think Meryn's had about all she can take of your kind of help. We can handle things from here." His voice spewed venom.

Lieutenant Gallagher stepped in front of him, dark eyes flashing. "Watch it, sir, or you'll find yourself on the receiving end of the same kind of *help* she's been given."

Drew stiffened. "Go ahead, arrest me. Fill your prisons with people giving out Bibles and exercising their constitutionally guaranteed right to free speech while terrorists run around blowing up buildings and killing people. Seems like a perfect use of tax-payer dollars."

"Drew." Meryn rested a hand on his arm. If he didn't calm down, he would talk himself into a jail cell.

He didn't take his eyes from the lieutenant, who stepped closer until their chests were nearly touching.

The major put a hand on the lieutenant's shoulder. "Thank you, Lieutenant. I'll handle this. We'll let you get back to your work."

The lieutenant threw a last, heated look at Drew before offering the major what appeared to be a mocking salute. He spun on his heel and left the room.

Drew's attention focused back in on Jesse.

The major turned to him. "Why don't you go too, Captain? I will escort them out of the building."

"Yes, sir." Jesse's gaze swept the room. He offered Ethan a brief nod before meeting Meryn's gaze.

She pressed a hand to her stomach as he strode from the room.

Drew touched her arm. His fingers still quivered with tension. "Let's get out of here."

Meryn nodded.

The major stepped back and held a hand toward the door. "I'll show you out."

They walked silently behind him through the winding hallways. When they reached the exit to the parking lot, the major held the door open for them. A brief smile crossed her lips as she passed by, and he answered with one of his own.

Meryn stepped outside and tipped back her face to the cool, fresh air. Never would she take the feel of sunshine and wind—or blessed freedom—for granted again.

CHAPTER THIRTY-EIGHT

Caleb caught up to Jesse halfway back to his quarters but didn't say a word as they walked. Once the door had shut behind them, Caleb did open his mouth as if to speak, but Jesse lifted a hand and headed straight into the washroom.

After emptying his stomach of the few bites he'd been able to get down at breakfast, he brushed his teeth, splashed cold water on his face, and took a deep breath before coming back into his room.

Caleb sat in his usual leather chair in front of the fireplace.

Jesse walked past him over to the mantel. Gripping the cool wood in both hands, he dropped his head down between his arms and concentrated on drawing in one cleansing mouthful of air after another.

Caleb gave him another minute before he spoke up. "She's okay, Jess."

"I know."

"In fact, she's more than okay. She's pretty remarkable. She barely made a sound through the whole thing. I've seen men twice her size hollering for mercy after ten lashes."

Jesse smiled grimly as he stared down at the smooth, dark cherry wood. "I know."

"And she has absolutely no interest in him."

His smile faded as his fingers tightened on the edge of the mantel. "I know."

Behind him, leather creaked as Caleb shifted in his chair. "All right, smart guy, since you know so much, tell me this. Did you feel something happen in there?"

He hesitated. "Yes."

"I've felt it before, with other Christians."

"Me too."

"So what is it? Do you know?"

Jesse turned around. "As profound as it is, it's also pretty simple. I was praying for strength for her, and I'm sure she was praying for strength for herself. So God gave her strength."

"That's it?"

"Isn't that enough?"

"Apparently it is." Caleb drummed his fingers on the arms of the chair. "How did you leave things with her?"

"Pretty up in the air. We were both concentrating on getting through today. Kind of hard to think much past that."

"But you're going to try and see her."

"How can I not?"

"It'll be risky."

"I know."

Caleb pressed his palms against the arms of the chair and rose. "Look, I don't pull rank on you very often, but—"

Jesse snorted. "You pull rank on me *all* the time."

"Hey." He lifted his hands. "Is it my fault you need to be reminded every five minutes who's in charge?"

"No, I guess not."

"In any case, I'm going to pull rank on you now, Captain." Caleb walked over to stand in front of him. "I am ordering you to ..."

Jesse raised an eyebrow.

Caleb let out a long breath. "To be careful."

"I will."

"Do you need to take some time off?"

"No. That's the last thing I need. What I need to do is work. I'll start by helping Hamilton set up the shooting range again. Then I'm available for whatever you want me to do. If I work hard enough, maybe I can stop thinking. Like about how, even if she has absolutely no interest in Drew, he's the one who's with her right now, and the one who can see her any time he wants." He clutched Caleb's arm. "Keep me busy, Cale. That's all I ask."

"I can do that." Caleb slapped him on the back. "Let's go."

CHAPTER THIRTY-NINE

There wasn't much the doctor could do for Meryn beyond cleaning the small, dot-like wounds, applying antiseptic, and bandaging the larger lacerations. Like Jesse had told her, both the instrument and the technique were designed to cause minimal damage to the skin, and none of the wounds needed stitches.

"Apply this every morning for the next few days." Rick held the tube up to show her before setting it on the table beside her bed. "And get lots of sleep, Meryn. Your body has been through a trauma and needs time to recover. Okay?"

"Okay." Meryn curled up on her side on the bed, facing Rick.

He pulled a plastic bottle out of his bag, twisted off the cap, and knocked two tablets into his hand before setting the bottle beside the tube of ointment. Holding out the tablets, he picked up the glass of water from the bedside table.

Wincing, Meryn propped herself up on one elbow, took the pills from him, and popped them into her mouth, reached for the water, and swallowed.

"Those are for pain. Take two of them every four hours for as long as you need to. They'll help you sleep too." The elderly doctor rested a hand on her head. "And call if you need me. Any time, day or night, all right?"

"I will."

He gathered his things and headed for the door. Before he left the room, he turned to Kate, who sat in the chair in the corner by the window. "She'll be fine, don't worry. Keep an eye on her, and call me if you have any questions or concerns."

Kate gave him a quick hug. When he had gone, she walked over to the dresser and withdrew a pink tank top from a drawer. "Want to lose that blue shirt?"

"Definitely." Meryn bit her lip as her friend undid the ties, tugged off the shirt, and helped her pull on the tank top.

"I'll burn this, if you don't mind." Kate held up the shirt.

"Be my guest." Meryn lay back down on her side.

Kate lifted the cloth bag Jesse had given her off the top of the dresser. "Here, Mer. I'll leave this with you." She set it down on the bed.

"Thanks, Kate. I think I'm going to sleep for a while."

"Okay." Kate pointed to the i-com sitting on the bedside table beside the medication. "I'll come up in a couple of hours to check on you, but message me if you need me before that, okay?"

"Okay."

"I take it you don't want me to send Drew up to say goodbye."

Meryn wrinkled her nose. "I don't think so. Although I did appreciate him coming to the base today."

"Even though he went after Jesse?"

"He was angry about what happened to me, so I can't be too upset with him about it. Jesse would have understood that too."

"And the major, otherwise Drew would probably be sitting in a cell right now, especially if that lieutenant had anything to say about it."

"Yeah, there's something wrong with that guy. He isn't quite right in the head."

"That was pretty clear. Anyway, get some rest and we'll talk later."

Meryn's eyes closed and she drifted off into a deep, dreamless sleep.

———◆———

When Meryn woke, long shadows fell across the room. Outside the window, ribbons of red and orange stretched across the sky. The mournful cry of a whippoorwill floated through the screen.

She struggled to sit, catching her bottom lip between her teeth at the slivers of pain that shot across her back. Her elbow bumped the white bag, and she reached gingerly for its handle. Her lavender sweater was on top of the other things in the bag, and she pulled it out, made a face, and tossed it over the foot of the bed. She really didn't care if she never saw that, or her black pants, again. Her purse was next, and she dropped it down on the floor before pulling Jesse's copy of *Moby Dick* from the bag.

She ran her hand over the smooth, leather cover. His hands had held it; his fingers had turned every page. Now that she was supposed to be on bed rest for a few days, maybe she'd actually be able to get past the first couple of paragraphs. She moved her i-com to one side and set the book on her bedside table.

The bag still felt heavy.

Meryn dug down inside of it. What else could he have sent home for her?

The familiar royal-blue T-shirt and flannel pyjama bottoms were folded neatly at the bottom. She choked back a laugh as she grabbed them.

They were wrapped around something solid.

She pulled the bundle into her lap, absently dropped the bag on the floor, and unfolded the pyjamas.

Her Bible.

She covered her mouth with one hand and squeezed her eyes shut as two tears slid down her cheeks. After a moment she opened her eyes, wiped the moisture away with the back of her hand, and lifted her Bible away from the pyjamas. Her fingers trembled as she opened the cover.

A piece of paper fluttered onto the bed beside her.

Meryn picked it up and read the words Jesse had written.

Hide this somewhere no one will ever find it. And know that, whatever stands between us, I will always find you. J.

Meryn tucked the note back inside the Bible and set the book beside her on the bed. Memories of the past seven days crashed through her mind. So much had happened. So much had changed that her weary brain couldn't begin to process it all. The only thought that crystallized was that she missed Jesse desperately and would give anything to feel his arms around her again.

Clenching her jaw, Meryn slid back the covers and stood up. She swayed on her feet for a few seconds before pulling Jesse's T-shirt on over the pink tank top. She tugged his pyjama bottoms up over the shorts she was wearing and lowered herself carefully back onto the bed. Lifting the bottom of the shirt up to her face, she inhaled the scent of him that still clung to it from when she had slept against him on the couch the night before.

When would she see him again? She was the one who had cautioned him against taking risks to see her. If he listened to her, it could be days, or even weeks, before he would make the attempt. And the major likely wouldn't encourage him to meet with her either. At the ache in her stomach, she bent forward.

A soft rap on the door brought her head up sharply, and she sucked in a breath at the pain the quick movement caused.

Meryn shoved the Bible under the blankets and wiped her face with her fingers, then called out, "Come in."

The door opened and Kate poked her head through the opening. "Up for some company?"

"If it's you, always."

Kate walked through the doorway. She carried a tray with a bowl and a teapot and a mug on it, which she set down on top of the dresser before walking over to the bed. Settling herself on the edge of it, she rested a hand on Meryn's leg. "How are you doing?"

"Better, I think. I slept for a bit. And I'm extremely glad to be home."

Kate tilted her head to one side. "Are you?"

"Of course. Why would you ask me that?"

"Because the air between you and the captain seemed pretty charged today. I don't know how much you actually saw him while you were on the base, or what went on between you, but it seemed like something had changed. Something big enough to make me wonder if you really would be happy to go home or if part of you might be sad to leave him."

Tears welled in Meryn's eyes again, but she blinked them back. "Oh, Kate. You're right. Nothing is the same." Her cheeks grew warm. "I saw a lot of him on the base, actually. They didn't have accommodations for female prisoners, so I ended up being held in his quarters."

Kate's eyebrows rose. "Really."

"Yes. Nothing happened. At least, nothing like what you're thinking. But so much happened, I don't even know how to begin telling you about

it. I will, soon, once I've had time to process it all. In the meantime ..."
Meryn reached under the blankets and pulled out Jesse's gift. "Look."

Kate inhaled sharply. "He gave you back your Bible."

Meryn found the piece of paper and held it out. "Read this."

Kate studied the note, then looked up, eyes glistening. "He really cares about you, Mer."

Meryn slipped the paper back inside the cover of the Bible and reverently set it back down on the bed beside her.

"What are you planning to do?"

"He wants us to be together."

"Of course he does. But that's not what I asked you. What do you want?"

Meryn chewed on her thumbnail before dropping her hand into her lap. "I ... I want that too."

Kate's eyes widened. "Now I really have to hear what happened in that room. But what about ...? I mean, you've been so adamant about not getting involved with anyone. Have you finally decided it's time to move on? Forget the past?"

Guilt niggled down deep in her stomach, but Meryn smothered it. She couldn't think about the past at the moment. She had enough to deal with in the present. "Yes. I guess I have."

Kate touched her knee. "That's good, Mer. It's been three years. It's time to let go and get on with your life. And you have a good, decent, incredibly gorgeous man who wants to help you do that. I say go for it."

Meryn laughed. "I think I might. It won't be easy, though. He's become a believer."

"I gathered that when he came here the other night to talk to us. He said he wanted to leave the army, but you convinced him he could do more good where he was. Which is true, but it does put him in a dangerous position, doesn't it?"

"Yes. Especially if he's caught with a Christian who also happens to be a convicted felon."

Kate smoothed the flowered bedspread with one hand. "Speaking of which, I admire you for having the courage to do it, but I've been going over and over it in my head, trying to understand why you wouldn't tell me you were smuggling those Bibles."

"I thought about it, honest. I almost did tell you a few times, but I couldn't bring myself to involve you. If something went wrong, it would only affect me. If you were arrested, your family would be devastated. They need you too much right now."

Kate cupped Meryn's chin. "You're my family too. So let's get a couple of things straight. One, not that I am encouraging you to break the law again, ever, but if there is a next time, please let me know what's going on. Even with the risk, I would have wanted to at least think about whether or not I could have helped you somehow. I don't like sitting around doing nothing, and I really don't like that you felt you had to do what you did alone, without any support. Okay?"

"Okay."

"And two, just so you know, you weren't the only one affected by your arrest, not by a long shot. Ethan and I were extremely upset, and so was Drew, and a lot of your other friends. Shane and Brendan won't take the news very well either. And I'm sure Jesse was not happy when he had to bring you in."

"He wasn't. He was furious. And I'm sure my brothers will be too. I have to call them in the next couple of days to tell them what happened, and I'm not looking forward to it."

"I don't blame you. Brendan, especially, will be beside himself. It's probably a good thing he's several provinces away."

Meryn had never thought of those thousands of kilometres of mountain ranges and fields of wheat between her and her brothers as a good thing, but maybe, in this case, her friend was right.

Kate shifted on the bed. "It's crazy what's going on. These new laws are making criminals out of ordinary citizens trying to do the right thing. And the punishments now ..." She shook her head. "We were all worried sick about you and what you were going through."

"I'm sorry I put you through that. That's the thing I regretted about breaking the law, that I had made you worry. And that I had disappointed ..."

"Jesse?"

"He was so angry when we got back to the base. He came storming into the room demanding to know what it was about the words 'stay out of trouble' that I didn't understand."

"Good question. I take it he got over it."

"Eventually."

"When will you see him again?"

"I don't know." Meryn's stomach clenched. "Likely not for a while. He said he'd message me when he thought he could get away."

Kate reached over and wiped away the moisture beneath Meryn's eye with her thumb. "Is that what this was about?"

"Yeah. It's silly, I know, but I suddenly started missing him like crazy."

"It's not silly at all, Mer. It's called love."

Meryn almost choked over her next breath. "I didn't say anything about love. We're just going to try this and see how it goes."

Kate grinned. "Yeah, okay. I get it. This is a big step for you. You want to take it slow."

"It is a big step. It's huge. And with all the obstacles we're going to face, slow seems like the right pace."

"We'll see how long that lasts." She stood up before Meryn could protest and retrieved the tray from the dresser. "I brought you some soup and a pot of tea. I'm guessing you haven't eaten much today, have you?"

Meryn thought back to the few sips of coffee and bites of toast she'd taken that morning. "No. And that does smell good."

"It's probably cold by now. Should I warm it up?"

"No, it's fine. I'm hungry enough, it won't matter."

Kate set the tray on Meryn's lap, then pulled back and looked at her. "What on earth are you wearing?"

Heat flared in her cheeks. "Jesse's pyjamas."

Kate pressed her lips together as if she was trying not to laugh. "What was I worried about? Clearly you've got this taking-it-slow thing all figured out."

CHAPTER FORTY

Over the next few days, Jesse worked himself nearly to exhaustion. He was up at six doing whatever he could find to do, the heavier and more manual the labour, the better. Around midnight, he'd shower and drop into bed, hoping to fall asleep seconds after his head hit the pillow. Anything to keep himself from thinking about Meryn and how much he missed her.

It wasn't working.

Every time he closed his eyes, her face appeared. When he did finally fall asleep, more often hours rather than seconds after he had crawled into bed—it was her blue eyes and the memory of the way she had slowly opened up to him that flowed through his dreams. By suppertime on the fourth day, wondering when he was going to see her again consumed all his thoughts.

Jesse picked his way through dinner in the officers' dining room.

Caleb dropped down on the bench beside Jesse and clapped him on the back. "What's up?"

He set down his fork. "I was thinking about setting up an obstacle course in the back field this evening. We could—"

"No."

His eyes narrowed. "No? You haven't even heard my idea. And I thought you wanted an obstacle course created at some point."

"At some point, yes. But not tonight. Save your brilliant ideas, and we'll use them in the next couple of weeks."

"What do you want me to do tonight, then?"

"Nothing."

"Nothing? But—"

"Jess, you're killing yourself. You've been working like a madman, not eating, not sleeping. Enough."

"I'm eating," Jesse protested weakly, then glanced down at the nearly full plate of food that had grown cold while he'd been playing with it over the last hour.

"Take this as friendly advice or as an order, I don't care. Go back to your quarters. Rest. Read. Whatever. The work will be there tomorrow, and after you've had a break, I promise not to discourage you in any way from doing it."

———•———

The evening stretched out before him like a long, straight road through the desert, with only scrub brush and sand for miles on either side. Jesse trudged back to his room, dreading the hours that would need to be filled before he could pull the blankets over his head and attempt to get some sleep. He wandered aimlessly around the room for a few minutes, picturing her there, in front of the couch reading, or curled up on her side on the bed, asleep, her cheeks flushed and her breathing soft and even.

The room echoed with the aching silence of her absence.

Jesse stopped in front of the picture that hung above his bed. He knew exactly how the sailors on that boat felt, being flung about by forces beyond their control. Only now he knew whose control those forces were in. For the first time in his life, he understood the words from the song he'd learned in Sunday school as peace flowed through him like a river. *Thank you.*

The tight knots in his stomach unwound.

At the sound of a knock on the door, he spun around and strode over to answer it.

Caleb stood in the hallway. "Let's go. I'll drive."

Jesse rolled his eyes. "Of course you will. Where are we going?" Should he follow him and not worry about their destination, just be glad for the distraction? Or decline because he'd be terrible company and Caleb was not likely to be willing to put up with that for much longer?

"Where do you want to go?"

Jesse cocked his head. Was that a trick question? Caleb knew there was only one place in the world Jesse wanted to be at the moment, but Caleb wouldn't be offering to drive there, would he?

"Well? Do you want to see her or not?"

Jesse's heart rate picked up. "Really?"

Caleb glanced down the hall in both directions, then planted both hands on the door frame and leaned in closer, lowering his voice. "Look, I know you're miserable. I'm really, really hoping that if you talk to Meryn, if you see for yourself that she's all right, it might help. As happy as I am that so much work has gotten done around here this week, I doubt you can take much more of this, and I know I can't. So let's go." Caleb dropped his hands and stepped back.

Jesse wasn't going to stand around waiting and risk Caleb changing his mind. Jesse came through the doorway, pulled the door shut, and waved a hand toward the exit. "Right behind you."

Caleb shot him a grin, then started down the hallway. "Somehow I didn't think it would take a whole lot of arm-twisting. And while you're there, you can tell her they've ruled that she can keep her store. She just has to report to us whenever she is getting in a new shipment of books, and she also has to submit to random searches of the building."

Relief flowed through Jesse. "That's great news. For a change." He followed Caleb out to the jeep and took his usual position in the passenger seat. This time he didn't mind. All he cared about was that he was going to see Meryn.

"So what are you going to do?"

Jesse shifted in his seat to face Caleb as he pulled through the gates of the base and onto the road. "About what?"

"The army. Are you staying or going?"

"Oh. I'm staying. For now."

"How exactly is that going to work?"

"What do you mean?"

Caleb looked at him.

Jesse ran his fingers up and down the seat belt that crossed over his chest. "I was going to leave. I wanted to, but when Meryn and I talked about it, we realized I might actually be able to do some good where I am, help the ... help people who find themselves in trouble or in need of assistance."

"Help the Christians, you mean."

He blew out a breath. "Yeah."

"The ones who claimed responsibility for 10/10 and whose religious practices are now considered hate crimes under the law you have sworn to uphold."

Jesse's fingers tightened around the seatbelt. "Come on, Cale. You've gotten to know these people. There's no way they blew up those mosques. Nothing in what the Bible teaches supports that in any way. And you know as well as I do that this whole hate crimes thing is beyond ridiculous. Even if I hadn't come to believe, I don't know if I would have been able to keep upholding a law that is so blatantly prejudiced and unjust. And I don't see how you can in good conscience either."

"Hey." Caleb smacked the steering wheel. "Don't turn on me. I'm on your side here."

"Really? It doesn't sound like it."

Caleb pulled over to the side of the road and jammed the jeep into Park. "I'm trying to show you how challenging it's going to be for you to stay in the army and pretend that nothing has changed, when the reality is that every single thing in your life is different now."

"Yeah, I kind of got that when, two days after becoming a believer, I had to do the most difficult thing I've ever had to do. I'm not under any illusions. I know exactly how hard it's going to be. I know it could, and probably will, cost me everything, including my life. And I don't care. I have finally come to realize that every gift and skill I may have been given, every choice I've been compelled to make over the years, hasn't been to advance my career. That would have been meaningless. Instead, it's been to fulfill my purpose for being on this planet. And right now, staying in the army and doing whatever I can to help the Christians is the reason I'm here. This is what I'm supposed to be doing. So I'm going to do it, with or without your support."

Caleb rubbed his eyes with a thumb and forefinger. When he dropped his hand and spoke, his voice was weary. "Jess, where have you been for the last thirty-five years? I couldn't care less that we don't have the same blood flowing through our veins. You are my brother and I love you. I will always have your back, and you will always have my support. Always."

Remorse washed over Jesse and he closed his eyes. When he opened them again, he reached out and clasped Caleb's arm. "I know that. I'm sorry. I love you too." Jesse let go and raked his fingers through his hair. "Everything that's going on has made me crazy, I know, but I have no right to take it out on you. You've never, not once, given me a reason to think you wouldn't be on my side, even if you don't completely agree with what I'm doing."

"What makes you think I don't agree?"

Jesse dropped his hand and stared at his friend.

Caleb exhaled. "The truth is, I was already thinking about getting out myself, before all of this happened. Ever since those bombings, and really for a lot longer than that, things have been going on in this country that make me extremely uncomfortable. The marginalization of any group in society has historically only led to galactically bad things happening. I may not be quite where you are, as far as buying into everything the Christians believe, but I don't want to be party to this legalized persecution either."

"What are you thinking?"

"Maybe you're right. Maybe leaving isn't the solution, at least not yet. If we stay, we might be able to use our positions to do something positive before we're found out and it all blows up in our faces." He offered Jesse a wry grin. "At least we'll be together. We'll be making our lives count for something, and, in all likelihood, we'll be able to go out in a blaze of glory. Like Butch Cassidy and the Sundance Kid."

"Are you sure, Cale? I don't want you giving up everything just for me."

"It's not just for you, but that is a big part of it, and that's okay. It's not because I'm into blindly following whatever path you might go down on a whim. It's because I trust you. If this is something you believe is worth doing, then it's worth doing, and I want to be a part of it. Besides, I promised Rory I'd watch your sorry tail and do my best to keep you out of trouble. Of course, I had no idea that was going to be a full-time occupation."

Jesse grinned and shrugged in apology.

Caleb nodded. "I have to figure out this Christianity thing on my own. I respected Rory more than anyone I ever knew, and I feel the same way about you, so if you both believe it, then I'm going to have to take a serious look at it and decide if I can accept it or not."

"Let me know if there's anything I can do to help with that."

"I will." Caleb punched him lightly in the shoulder. "Now can we go to Meryn's place or what?"

"If you insist."

"If it will help you get your head on straight, I do."

When they had nearly reached the lane that led to Meryn's house, Caleb pulled onto the shoulder again and turned off the vehicle. "I'll let you out here. I signed us up for patrol duty around town tonight, so no one would wonder why we were leaving the base this late. I'll go drive around for a while, make sure everything's quiet, but I'll be back to pick you up in half an hour. I'll park here again and flash the lights a couple of times, and if you know what's good for you, you'll come right away."

Jesse reached for the door handle. "I will. Thanks, Cale."

"Give her a big kiss for me."

Jesse shot his friend a dark look.

Caleb pointed a finger at him. "Half an hour. The more careful we are, the longer we'll be able to keep this thing going."

"Got it." Jesse climbed out of the vehicle. After the agony of the last four days, even half an hour with Meryn sounded like a taste of heaven. He wasn't about to complain. He picked up his pace as he made his way up the driveway.

He wasn't about to waste a single second of it either.

CHAPTER FORTY-ONE

Meryn dried the last of the supper dishes and set the plate on the pile in the cupboard. After hanging the towel over the stove handle, she turned to Kate, who was wiping down the sink. "I think I'm going to go for a walk. I could use some fresh air."

"Are you sure you're up to it?"

"Yes, I'm fine. I won't go far."

"Do you want me to come with you?"

Meryn squeezed her friend's shoulder. "No, go spend some time with your family. I won't be long."

Meryn slid her silver trench coat off a hanger in the front closet and pulled it on carefully. Her back was still tender, but much better than it had been the day she'd come home from the base. She buttoned the coat up over Jesse's pyjamas. Kate had washed them a couple of days ago, and Meryn could no longer catch the faint citrus smell of Jesse's musk on them. This afternoon her heart had been so heavy with thoughts of him that she'd slipped them on, hoping to feel as close to him as she had the nights she had worn them in his quarters.

She slid her feet into a pair of sandals and opened the screen door. The pungent scents of pine needles and impending rain mingled in the air.

Spring.

She inhaled deeply before making her way down the porch steps and across the front yard, dappled with shadows. Patches of moonlight streamed through the branches of the maple trees as she made her way to her favourite lookout spot. When she reached the cedar-rail fence at the summit of the small hill that sloped down to the pond, she stopped and folded her arms across the top rail. At the bottom of the hill, moonlight shimmered across the surface of the water. Meryn drank in the sight of it, lifting her face to let the cool evening breeze brush lightly across her skin.

A twig snapped behind her, and she whirled around.

"I'm sorry." A tall figure, shrouded in the shadow of a large oak tree, stepped into the light. "I didn't mean to startle you."

"Jesse." Meryn pressed her hand to her chest. "I thought you weren't going to come here."

"So did I." He moved closer.

Her heart squeezed when moonlight fell across his face, illuminating the features that had hovered in her mind for days now.

"But I couldn't stay away."

"I'm glad you couldn't."

"Me too." Jesse reached the fence and rested an elbow on it. "I had to see you, Meryn. I had to know if you were okay. Are you?"

She gave him a shaky smile. "Yes. I'm fine. Better every day. Rick gave me these wonderful little pills that make everything seem right with the world, and Kate's been waiting on me hand and foot. Ethan's here too, and Matthew and Gracie. I can never feel too down when they're around, so it's all good. Almost all, anyway."

He searched her face. "What isn't good?"

Her gaze dropped to the ground. "I've been missing you."

Jesse moved down the fence until he stood in front of her. He slid two fingers under her chin and lifted her face until she looked up at him. "I've been missing you too. More than I can say. In fact, I've been moping around the base so much, Caleb dropped me off here and ordered me to spend half an hour with you so I could 'get my head on straight.'"

"Well, God bless Caleb."

"My sentiments exactly." He started to drop his hand.

She grabbed it and pressed it between both of hers. "Jesse, thank you for giving me back my Bible. I can't tell you how much that means to me."

"You're welcome. Hide it well."

"I will." Her knees weakened, more from the sight of him than from the lingering effects of what had happened to her. In any case, she had to reach out and grip the top rail to steady herself. "I have some news."

He watched her closely. "Come and sit down and tell me." He tugged on her hand and guided her through the opening in the fence and over to the wrought-iron bench that overlooked the pond.

The light from the pole in the farmyard cast a warm glow over them as she settled onto the bench and turned to face him. Was he really here?

Their arms rested along the top of the bench, and Jesse entwined his fingers through hers. "Before you tell me your news, I have some news for you. They've ruled that you can keep the store."

"Really?"

"Yes. There are a couple of restrictions, like you have to let us know when you're getting a shipment of books in, and there will be periodic, unannounced searches of the store, but you can open back up whenever you're ready."

Meryn squeezed his hand, happiness welling in her chest at the un-expected gift. "I'm sure the testimony you gave on my behalf had some-thing to do with that. Thank you."

"It was the least I could do." He brushed a strand of hair back from her face. "So what did you want to tell me?"

She shifted. "I video chatted with Shane and Brendan a couple of days ago to tell them about everything that's happened."

"What did they say?"

"They were a little upset."

"Just a little?"

"Maybe more than a little. Shane's usually pretty calm, but he did lose it a bit. Brendan went ballistic, but he's prone to doing that. Anyway, my news is that they got talking to each other after that and decided they are both going to move to Kingston. When Shane called to tell me, I told him I didn't want them to do that just for me, but he said they'd both been thinking about it ever since the bombings. That's one good thing that can come out of horrific events like that, I guess. They make people realize what's truly important in life—God and family—and how close they want to be to both."

"I guess." His fingers tightened around hers. "I'm glad they're coming back. I've hated the idea of you having no family around."

"There's always my sister."

He shook her hand lightly. "You're hilarious. I meant none that would actually be there for you and look out for you."

"You'll really like my brothers. They want to meet you, so as soon as—"

His head jerked. "You told them about me?"

Her forehead wrinkled. "Well, I ... I mean, your name might have come up. In passing."

"In passing." He grinned, then a shadow fell across his face. "Did you tell them it was me that ...?"

Meryn ran a hand over the smooth metal of the bench. "Shane asked me, and I didn't want to lie, so yes. But I also told them that you didn't want to do it, that you had to so you could convince everyone you were still loyal to the army."

"And did your brothers buy that?"

She bit her lip. It might be better not to tell him exactly what their response to her attempts to defend him was.

"I didn't think so. I'm not surprised they want to meet me, then. No doubt there are a few other things they'd like to do to me." Jesse rubbed his thumb over the back of her hand. "But I don't blame them for being furious. I'd feel the same way if I had a sister and this happened to her." He pressed the fingers of his free hand to his forehead. "I keep going over and over everything, asking myself if we could have done anything differently. If there was any way you could have avoided going through that. Maybe if I had—"

Meryn touched the knee of his faded jeans. "Don't. You'll drive yourself crazy. There was no other way, not without one or both of us going on the run and having to spend the rest of our lives looking over our shoulders. We did what we had to do, and now it's over."

"I guess you're right."

"When they meet you, they'll see that everything I told them about you is true."

"Everything? That doesn't sound like a passing mention."

"I might have said something about you being a pretty great guy too."

"And?"

She smiled. "What, are you feeling a little insecure tonight? Do you really need to hear every little detail of what I told them?"

"I think I do, yes."

Meryn pulled their clasped hands onto her bent knee. In the light reflecting down on them, Jesse's eyes softened as he watched her, and her stomach tightened. "All right, here goes. I said that you are kind and intelligent, and that you have a great sense of humour. I also told them you are strong and loyal and good, and that you are one of the bravest men I have ever known. There may have been one or two other things, but I think that was ..."

His look grew so intense she could almost feel it brushing across her cheek. "Meryn." His husky voice sent shivers skittering up and down her spine.

"Yes?"

He opened his mouth as if he was going to say something, then closed it again. He pulled her hand to his lips and kissed her fingers. "Did I mention how much I've missed you?"

"I think you did, yes." She offered him a sheepish smile. "And I totally get it. The day I came home I was sitting on the bed thinking about everything that happened, and I suddenly burst into tears, because I was missing you so much. And whenever I want to feel close to you, I go and put on your pyjamas again."

His lips twitched.

"What?"

"I'm just enjoying how much you've embraced this whole transparency thing."

"I know." She wrinkled her nose. "Look what you've done to me. I've become so transparent, I feel like I'm made of glass now."

Jesse chuckled.

"And about my brothers, if it's any consolation, they're far more furious with Annaliese than they are with you."

His smile faded. "That I definitely understand."

A heaviness settled in her stomach, and she clutched his arm. "Jesse, if my sister even suspects that we're ..."

"Seeing each other?"

She nodded. "You should know that she will come after you full-force. Our whole lives, she has always tried to take everything I have. That's the reason I never told her about ..."

His eyes narrowed. "About what?"

Meryn fished for a response that would satisfy him. "Anyone I cared about."

For a few seconds he looked at her as if he knew she'd taken an abrupt turn from where she had been headed, then the corners of his mouth turned up. "Pretty long list, was it?"

Her shoulders relaxed. "Not very, no. But she always found out about it and succeeded in taking whomever it was away from me."

"Well, she is doomed to failure if she comes after me. I wouldn't spend two seconds with a woman who could slap her little sister across the face or lock her in a chicken coop or"—his face hardened—"turn her over to the authorities. In fact, I told Ethan if I was ever in the same room as her again, I might rip her head off."

"What did he say to that?"

"That he'd like a front row seat to that show."

Meryn started to laugh, then pressed a hand to her mouth. "I shouldn't laugh. That's terrible."

"Why? She deserves a lot more than that for what she's done to you. You have every right to hate her."

"I don't hate her, Jesse. Thanks to you."

He blinked. "Me?"

"Yes. When I found out it was my sister who betrayed me, it did hurt. A lot. My first instinct was to be angry and bitter, and I was, for a couple of days. But then I remembered what you said the night someone threw the brick through my store window, about forgiveness being the light that counteracts the darkness of hatred and bitterness and pain. And you're right. So as hard as it is, I choose the light. I choose to forgive her. Besides, she's still my sister. Maybe someday she'll come to regret everything she's done and we can actually be a family."

Jesse pressed his lips together, as if he had more to say on the subject but was trying to restrain himself. Then he let out a breath. "You're pretty amazing, do you know that? I don't know if I can manage not to hate your sister, and I definitely don't know if I can forgive her, but I promise I'll try, for your sake."

"Thank you."

"In any case, you have absolutely nothing to worry about. Annaliese's cold, soulless beauty doesn't attract me. It makes me want to run in the opposite direction. Besides ..." He reached out and stroked her hair. "I told you before, I'm strictly a brunette man."

The heaviness in her stomach dissipated, replaced with a quivering rush of warmth.

Jesse rested his fingers on her cheek. "So if your sister comes after everyone you care about, and you're worried she's going to come after me, are you saying you care about me, Meryn O'Reilly?" His fingers moved slowly up and down the side of her face.

The breath she'd been drawing in got trapped in her throat. "More than I should, probably."

The glint in his eye gave her a glimpse of the mischievous little boy who'd followed his older brother and his friend into one scrape after another. "Why, is there a limit? If so, I'm pretty sure I exceeded it a while back."

Meryn shook her head. "No, there's no limit. Apparently."

"I'm glad to hear it."

When he dropped his gaze and lowered his hand to lift the collar of her silver coat, her pulse jumped erratically.

"I see you're wearing my pyjamas now."

"Yes."

He stood up, took both of her hands in his, and pulled her to her feet. He let go of her and reached for the top button of her coat. "May I?"

Her breathing grew shallow, but she nodded.

Jesse undid the buttons of the coat and slid it down over her shoulders and arms. He tossed it onto the bench behind him and stood back to look at her. He shook his head. "Man, I love you in those pyjamas. If we ever get married, you won't have to bother with any of that fancy lingerie on our wedding night."

She ignored the thorn of guilt that pricked her chest at his words. She would not let the past ruin these fleeting moments they had together. "I'll keep that in mind."

He studied her. "A few seconds of panic there, but you stayed with me. That's progress." He motioned to what she was wearing. "Does this mean you were wanting to feel close to me earlier?"

"It's dangerous to tell you anything, isn't it?"

He grinned. "It may come back to haunt you, yes. But were you?"

"Yes."

Jesse held out his arms. "I'm right here. For the next"—he glanced down at his watch and made a face—"three or four minutes, you don't have to just *feel* close to me, you can *be* close to me."

Meryn wrapped her arms around his waist.

He hooked one arm around her neck and pulled her head to his chest with his other hand. He held her for a moment, then he bent down and spoke softly in her ear. "If it helps, you don't feel like glass, all hard and cold. Pretty much the opposite, in fact."

She raised her head.

Jesse pulled back his arm and slid his hands along her jaw. Slowly, slowly, he leaned in and pressed his lips to hers.

Meryn gave in to the feel of his mouth, his strong hands cupping her face. He moved his hand to the back of her head and pulled her closer. She clung to him as the world spun around her, this dizziness one she would gladly lose herself in forever.

He lifted his head. When he spoke, his voice was breathless. "Wow. Some things really are worth waiting—and risking everything—for." His gaze shifted to the road over her shoulder, and he grimaced. "Caleb's here. I have to go. But let's not leave things up in the air again. Let's plan a time to meet. Soon." He rested his forehead on hers. "What do you say? Wednesday night, eight o'clock, at the place you told me about?"

"Wednesday night. I'll be there."

"You'd better be." He kissed her again and then, with a reluctant groan, let his hands slide from her face as he stepped back. "We'll work this out, Meryn, I promise. It'll be an adventure."

He turned and jogged toward the dim outline of a jeep parked on the side of the road.

A smile crossed her face. An adventure.

So much had happened in the months following 10/10, in her life, in her country, and in the world. She hadn't chosen any of it, but God had chosen her to be a part of it. The journey hadn't been easy, but the moments of joy made the challenges worthwhile.

The headlights of the jeep came on, and the major pulled onto the road.

Meryn's gaze remained fixed on the vehicle until the taillights were swallowed up by the night. She picked her trench coat up from the bench and slung it over her shoulders.

A cloud drifted across the moon.

Gravel crunched beneath her sandals as she hurried across the driveway and started up the steps to the porch.

Wind rustled the long grass at the edge of the strand of trees on the far side of the lawn.

She stopped and turned slowly, eyes probing the darkness.

No breeze stirred the cool night air.

The back of her neck prickled. Meryn tilted her head, straining to hear any other out-of-place sound, but all that filled her ears was the staccato rhythm of her pulse pounding.

A squirrel? She continued up the steps, clutching the railing. A raccoon, more likely. Still, her steps quickened.

She crossed the porch. When she grasped the handle of the screen door, images exploded in her mind like deafening, red-tinged fireworks—a brick exploding through glass, the sharp tip of a knife sliding into her skin, venomous words scrawled across paper, the cold, round barrel of a gun pressed to her head, cords of a whip dripping with blood.

Meryn dragged trembling fingers back and forth across her forehead, trying to erase the blinding memories.

That was out there. This was her home.

She was safe here.

Safe. The word—the same one written on the paper taped to the brick and spoken by the man with the knife—sent pinpricks of ice across her skin. One hand still clutching the door handle, Meryn looked back at the darkness. Like it had that night in Jesse's quarters, it seemed to have become a living thing, mocking her.

With a shudder, she turned away and pulled open the screen door. She *was* safe here.

Wasn't she?

Sara Davison is the author of the romantic suspense novels The Watcher and The Seven Trilogy. She has been a finalist for eight national writing awards, including the Word Award for Best New Canadian Christian author, a Carol, and two Daphne du Maurier Awards, and is a Word and Cascade Award winner. Sara has a degree in English Literature and currently resides in Ontario, Canada with her husband Michael and their three children, all of whom she (literally) looks up to.

www.SaraDavison.org

ACKNOWLEDGMENTS

It's always a challenge for a fiction writer to craft an acknowledgments page. It's not because we're not grateful for every person, every opportunity, every open door, every word of encouragement that has brought us to this place. We are. It's because, no matter how unique and creative the end result may be, the journey is essentially the same. So there is no making stuff up here, there's just stating the facts. And the facts are these: None of us makes it alone. Countless people are needed along the way to bring a book from idea to outline to rough draft to polished final version and into the hands of readers. Here are some of the many who have travelled this road with me and to whom I am forever indebted.

My deepest thanks always to my husband, Michael, and children, Luke, Julia, and Seth. You put up with more macaroni and cheese, hot dog, and scrambled egg dinners than any family should have to, and you do it without complaining. Thank you for your unwavering support and your unswerving conviction that I can accomplish far more than I think I can. With you on my side, I find myself daring to believe that you're right.

To my parents, sisters, nieces, nephew, and extended family and friends: I continue to be humbled and amazed that you read my books and ask for more. And I appreciate that you make everyone you know read them too. You have kept me going at times when I was ready to quit and find a real job, and I love you more than you can know.

To the members of my writer's groups, The Word Guild, and my book club: I love being with you and sharing our mutual passion for God and for words. What an encouragement you are to me.

To those, bless them, who read early, very rough drafts and somehow managed to see tiny sparks of diamond shining through the layers of dirt: You have my undying thanks. Special mention to Simon Presland, whose belief in me and in my work has given me the confidence to calmly handle the noes and doggedly persevere until they turn to yeses. I am grateful for you and for our friendship.

To my wonderful former agent, Alice Crider: I cannot tell you how thankful I am that you took a risk on an unknown writer from somewhere up in the wilds of Canada. Your patience, persistence, and encouragement were gifts from God to me, and as much as I wish you well in your new position, I will miss you. To my new agent, Sarah Joy Freese: I look forward to getting to know you better and walking the next leg of this journey together. Special thanks to Greg Johnson and all the wonderful people at Wordserve Literary. Thank you for dedicating your time and efforts to helping authors get the words God has given them out there for others to read. You are deeply appreciated!

And to Sherrie and Christina and all the amazing people at Ashberry Lane Publishing: Words cannot express to you my gratitude for your willingness to take a chance on me and my work. We may live at the opposite ends of different countries, but we are kindred spirits at heart. You are truly a joy to work with. I love being part of the family and look forward to many adventures ahead!

DISCUSSION QUESTIONS

1. Do you believe the church in North America is prepared for the type of persecution that Christians already face in other parts of the world? Why or why not? What can we do to prepare?

2. Do you have a Lieutenant Gallagher in your life, someone who resents you and all you have accomplished? How do you handle that? How can you show the love of God to someone who treats you badly?

3. Romans 12:20 says, "On the contrary: 'If your enemy is hungry, feed him; if he is thirsty, give him something to drink. In doing this, you will heap burning coals on his head.'" What does the concept of "heaping coals" mean in this verse? When Kate gives the jam to the soldiers and says she is doing it to heap coals on their heads, is she interpreting this passage correctly? What can be accomplished when we treat our enemies the way God commands us to in this verse?

4. If your Bible was ever taken from you, what would you do? Does the possibility of such a thing happening drive you to want to study or memorize the Word more while you have it? How else can you prepare for such a loss?

5. Do you agree with Jesse's assertion that the ray of light that

counteracts the darkness of pain is forgiveness? What does refusing to forgive others do to us? To our relationships with others? To our relationship with God? What can forgiveness accomplish?

6. Meryn breaks the law when she decides to order and distribute Bibles. Do you believe there is a time for civil disobedience? Under what circumstances would you consider breaking the law justified? Would you be willing to take the kind of risks that Meryn and Jesse both feel called to take?

7. When Meryn attempts to leave the store before the soldiers come, she senses the Holy Spirit telling her she is to stay and face the consequences of what she has done. Do you believe God communicates to people like this today? In what other ways does God communicate to us?

8. When Jesse asks Meryn why God is allowing all the chaos and confusion to take place in the world, she responds by saying, "God isn't *letting* this happen. God is *making* this happen." Do you believe this statement is true? How do you feel about the idea that God is sovereign and in control of *all* things? Do you agree or disagree, and why?

9. Meryn tells Jesse that God is pursuing him, because he loves Jesse and wants him for his own. Do you believe that God pursues people that relentlessly? If so, what part does our free will play in the salvation process?

10. In the middle of her sentence being carried out, Meryn cries out to God, and she receives supernatural peace and the courage and strength to endure what she is going through. Has anything like this ever happened to you or to someone you know during a crisis or difficult time in life? What did that look like? How did it affect your faith?

THE
DARKNESS
DEEPENS
the seven trilogy
book two

SARA DAVISON

The Darkness Deepens
Book Two

Their Secrets Protect Them ... But Secrets are Hard to Keep

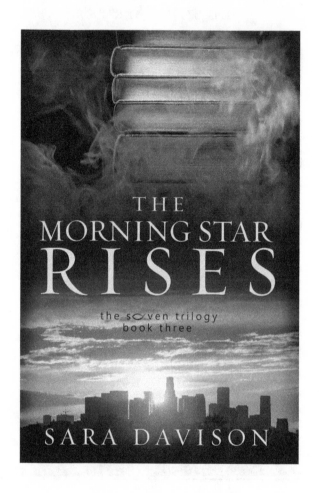

The Morning Star Rises
Book Three

In the midst of all the fear and confusion,
only one thing is clear …
This isn't over yet.

CPSIA information can be obtained
at www.ICGtesting.com
Printed in the USA
BVHW071419120620
581245BV00001B/35